P

Crimson Snow by Jeanne M. Dams
Agatha Award Winner

❧

"Dams develops the plot with her usual attention to detail.... Regular series readers who enjoy the author's subtle observations on life at the turn of the twentieth century—religion, sexual mores, class structure—will not be disappointed. A typically good entry in the series."

—*Booklist*

"Dams creates the atmosphere of that transitional time with newly flickering electric street lights and a factory switching from the manufacture of carriages to that of motor cars.... Casting an immigrant maid as heroine allows for much social observation across classes, and adds interest to this portrait of American society in a small city over a hundred years ago."

—*The Historical Novels Review*

"Dams brings the period alive as the captivating Hilda solves a murder and her own problems too."

—*Kirkus Reviews*

"Mystery and romance all wrapped up in one delicious story.... Cozy mystery fans will love this book, with characters that go right to your heart. It will have you clamoring for more!"

—*Cozy Library*

"Beautifully researched and impeccably crafted. Highly recommended."

—*Chicago Tribune*

"Based on a real, unsolved case from 1904, the novel seamlessly integrates historical details with a suspenseful plot."

—*Publishers Weekly*

INDIGO CHRISTMAS

Also by Jeanne M. Dams:

Indigo Christmas

A Hilda Johansson Mystery

Jeanne M. Dams

PERSEVERANCE PRESS / JOHN DANIEL & COMPANY
PALO ALTO / MCKINLEYVILLE, CALIFORNIA / MMVIII

A PERSEVERANCE PRESS BOOK
Published by John Daniel & Company
A division of Daniel & Daniel, Publishers, Inc.
Post Office Box 2790
McKinleyville, California 95519
www.danielpublishing.com/perseverance

Book design by Eric Larson, Studio E Books, Santa Barbara
www.studio-e-books.com

Cover painting: Linda Weatherly S.

10 9 8 7 6 5 4 3 2 1

LIBRARY OF CONGRESS CATALOGING-IN-PUBLICATION DATA
Dams, Jeanne M.
Indigo Christmas : a Hilda Johansson mystery / by Jeanne M. Dams.
    p. cm.
ISBN-13: 978-1-880284-95-7 (pbk. : alk. paper)
ISBN-10: 1-880284-95-2 (pbk. : alk. paper)
  1. Johansson, Hilda (Fictitious character)—Fiction. 2. Women private investigators—Fiction. 3. South Bend (Ind.)—Fiction. 4. Swedish Americans—Fiction. I. Title.
PS3554.A498I63 2008
813'.54—dc22
                    2008012296

*To the immigrants over the centuries
who have made this country what it is*

INDIGO CHRISTMAS

The Louisiana Purchase Exposition, by general verdict the greatest of all world's fairs, will close with fitting ceremonials at midnight.

—South Bend *Tribune*
December 1, 1904

1

HILDA PUSHED ASIDE her breakfast plate and put down the South Bend *Tribune*. There was nothing very interesting in its pages. Back in her servant days in the Studebaker mansion, the butler had not allowed her to read the papers. Of course she had done so anyway, behind his back, and the thrill of the illicit had lent glamour to even the most ordinary of stories. Now that she was married and a lady, and there was no one to stop her reading anything she chose, she found the prose boring.

The fair in St. Louis was closing today. That wasn't news. The *Tribune* was still exultant about the overwhelming Republican victory, nationally and statewide, some three weeks before. That wasn't news, either, nor did Hilda consider it cause for celebration, staunch Democrat that she was. A death in a barn fire a few weeks ago was probably a murder, according to the *Tribune*, though the coroner had ruled it death by misadventure. Hilda had never heard of the dead man and found the details of the story uninteresting.

She sighed again and reached for her coffee cup. It was empty, and the pot—she felt its silver side—was cold. She pushed back her chair, picked up the pot, and headed for the kitchen.

Mrs. O'Rourke, the cook, looked up from her breadboard with a frown. "Is something wrong, ma'am?"

"Nothing, Mrs. O'Rourke. I need more coffee."

The cook glanced at the signal box on the wall. "I didn't hear ye ring, ma'am."

"Oh. Oh! Yes—well—this time I preferred to come to the kitchen. To remind you that there will be visitors for tea."

The cook's face showed what she thought of that excuse. "Yes, ma'am. Four o'clock, tea and cakes for three. The coffee's all gone, ma'am. I'll make more and bring it in to ye."

"Yes," said Hilda firmly. "And don't forget the egg shells."

The reminder, like that about the tea, was unnecessary, and the cook bridled. Mrs. O'Rourke never forgot the egg shells. She made superb coffee, once Hilda had taught her the Swedish way of doing it. She was a fine cook. Hilda could never complain about any meal that came out of Mrs. O'Rourke's kitchen. Not that she would have dared complain, anyway. The cook kept Hilda firmly in her place—which was *out* of the kitchen. Her husband, the coachman/gardener/handyman, was nearly as tyrannical in his various realms as his wife in hers.

Hilda retreated to the dining room. It was a pleasant room, paneled in dark wood with a built-in sideboard. Not as big as even the family dining room at the Studebakers' Tippecanoe Place, it was magnificent compared with Hilda's home back in Sweden. Hilda was still trying to get used to such opulence.

Upstairs she could hear water running, as little Eileen O'Hara cleaned the master bathroom. There was no real need to clean the other one, since Hilda and Patrick had had no guests in the eight months they had lived in the house, but doubtless Eileen, who was conscientious, would dust the fixtures and the window sill, shake out the curtains, mop the floor.

Hilda would have liked to go up and help Eileen, and have a good chat while she did it, but it wasn't the done thing for the lady of the house to gossip with the servants. And Eileen might be shy and tongue-tied, and might think Hilda was there to criticize her work.

Mrs. O'Rourke brought the fresh coffee. Hilda sipped it while she stared out the window. It was snowing again. It had started last week, just after Thanksgiving, and had kept it up in snatches ever since. Today it looked likely to continue at least through the day. Huge, wet flakes floated down to cover every twig, every branch with white icing. The oak trees still had most of their leaves; Hilda hoped the weight of the snow wouldn't bring branches down.

She briefly considered going out for a walk. The snow was pretty, and she liked it. As a child in Sweden, she had loved sledding and building snow castles with her brothers and sisters.

But she wasn't a child anymore, and her brothers and sisters had their work to do. They could not, in the middle of a weekday, frivol about in the snow.

Hilda had no work to do. She had nothing whatever to do except read (but there were no new books or magazines in the house), or go shopping (for what?), or do needlework (which she detested), or call on the neighbors. But the neighbors weren't especially friendly, and morning wasn't the time for calls. She could, she supposed, go to the library to see if there were any new stories about Sherlock Holmes, her favorite, but it was a long walk on snow-covered sidewalks, and she didn't want to get the horses out on slippery streets.

She wandered to the parlor, picked up last month's *Ladies' Home Journal*, and began to leaf through the advertisements for scouring powder and corsets.

By four o'clock she was in such a frenzy of boredom that she nearly answered the doorbell herself, but remembered in time that greeting callers was the maid's job. When Eileen had taken their cloaks and shown them into the parlor, though, she gave one of them an ardent welcome.

"Aunt Molly! It is so good to see you!" Hilda threw her arms around Patrick's diminutive aunt, who smiled and raised an eyebrow.

"It's only been a week, my dear."

"I know, but—oh, I am sorry. This is your friend?"

"Hilda, let me present Mrs. Elbel. You know, of course, about her husband's family, so important in South Bend musical circles. Dorothea, this is Mrs. Cavanaugh, my nephew's wife. I've wanted the two of you to meet for some time."

Hilda took the woman's gloved hand. "I am very happy to

meet you, but I am sorry it is such a cold day for a visit. Will the horses be all right?"

"The coachman's taking them back home," said Aunt Molly. "It's just down the street, and they do like their own stable in this sort of weather. That's a lovely fire you have there."

Hilda was reminded of her manners. "Yes, do please sit down and warm yourselves." She pulled the bell cord, feeling very self-conscious about it, and sat down primly on the fashionably hard settee. Looking at the clothes worn by her callers, she was unpleasantly reminded that she had not changed into the elaborate "tea gown" suitable for such entertaining. Ill at ease, she was suddenly unable to think of a word to say.

Aunt Molly took the lead. Characteristically, she didn't waste time on small talk. "Now, Hilda, my dear, it has seemed to me that you need something to occupy your time. Mrs. Elbel, as I've told you, has organized a number of charitable efforts in town. Her latest endeavor has to do with the welfare of some of the boys in South Bend."

Mrs. Elbel took up the narrative. "Mrs. Malloy has told me you have a young brother—thirteen, is he?"

"Fourteen in February, ma'am—Mrs. Elbel."

"And you're said to like boys and get along well with them."

Hilda thought the woman sounded as though boys were a species of insect. "Yes, I do. Erik was always my favorite when we were growing up."

"You have an advantage, then, that I have not. I have only daughters, and I love them dearly, but they do not help one to understand boys. At any rate, you probably know that there are many boys in this city, especially the foreigners, who get into far too much trouble. We are trying to start a club for them to give them good, wholesome activities after school. Ball games, er—marbles and that sort of thing."

Hilda frowned. "Many of the children of immigrants do not go to school. They work all day and have no time for games."

"They seem to have plenty of time for hooliganism! They

are a very undesirable element in this community, and something must be done to civilize them!"

Molly Malloy intervened. "Hilda, you'd be very good at working with these children. I've seen you with Erik and his friends. Will you consider helping to form the club?"

The arrival of tea allowed Hilda to consider her answer. She didn't want to be rude to Aunt Molly, but she didn't care at all for Mrs. Elbel's attitude. Undesirable element, indeed!

She poured out the tea and handed round the platters of tiny sandwiches and dainty little cakes, and when her duties as hostess were completed, she sat back. "I do like boys, as Aunt Molly says. And they like me. I might be able to help them in some way, but it will not be easy. I also know about the problems of immigrants, you see."

"Yes, of course." Mrs. Elbel studied her teacup for a moment. "Mrs. Cavanaugh, I hope you don't think I was—er—condescending about the boys."

Since that was exactly what Hilda did think, she kept silent.

"I know that they have problems I may not always understand," her guest pursued. "That is exactly why I need your help. You—your background—" She paused. "Mrs. Cavanaugh, may I be frank?"

Hilda nodded, her lips set.

"I hope I won't offend you, but you come from much the same background as some of these boys. You have risen above it. You now have the time, and the resources, to help us address some of the evils of modern society. Will you do it?"

Hilda gritted her teeth. Risen above it! There was nothing in her background to be ashamed of, nothing to "rise above."

However, the woman had come to ask her help. That showed some sense, even if Aunt Molly had been the guiding spirit. She ought to say yes—although—

The doorbell rang. Voices were raised in the hall, Eileen expostulating with someone whose voice Hilda knew well. She rose just as a woman burst into the parlor.

Dripping wet, her boots leaving muddy tracks on the carpet, Norah O'Neill ran across the room holding out her hands to Hilda. "Oh, Hilda, oh, ye've got to help me! Sean's been arrested for murder!"

2

"**N**ORAH! TELL ME! No—take off your wet things and sit down. You should not be running now, and you must not get a chill." Hilda was pulling off Norah's shawl as she spoke, and leading her to a chair by the fire. Heavily pregnant, Norah sank into the chair and dashed tears from her eyes with the heels of her hands.

"I'm sorry—ye've got company—but somebody's got to do something!" The distraught woman began to sob.

Dorothea Elbel looked somewhat helplessly at Molly Malloy. "I should go, unless there's something…"

Aunt Molly pulled the bell cord. "Hilda and Patrick are on the telephone. We can fetch my carriage to take you home. I must stay to help. I'm sure you understand. Oh, Eileen, would you be good enough to ring my house and ask Donald to bring the carriage round? And please get some fresh tea for Hilda's friend, there's a good girl."

"Has something happened, ma'am?" Eileen ventured.

"This young woman is in trouble, and she needs our help. Quickly, Eileen!"

Eileen vanished. Hilda, meanwhile, had taken off Norah's wet boots and set them on the hearth, and was chafing her hands. "Norah, stop crying and tell me everything."

Norah continued to sob.

"My child," said Aunt Molly, putting her hand on Norah's shoulder, "you *must* stop crying. This is doing your baby no good, you know."

Mrs. Elbel stifled a gasp. Norah's condition was perfectly

obvious to anyone with eyes in her head, but it was considered improper to notice babies until they had actually made their appearance in the world.

"If your husband is in difficulties," Aunt Molly went on, "the last thing he needs is for you and the baby to be in difficulties, too. Now take this handkerchief, dry your eyes and blow your nose, and tell us."

Molly Malloy might be a tiny woman, but she had a way of imposing her will. Norah pulled herself together, mopped up with the proffered handkerchief, and sat back to tell her story, the occasional hiccup interrupting.

"It happened just now. I was at home when I heard, and I ran all the way."

"That was a very foolish thing to do in your condition, my dear," said Aunt Molly. "You must promise me you will never do such a thing again. Now go on. You were at home."

"Well, ye know I'm not workin' now, bein' so near my time."

Hilda nodded. The Hibberd family, who employed Norah as maid, were unusually considerate. Many servants worked right up until the labor pains started. Norah and Sean could ill afford to lose her wages, but a first pregnancy can be tricky, and they were taking no chances.

"So I was home, sewin' things for the baby, when me brother Flynn came poundin' on the door. He works with Sean, ye know. And I wondered what he was doin', leavin' work in the middle of the day, and in such a storm, too. And he told me—" Here Norah threatened to break down again, but Aunt Molly gave her a cup of fresh, hot tea and a stern look. Norah sipped, sniffed, and went on.

"He said there's been a man killed, on a farm just out of town. It was a while ago, in November, and everyone thought it was an accident. Burned up in a fire, he did. But somebody started askin' questions, and now the police think it was maybe murder, and they've taken Sean away!"

"Now, you're not to cry again," said Aunt Molly briskly.

"Dorothea, I believe the carriage is here. So sorry you have to leave. I'll talk to you again soon. Hilda, we need to get this child into some dry clothes. Have you anything that will fit her?"

"There is the kimono you gave me, but it is silk and not very warm."

"It'll be warmer than these wet things. Let's get her to your bedroom. Is there a fire there?"

"Yes, a small one."

"It can be built up. Now, Norah."

Norah allowed a few tears to track down her cheeks as she obediently went upstairs, but she didn't sob. She didn't dare to. Molly Malloy was the dead spit of Norah's great-granny back in Ireland, who had terrorized the whole family even in her nineties. When they had attained the bedroom, Norah obediently suffered herself to be undressed, dried off, wrapped in Hilda's silk kimono and a warm shawl, and settled in a cozy armchair before the fire.

Eileen was sent for once again, to build up the fire and take Norah's wet things to dry, and as she went downstairs to fill the coal scuttle, Hilda called after her. "Eileen, if you can find it, bring up this morning's *Tribune* when you come back." She turned to Aunt Molly and said quietly, "There was a story in it, I think about this death. I want to read it carefully. It might tell me something new."

Norah heard and was instantly combative. "It won't tell you anything about Sean doin' it, cause he didn't!"

"Norah Murphy, do you think I would not have noticed if Sean's name had been in the newspaper? Do not be foolish! Of course the *Tribune* did not say he did it. I want to read what it did say, and see if there is anything that will give me an idea."

Norah tried to get to her feet. "Then ye'll do it? Ye'll find out? And me name's O'Neill, now." She was plainly feeling a little better.

"You should not try to get up," reproved Hilda. "I will do what I can. I do not even know where the farm is."

"If the fire was the one I recall," Molly put in, "it's actually quite close to Mr. Malloy's property. You know where that is, Hilda, just south of the city limits. The city has grown so, Mr. Malloy is thinking about selling the land for building. It's good rich soil, though—'twould be a pity to cover it with houses."

Hilda frowned. "Why would the police think Sean might be involved in a murder out of town?" she asked Norah. "He has his work to do. He does not travel around the county."

"See, that's it. He was workin' out there, just for two days. Me cousin Barry was helpin' build a new barn for a relation, and they needed more men, and o' course Sean went when they asked. Barry's family." Norah was getting teary again. "But if I'd known what was goin' to happen, I'd have made him stay at home!"

"But what *did* happen? Norah, if you cry again I will leave the room!" Hilda stamped her foot.

"An' you'd cry too, if it was your man in jail!"

"I would not! I would find out what had really happened! And so I will for you, if you will stop being foolish and *tell* me!"

Norah gave a last sniff and glared at Hilda. "Foolish, am I? It's the police who are being foolish. There's not one single thing to tie Sean to the man's death, not one thing, except he's Irish an' ye know how they treat the Irish. An' ye don't need to look at me that way. I'm tellin' ye all I know. Sean was workin' there that day, the day the man died."

"Not on the man's farm?"

"No, the next farm."

Eileen returned with the coal and Hilda's newspaper. As the fire grew warmer, Norah settled more comfortably into her narrative. "See, it's raw land yet, but me cousin Barry's cousin on his mother's side, he came into a bit of money and bought the land. And come spring he's going to start farming it, but first he needs a barn."

Hilda nodded. That made sense. You had to have a place to keep the animals and to store the crops. City people might think a house came first, but Hilda's family had been farmers in Sweden, and she knew the vital importance of a barn.

"So he needed a barn," she prompted.

"So o' course he got family to help. I reckon there's enough strong Irishmen around these parts to build a dozen barns. Most of the women went, too, with food, but Sean wouldn't let me go. He said it was too much work an' standin' for me now, as tired as I get these days." Norah sniffled again at that, but a black look from Hilda stopped her tears.

"So they was almost done with what they could do that day, an' the walls was framed and the roof on, an' anyway it was gettin' too dark to see. So they was all gettin' ready to set down to their supper when somebody smelled smoke. And they looked over across the fields an' saw flames, an' thick smoke risin', an' they thought it was a brush pile burnin'. But that was dangerous-like, what with the dry weather we'd had. The grass could've caught, an' there's some swamp land out there with mucky soil; a fire can burn along under the ground for weeks.

"So some of the men went runnin', thinking to stomp out the brush fire if they could, or throw dirt on it maybe. They hadn't got no water; Barry's cousin hasn't dug his well yet. But when they got close enough, they saw it wasn't brush atall, but the barn on the neighbor's property."

Hilda shook her head sadly. A barn fire was hard to fight even with plenty of water. With none, or what little the men could have pumped from the well on the older farm, there was no hope at all.

Norah nodded at Hilda's unspoken comment. "Nothin' they could do but watch it burn. It was too bad by the time they got there to even see if they could get the animals out. But the way it turned out, there wasn't no animals inside. The fire brigade came, after a bit. Somebody in town saw the smoke an' turned in the alarm, an' they got out with a pumper wagon as fast as they could, but the barn was far past savin' by that time and they could see no animals hadn't tried to get out. There was only the man, though they didn't know that till later."

Hilda shuddered, and Aunt Molly put a hand on her arm. "Who was the man, my dear? The owner of the farm?"

"I don't know. I never heard. And Sean was sad and sorry

about it when he heard, like everybody, but it wasn't nothin' to do with them, really."

"Jenkins," Hilda said. She had picked up the newspaper and was scanning the front page. "James Jenkins. He was a hired hand on the farm, it says here, not the owner. He sometimes slept in the barn." She skimmed the rest of the story. "The coroner said it was an accident, but his brother—Mr. Jenkins's brother Robert—is certain it was murder. He says Mr. Jenkins was robbed and then murdered. His billfold was not found on his body."

She looked up from the paper. "Norah," she said slowly, "why did the police arrest Sean?"

Norah threatened to dissolve again into tears. "Are ye sayin' Sean robbed and killed that man? Hilda Johansson, I never thought you'd end up as bad as the police! I told you, he's Irish and the police always—"

Hilda looked Norah squarely in the eye. "They were all Irish, Norah. Everyone there that day was Irish, except some of the firemen. You said so yourself. You will not dare to accuse me of hating the Irish. I have married into an Irish family. I know they are good people. You will tell me, Norah, why of all the Irishmen at the scene of the fire, the police have arrested Sean." She held the gaze.

It was Norah who broke the eye contact. She looked down at her lap. "It's nothin' atall, only the police takin' a little thing an' blowin' it up. It doesn't mean nothin'."

"What little thing?

Norah shut her mouth firmly.

Hilda was relentless. "What little thing?"

"The billfold." Norah's voice was almost inaudible.

"What did you say?"

"The billfold!" Norah turned defiant. "Sean found a man's billfold outside the barn. It wasn't burnt, and it was a good one. Not new, but good leather, and Sean hadn't but an old cheap one as was fallin' apart. He asked if it belonged to anybody there, asked even the firemen, and when it wasn't nobody's, he kept it."

Hilda had to swallow before she could ask the next question. "Was there any money in it?"

"Not a penny! Sean said so, and I believe him. I never thought ye'd be like the others, thinkin' my man's a thief...." She sank back, exhausted, and put a hand to her head.

Hilda sat down on the bed, suddenly weary. "Norah, I know that you are nearly out of your mind with worry and with—well, in a time when women can get—odd—but when you are not out of your mind, you know that you are my friend, and that I trust you and Sean. But you must see that if this billfold belonged to the dead man, and Sean has it now, the police, who are not your friends and do not know and trust you, have a very good reason to put Sean in jail. And to keep him there."

*Thank God every morning when you get up
that you have something to do that day which
must be done, whether you like it or not.*

　　—Charles Kingsley
　　　Westward Ho!, 1855

3

ORAH WOULD HAVE broken down completely at that but for Aunt Molly's firmness. "Now, my dear, you must not cry again," she said, gently lifting Norah's chin. "Look at me, Norah. Tears and sobs serve no purpose, except to make your headache worse. Oh, I can see that you have a headache. And I am very serious when I say a storm of weeping could harm your baby. Take deep breaths now—that's it—and Hilda, have you any headache powders? Oh, of course you do, I was forgetting the bad headaches you get yourself. And you and I could do with a drop of brandy, if there's such a thing in the house."

"In the kitchen, maybe, I t'ink." Only in moments of extreme stress did Hilda revert to the Swedish accent she had taken such pains to eradicate. "I will go and look, *ja?*"

"Eileen can do that," said Molly gently. "If you'll just ring the bell?"

Hilda bit her lip. Once more she had betrayed her unfamiliarity with the world of the well-to-do. This was no time to worry over whether she would ever fit in. She rang the bell.

Eileen entered the room instantly, carrying a tray with decanters and glasses. "Cook thought you might want this, ma'am," she said. "I was just goin' to bring it in."

So she had been listening at the door. Hilda shrugged. She had often done the same thing. One of the few rewards of servanthood was knowing everything that went on. "T'ank you, Eileen," she said with dignity. "And please t'ank—thank—Mrs. O'Rourke for me. It was very thoughtful of you both. And please bring also some water, and my headache powders. You know where they are?"

Eileen bobbed a curtsey and nodded. Aunt Molly hid a smile. Hilda was learning to deal with servants, if slowly. And if she sounded, at times, just a little like Mrs. Studebaker, her former employer—well, that did no one any harm.

Hilda, after years spent in the teetotal Studebaker household, was also learning to drink a little. She could now handle a glass of wine with a festive meal. Brandy was much stronger, she knew, so after an encouraging nod from Aunt Molly she poured only a thimbleful into each glass, added water, and handed one to Molly. "Patrick has told me this is good medicine when people are in distress. I have not tasted it, but maybe it will be good for us. Norah, you may not have any. It will make your head worse, but this—" as Eileen returned with a small box "—this will make it better. You will not like the taste, but it is good for the head." Stirring up one of the doses of powder in a glass of water, she handed it to Norah, who sipped and made a face. "Yes, I know," said Hilda, "but drink it all and your headache will go away."

Hilda took a sip out of her own glass, and made a face in turn. "Ooh! It tastes like medicine, and it burns!"

"Yes, dear," said Aunt Molly. "One would expect medicine to taste like medicine. And as for the burning, take another sip. It will warm you inside."

Outside the house, early December darkness had taken possession of the world, but the darkness was gentled by the snow. The sounds that could be heard were soft sounds, the occasional thud of horses' hooves on the snow-covered street, the sweet jingle of sleigh bells, the laughter of distant children playing in the snow. In the room the firelight cast a glow over Norah as she sat before it. A coal dropped from the grate, landing almost noiselessly on ashes.

Hilda roused herself. "It is getting late. Patrick will be home soon. Norah, you will stay for supper with us, and after supper we will all talk about what is to be done."

"But Sean—"

"Sean will do very well where he is for one night," said Aunt Molly. "I'd like to know the Irishman who can't deal with a night in jail! Patrick can telephone to the police station to tell them you're well and safe, and they'll tell Sean, and that will relieve his mind. Now, shall we see if your clothing is dry enough to wear? Or would you rather stay as you are and have a tray sent up to you?"

"I'll dress, thank you, Mrs. Malloy." The older woman's matter-of-fact attitude was steadying Norah.

"Child, you might as well call me Aunt Molly. I'm sure to be at least a shirt-tail cousin, if we go back far enough. And you're next thing to a sister to Hilda. Who is my niece, so that makes you my aunt, as well. Now, then." She glanced at Hilda, who had already reached for the bell to summon Eileen about Norah's clothes.

Molly smiled to herself. Yes, Hilda was learning.

When Eileen came with the dry clothes, Molly asked her to telephone her home saying she, Molly, would be out to dinner. Then leaving Eileen to help Norah dress, Hilda and Molly walked slowly down the stairs together. "This," Hilda articulated carefully, "is a terrible thing, Aunt Molly."

"It is." Molly sighed. "I'm a little bit worried about Norah. Her color isn't good. When she came I thought it was just the cold, but she's warm now, and still pale. Perhaps it's uneasiness about the baby, or about Sean. I confess, my dear, that things look very black for Sean."

"I believe Norah," said Hilda, "and I believe Sean. Or—oh, Aunt Molly, I *want* to believe Sean. I believe that he did not kill anyone. But—they are very poor, and with the baby coming—if there *was* money in that billfold, Sean might have been tempted to take it. And if he did, and the police find it out…" She gulped. She was not going to break down in tears like Norah. That would help no one. But she was very afraid.

"There is no merit in speculation, Hilda. We must have facts. And I confess I do not see where we are to find them. We do not know for certain that the man was indeed killed rather than dying accidentally in the fire."

"The police must believe that is true, or they would not have arrested Sean."

"We do not even know that, my dear. They might have arrested him for theft. Norah knows only a little, and she is very upset. She may not have told us everything she knows, either because she is afraid or because she did not remember."

"It is true. She is hiding something, I think. But maybe we have asked her enough questions for now? She needs to rest."

"For now, yes. We must do all we can to keep her quiet and happy, though how she can be happy... However, we will talk to her again later. It may help her to talk about it calmly. And we must try to get what facts we can from other sources."

"I have time!" said Hilda. "I have all the time I need! I can go and talk to—"

And there she stopped. Talk to whom?

Hilda had become embroiled, often against her will, in the investigation of several crimes while she worked as housemaid to the Studebakers. She hadn't found it easy. The strict rules governing a servant's life and conduct had drastically limited her freedom. She had, however, had easy access to the vast network of servants and tradesmen who always knew more about the activities of their upper-class employers and customers than those worthies ever suspected.

With her marriage, Hilda's life had changed. Owing to the kindness of Patrick's uncle Dan Malloy, Patrick was making a great deal of money as partner in a successful business. No longer a fireman, struggling to make ends meet, he could afford to buy Hilda anything her heart desired. He and Hilda were now a part of that upper class they used to serve. They lived in a fine house in the best part of town. They had servants of their own.

Uncle Dan, a gregarious Irishman and sometime politician, had seen to it that Patrick met important men in town, and Patrick, who could charm a bird out of a tree, had adapted easily to his new life.

Hilda hadn't fared so well. The wives of those important men remembered Hilda as the maid who had taken their cloaks when they called upon the Studebakers, and they were not prepared now to treat her as an equal. It was all very well, they supposed, for a young Irishman to make his way up the ladder. Men were supposed to be ambitious. But for a servant girl to consider herself a lady—well, times were changing, but the wealthy ladies hoped they weren't changing quite that fast. *Some* standards must be maintained.

So the ladies like Mrs. Elbel called on Hilda only when they wanted her help with a project, and only when prompted by Molly Malloy. If Hilda tried to return their calls, they were "not at home."

The servants and tradesmen with whom she used to be on such easy terms were no better. At some deep level, they felt Hilda had betrayed them. Marry an upstart Irishman who'd come into money! Leave her old friends behind for la-di-da new ones! Well, *they* still had to work for their bread. *They* had no time to waste talking to a fine lady who came to show off her clothes and her jewels and look down on them (or so they interpreted her actions). They had better things to do with their precious free time, thank you very much.

Hilda stopped and looked at Aunt Molly, dismay written across her face. "But—there is no one now—I am alone!"

Molly gripped her hand. "You are *not* alone, Hilda Cavanaugh! It will be harder for you, yes, but you have your family still. And by that I mean, of course, Patrick's family as well."

"They do not like me. Mother Cavanaugh hates me."

"No, Hilda, she does not. I am a mother of sons. I understand what she feels. She fears you. She fears you will take Patrick away from her, shake his religious convictions, change him. You must find a way to show her that his love for you does not change or diminish his love for her, and that your way of practicing your faith will not interfere with his different way. And one path to her trust will be to approach her for help in this matter."

"The last time I tried to do that," Hilda began, but the front door opened and Patrick walked in, with snow on his shoulders but a broad smile on his face and a small package in his hand.

"I thought I'd turn to a snowman, just walkin' from Uncle Dan's carriage to the door!" he exclaimed. "I've brought you a present, darlin' girl." He held out his arms and Hilda ran to them, heedless of the snow.

"Oh, Patrick, I am so glad to see you!" She buried her face in his cold, wet shoulder.

His mood changed immediately to match hers. "Darlin', I'm getting you all wet. Let me take off my coat and then tell me what's wrong. Hello, Aunt Molly. I didn't see you standing there."

"Patrick, dear, come into the parlor. Something very serious has happened, and we need to discuss it."

Hilda hung Patrick's coat and hat and muffler on the elaborate hall rack. Hilda was very proud of that hall rack, with its marble-framed mirror, its shiny brass hooks, its bench seat that opened to store boots and rubbers. Now she scarcely glanced at it, but followed Patrick and Molly into the parlor, where Eileen had lit the gas lamps and built a roaring fire in the grate.

Patrick dropped down on the plush settee with a little grunt of relief and pulled Hilda down next to him. "This is what I was wantin' all the way home in the carriage," he said. "Warmth, comfort, and me darlin' girl beside me. Now, love, tell me."

Already Hilda was less upset. Patrick was here. Things would be all right. "It is Norah," she said, keeping her hand in his. "She is upstairs."

"Not trouble with—she's not—"

"No." Hilda blushed. A forthcoming baby was not a subject she could discuss with her husband. Not yet. "No, she is—in good health, only tired and worried. It is Sean she is worried about, Patrick. He has been arrested, and we fear it may be for murder."

4

The Citizens' Bank, of North Liberty, this county, failed to open its doors this morning.

—South Bend *Tribune*
December 1, 1904

"D IVIL TAKE US!"

"Patrick!" said Hilda and Molly in unison.

"Sorry, darlin'. Sorry, Aunt Molly. But ye're never tellin' me Sean O'Neill killed someone, for I'll not believe it. Sean's the only Irishman I've ever known without a temper. It's a joke in the family. Aunt Molly, you know yourself he'll walk away from a brawl, if he can't get everyone to calm themselves down." In his agitation Patrick dropped Hilda's hand, stood, and began to stride around the room.

"Sit down, Patrick, dear," said Molly. She said it very quietly, but Patrick, looking abashed, sat. "We believe as you do. But you know very well that what we believe in the matter is of little consequence. It is what the police believe that is important, and we do not yet know what they are thinking."

"Well, then, I'm for findin' out! I still have friends—"

"Hush, Patrick," said Molly urgently. "Norah is coming down."

Norah entered the room on Eileen's supporting arm. She was still pale, but composed. She greeted Patrick with a half smile as he rose. "And it's pleased I am to see you, Patrick."

He would have spoken, but Molly got in first. "Norah, dear, we're glad you're feeling better. Now sit, child, and we'll talk of pleasant things until we've had our dinner. Then we will decide how best to solve your problem. Patrick, how was business today?"

Molly had a gift for making a mountain into a molehill, or at least making her family believe that the transformation was possible. Patrick followed her lead. "Slow today. It's only to be expected with the weather what it is. And times are hard. Seems we hear every day about another bank failin'. But Christmas is comin' and things'll pick up. We've got lots of new stock in— Hilda, darlin', there's some fine new dress goods, one in a color they call indigo, kind of a purpley-blue that'd go lovely with your eyes. And you haven't looked at my present I brought you."

"I am not sure," she began in a low tone, with a glance at Norah.

Norah saw the glance. "Open it, Hilda," she said, with an attempt at interest. "I want to see, too."

Hilda was still clutching the small paper-wrapped parcel, so she pulled it open. Lace cascaded into her lap, many yards of exquisite Valenciennes edging. "Ooh!" she said. "Look, Norah, how beautiful! There is enough to share. Let me give you some for—for anything you might be making just now. You are so much better at sewing than I am. You could make something very pretty with this."

Molly decided the time for euphemism had passed. "It will make a beautiful christening robe, Norah. Unless you have one already?"

The shadow lifted from Norah's face for a moment. "I've made the robe. Mrs. Hibberd gave me a piece of white silk she didn't need. But I haven't trimmed it yet." She fingered the lace Hilda had dropped in her lap. "But this is too fine-looking. I can't take such a costly gift."

"There is so much," said Hilda persuasively. "Take what you need, and then we can decide together what is to be done with the rest."

Dinner was announced, and though Norah ate little, she tried to take part in the conversation about clothes and the weather and whatever other common, everyday subjects Molly could think to introduce. Nevertheless, the atmosphere was strained, and everyone was glad when it was over and they retired with coffee to the drawing room.

"Now, Norah, dear," said Molly briskly, "it is time to make

some plans. Hilda and Patrick and I have been thinking about what is best to do, and we have some ideas."

Hilda looked at her blankly. She had, in fact, no ideas at all.

"The first thing is to get Sean home to you. That should be easy to do. I fear we can do nothing tonight, but you will be safe and comfortable here, and he will be safe in the jail, if not comfortable. Tomorrow Mr. Malloy will talk to his lawyer, and to the mayor if necessary, and will pay whatever bail is set. That will make everyone feel better."

"Do you—will it really be that easy?" asked Norah, unbelieving.

"I think so, dear. Without offending your modesty, I think I can say it is perfectly plain to anyone that you need him with you now. And since we know he had nothing to do with the poor man's death, there cannot be any evidence that he did. An upright judge will see that, and will grant him bail."

"But—but the billfold—"

"The billfold may be regarded as evidence of theft, but no more."

Patrick, who had heard none of the details, looked baffled. Hilda sketched out the story for him (in the most optimistic terms, for Norah's sake), but he was very sober when she had finished.

"We need to find out what the police are thinkin'," he said.

"Yes," said Hilda, nodding sharply. "And that is your job. You have friends in the police. I cannot go to talk to the police anymore. The police station is no place for a lady." She looked down at her dark green wool gown with something like loathing. "I cannot talk to servants. I can do *nothing*!"

She stopped at the hurt look on Patrick's face. She had not meant to sound so vehement. She and Patrick had never talked about her new social status, or lack of it. And now, with outsiders present, was no time to talk of it, either. She tried to say with a beseeching look that she was sorry, she hadn't meant to sound discontented, but Patrick wouldn't look at her.

Norah saved the situation. "You can think," she said. "You've always said you had the best brains of any of us. Fair sick I got of yer braggin' about it, but it's maybe true. You've figured yer way out of a lot of pickles, and got others out of 'em, too. I reckon this is a big enough pickle to test them fine brains you claim you've got."

"But I need to ask questions, and talk to people, and—oh!"

"Ye've thought of somethin'," said Norah.

"Yes. Aunt Molly, the boys!"

A smile spread across Molly's face. "The boys. Yes."

"If ye'd care to tell the rest of us what ye're talkin' about," said Patrick plaintively.

Hilda turned to him, her face alight. "Mrs. Elbel came here this afternoon to ask me to help do something for immigrant boys. I did not like her very much—I am sorry, Aunt Molly, but she was not polite—and I was going to say no, but now I will go to her and say yes. Boys get everywhere and know everything. They are like servants—if they are quiet, no one heeds them. Erik will help. The boys will find out things for me, and I will use my brain, and I will solve the problem!"

Patrick looked at Molly. There were so many ifs in Hilda's scheme...but when she believed she could do something, it really was rather remarkable how often the thing got done.

Norah said as much. "I've never known how ye do it, but somehow ye do, more often than not. And if ye can pull it off this time, I'll—I'll name the baby after you!"

Hilda began to laugh. The tension had to be released somehow. "Hilda! A fine name for an Irish girl, I do not think. And what if it is a boy?"

"Then we'll name him Sean. That's Irish for John—for your last name. Your old last name, I mean. It'll please his father, too; he'll think I'm namin' the boy after him. And it'll not be Hilda for a girl. It'll be Fiona."

Hilda frowned.

"Because," said Norah, looking at Hilda's hair, "*Fiona* means fair. And you're the fairest girl I ever knew—and fair the other way, too."

"And that, child, is a compliment worth having," said Aunt Molly. "Norah has said you are fair of hair, and just of mind and heart."

Just for one moment Hilda wanted to hug her friend, hard, but she felt tears in her own eyes and feared they would overflow at any show of sentiment. And then she might make Norah cry, too. So she sniffed, instead. "It is true that I do not like unfairness. But I do not think my family will understand if I tell them a baby named Fiona is named after me. You are fanciful, Norah, like all the Irish. You will be telling me stories about the Little People next."

"Ooh, Hilda, ye make me so mad! Can't even take a compliment seriously! See if I ever pay you another one!"

And they were off, bickering amicably until bedtime.

Aunt Molly left after she had seen Norah tucked into the spare-room bed with a glass of hot milk and a plate of soda crackers in case she woke up hungry. Hilda and Patrick went up to bed, but they were too restless to go to sleep.

"I hope it does not snow tomorrow," said Hilda as she buttoned her long-sleeved nightgown. It was beautifully trimmed with lace, as befitted a bride, but was made of good warm wool flannel. Hilda the Swede knew all about cold winters.

"Why? Do you need to go out?" Shivering, Patrick pulled his nightshirt on over his head and dived into bed.

"Patrick! You know I must go out." She unpinned her coronet braids and began to brush her long blond hair. "I must find Erik and talk to him, and call on Mrs. Elbel and tell her I will work with the boys, and talk to some of Erik's friends, and you—you must talk to the police. And to your fireman friends, too, to learn about the fire and how it started."

"I have to go to work, darlin'."

"Uncle Dan will let you take some time off. Aunt Molly will tell him all about Norah's trouble, and he will understand." She climbed into the big brass bed and pulled the comforter up to her nose.

"That he will. He's a good man, Uncle Dan. But Hilda—"

Patrick propped himself up on one elbow and turned to Hilda. "Do you think Sean really didn't take that money?"

"Oh, Patrick, I want to believe that he did not. But—"

"Yes. That's the trouble, isn't it? I'll never believe Sean killed a man. Never mind that he's my cousin. I've hundreds of cousins, thousands, maybe, and some of 'em would kill if they had to." He was silent, both of them thinking of his cousin Clancy, son of Uncle Dan and Aunt Molly, who had abetted a major crime and been virtually exiled from the family.

"But if some of 'em would, so I know most wouldn't, and Sean's one of the *wouldn't* crowd. Stealin', though, that's another thing. With not much money comin' in and a new mouth to feed soon...and if he did take that money, he's in big trouble, no matter what."

"I know, Patrick. I have thought of all that." She yawned in spite of herself. "That is why, in the morning, we must...we will...if it does not snow..." She turned and nestled her head into Patrick's shoulder. "Tomorrow..."

Patrick stretched his arm around her, kissed the top of her head, and in minutes was asleep himself.

Outside the snow fell, gently, silently.

5

A grievous burthen was thy birth to me.

—William Shakespeare
King Richard III, 1593

THE SCREAM RESOUNDED throughout the house. Hilda sat bolt upright. "Patrick! What is it?"

Patrick, still half-asleep, threw back the covers and shivered in the cold. "Don't know. Nothin' good. You stay here."

Hilda was not about to be left alone. She pulled a robe over her gown and followed him into the hall.

There were more cries, muffled now, more like sobs. They came from the spare room, where Norah slept. "She's maybe cryin' in her sleep," said Patrick.

Struck by sudden apprehension, Hilda put out her hand. "Patrick, let me go in. You summon Eileen—and Mrs. O'Rourke. I t'ink maybe—"

The hallway was pitch dark, but Hilda felt her way to Norah's door, tapped on it, and went in.

The draperies weren't quite closed, and the light reflected from the snow was enough that Hilda could see her friend, sitting up in bed and sobbing.

Hilda went to her. "Norah, you are not to cry! You know Aunt Molly said—"

"It's the baby! It's comin', and I think I'm bleedin', and I'm so scared!"

Hilda's throat was suddenly dry, but she kept her head. She had been present at the birth of her younger siblings, and knew something about the matter. "We need light," she said firmly.

"Don't leave me!"

"Of course not!" Hilda went to the window and pulled the

draperies open wide. She found the matches and lit the gas fixture on the wall. "Now let us see."

She pulled the covers back and inspected the bed. "There is almost no blood," she said. "You are all right."

"But I felt somethin' gush out of me—"

"Yes. It is normal. It means the baby is on the way. We must send for the doctor."

Norah lay back down and moaned.

"Is the pain bad?"

"No. Just like a bad backache, most of the time. But it's too soon, Hilda! The doctor said another two weeks—"

"Doctors do not always know everything, Norah—as you should know, with all your brothers and sisters. Babies come when they will." Hilda wished fervently that this one hadn't decided to come just now, but apparently it had, and they must all cope.

Mrs. O'Rourke bustled in, followed by Eileen, wide-eyed.

"Now, then, Miss Norah, let's see what we have here. Excuse me, madam." The cook, plainly in her element, elbowed Hilda aside and took charge. She prodded Norah's swollen belly and examined her.

"I will tell Patrick to phone for the doctor," said Hilda.

"There's no need for that just yet, madam," said Mrs. O'Rourke with authority, "if you don't mind my sayin' so. I've had twelve of me own, and helped with as many more, and this one's not comin' yet awhile."

"But it is maybe two weeks early, and an early baby—" Hilda broke off, not wanting to alarm Norah.

"'Tis a fine big baby, ready for the world," said Mrs. O'Rourke. "And the way that snow's comin' down, the doctor'd not thank you for callin' him out of his bed just yet. You go and get some sleep, madam. I can tend to things here. I'll let you know when it's time. Eileen, you go down and start boilin' water."

Hilda hesitated. "Norah, will you be all right?"

Norah had been calmed by Mrs. O'Rourke's confidence. She nodded. "I'm sorry I woke everybody up in the middle of the night, but—"

"Now, you can't be expected to know, not when it's your first," said the cook comfortingly. "You rest, Miss Norah. You'll be workin' hard enough in a few hours."

Hilda squeezed Norah's hand and left her to the cook's ministrations.

Patrick was hovering in the hall outside. "It's the baby, isn't it? Is it bad? Will she be all right? Should we send for her mother?"

"Cook says she will do well, and the baby will not come for some time. Patrick, I want some coffee."

They went to the kitchen, where Eileen was busy putting large pots of water on to boil. "What's that for?" Patrick asked.

"I do not know," Hilda admitted, "but one boils water, always, when a baby is coming. Eileen, leave some space on the range for a coffee pot, please."

She busied herself with grinding coffee and cracking an egg, and then she and Patrick were glad to sit down in the warm kitchen. Outside the snow lay thick on the window sills, but it seemed to have stopped falling.

"I wonder if someone has told Mrs. Murphy about Sean's arrest."

"Sure to've done," said Patrick. "News travels fast in an Irish family."

"Will she know that Norah came here?"

Patrick wasn't so sure about that. "Maybe not, unless Norah said where she was goin' when she left her house."

"We should have sent word, Patrick! *Herre Gud*, but I never thought. If Mrs. Murphy knows, she will be angry, maybe, that Norah came to me instead of to her. And if she does not know, she will be worried. I think we had better ask Mr. O'Rourke to go and get her."

"And I think you're right. I'll see to it as soon as I've had some coffee. It smells good, darlin', for all I grew up with tea."

After Patrick had dispatched a none-too-pleased coachman out into the snow, he came back inside and fell asleep on the settee. Hilda was too restless to sleep, and she needed in any case to be awake to greet Mrs. Murphy when she arrived. She prowled around the parlor, picked up a book and put it down, and built up the fire.

There was no noise from upstairs. Evidently Mrs. O'Rourke was right, and the urgent part of the business was yet to come. Hilda paced, her thoughts a tangled web of worries. Worry for Norah and her baby. Worry about Sean. Worry on her own account, her uncertainties, her inability to fit into her new position...

The doorbell rang and Hilda ran to answer it. The woman at the door looked much as Hilda's mother used to look back in Sweden: tattered, worn from work, but proud. Her black shawl was darned, but clean. Her boots were neatly polished, if wet with snow, but her hair was roughly and hastily pinned up. Her face bore an expression compounded of worry, anger, and fear.

"Mrs. Murphy, come in and be warm. Let me take your shawl. Norah is fine. She is asleep, I think maybe."

"You never left her alone!" There was hostility in her voice.

"No! My—Mrs. O'Rourke and Eileen O'Hara are with her. Mrs. O'Rourke has had many children and is capable, I think. You will want to go straight up to Norah?"

Mrs. Murphy nodded stiffly, and Hilda led the way.

"I am sorry we did not let you know that she was here," said Hilda. The remark met a wall of silence. Hilda tried again. "I think she came to me without thinking, because I have investigated—" No, it wasn't wise to mention crime. Mrs. Murphy might think that Hilda believed Sean to be guilty. "Because she and I have found out—"

"You've led my daughter into trouble before now, with your pryin' into what's no business of a good girl! And now she comes runnin' to you instead of her mother!"

"Mrs. Murphy, I cannot help where she runs! It is not fair that you—"

The door to the spare room opened and Mrs. O'Rourke stepped into the hall, hands on hips. "And I'd be thankin' you both not to shout!" she said in a furious whisper. "Savin' your presence, madam. I've just got her to sleep, and she needs the rest. Maureen, you can come in, but mind you don't wake her. She'll wake soon enough when the babe gets impatient."

Mrs. Murphy went in, Mrs. O'Rourke shut the door, and Hilda, feeling thoroughly snubbed, went down to the kitchen to make a pot of tea. She was trying hard not to lose her temper. Mrs. Murphy was frightened and upset. Her rudeness was understandable. And Mrs. O'Rourke—well, she was a part of Mrs. Murphy's world. Plainly they knew each other well.

They both belonged to the class, to the world Hilda had left forever.

She took an obscure pleasure in the menial duty of tea-making.

When she had delivered it upstairs, where it was received with thanks but scant ceremony, she went back down to the parlor and collapsed into a chair with a long sigh.

"Mmm?" said Patrick, half-waking. "Norah's ma get here?"

"She is upstairs. I am very tired."

"Why don't ye get back to bed, darlin'? I can stay here, in case somebody needs somethin'."

"I think first I should phone Aunt Molly. Or perhaps you should. It is nearly morning, and it is important for Sean to get out of jail without delay. Norah needs him."

Patrick sat up. "Darlin' girl, nothin's goin' to happen about that till a judge is awake, and maybe a lawyer, maybe the mayor. Even Uncle Dan can't make 'em hurry up in the middle of the night. It's not yet gone five. You go to sleep and let me do the worryin' for a bit. Here, you're not cryin'?"

Hilda dashed the tears from her cheeks. "It is—you are—I do not know why I am crying, but I will go to bed." Hilda dared not say that she was crying out of sheer relief. She would break down completely if she talked about the long years before her marriage, when she had had no one to take charge, to look after her, give her respite. For years she had worked hard, carried her own burdens and often those of others. Now there was Patrick. Patrick, who would shoulder the load when it was too much for her, who would tell her what to do when she was floundering.

He kissed her, then pushed her toward the stairs. "Off with ye, then."

Of course, she thought as she climbed the stairs, he often told her what to do when she neither needed nor wanted to be told. Then they would argue, and she would do what she wanted. Never yet had she admitted that he was sometimes right.

There was no sound from the guest room save for faint snores. Mrs. O'Rourke must have fallen asleep, Hilda assumed. It appeared that all was well so far.

Weary to the bone, and secure knowing that Patrick was ready for an emergency, Hilda tumbled into bed and was instantly asleep.

∽

"Darlin' girl, it's sorry I am to wake you, but there's things I think you'll maybe want to do."

Hilda opened her eyes and looked blearily at Patrick. Just for a moment, she had no idea where she was, who she was, who this man was. She had been dreaming of a pleasant summer day. Why was the room so gray and cold?

"I brought coffee." Patrick brought it close to her nose, and the mists began to clear.

"I did not—I was—what time is it?" She sat up and reached for the cup.

"Gone nine. You haven't slept near enough, but things are movin' and I need to be off."

"Off? Where?"

"To talk to me friends about Sean. And speakin' of Sean—he's here."

Awareness came flooding back, and Hilda groaned. "Sean. The police. Norah—the baby! How are they?"

Patrick grimaced. "Nobody'll tell me anything, just that 'they're doin' fine,' but I reckon nothing much has happened yet. Sean went in to see Norah, but they only let him stay for a minute."

"Of course! It is not proper for men to be there when a baby is coming! Patrick, this is good coffee, but I must get up." She handed him the coffee cup and pushed back the covers. "Brrr!"

Patrick handed her her robe. "I'm sorry there's no fire, but Eileen's been busy with Norah, and I've been busy with Sean."

"It does not matter. I am a Swede. I will dress quickly and come down. And do not let Sean leave before I can see him!"

"No chance of that. He's hanging about chewin' his finger-nails and lookin' like a sick cow," said Patrick with the casual rudeness of a relative. "I'll go and see to the parlor fire, and then I'm off."

Hilda found Sean in the kitchen, and if he didn't look exactly like a sick cow, there was a certain resemblance. The moment he saw Hilda, he rushed to her. "Is there any news? What's happening?"

"Nothing exciting is yet happening, if you mean Norah. Sit down, Sean. I want to talk to you."

He sat.

"How much money did you steal, Sean?" She had decided shock was the best approach.

He looked dully at her. "Steal? What do you mean?"

"From the billfold."

"The—oh. It was empty. I've told everyone, over and over. Hilda, is she going to be all right? It's taking a long time."

Hilda decided he was either the world's best liar, or too tired and frazzled to tell anything but the truth. On the whole, she believed him, and she felt great relief. "Good. I did not think you would steal, but I know times are hard. And do not worry. It is normal for a first baby to take a long time. Now, what would you like for breakfast?"

He looked at her as if he had forgotten what "breakfast" meant, but Hilda was hungry, so she fried eggs and made toast. She wasn't the world's best cook, but Mrs. O'Rourke was other-wise occupied. The meal was edible. Sean ate without noticing.

"D'ye think I could go up and see her, just for a minute?"

"No. They will tell us when it is time to send for the doctor. Sean, I want you to tell me exactly what happened, that day at the fire."

"The police've asked me that, fifty times anyway. There's nothin' to tell. We was workin', and we saw the fire, and went to see what it was and if we could stop it. We couldn't, so we watched it burn for a while, and then when the fire brigade came we went to our supper, and high time, too. And I saw the billfold lyin' on the ground and picked it up, thinkin' it belonged to somebody in our gang, or maybe one of the firemen. So I asked around, and it didn't, and I took it home 'cause it was too nice to throw away. And that's all."

"Where exactly did you find it?"

"On the ground. I don't know."

"Who told the police you had it?"

"How would I know that? Are you sure she's all right?"

Hilda gave it up. Perhaps when Norah's ordeal was over, she could get some sense out of Sean, but meanwhile all his attention was focused on that room upstairs. "Come into the parlor if you have finished eating. It is more comfortable. I will go up and ask about Norah."

Norah was awake and uncomfortable, but not yet in severe pain. Mrs. O'Rourke and Mrs. Murphy were getting along famously, telling each other stories of babies over the years, difficult labors, easy labors—"just popped out like a little greased pig, bless his heart"—unexpected twins. Hilda wasn't sure some of the stories were encouraging for Norah just now, but she didn't dare say anything. This might be a room in her own house, but right now it was ruled by two other women. Little Eileen was sent on one errand after another, many of them unnecessary, to Hilda's way of thinking. She suspected the cook was greatly enjoying her time of glory.

Hilda stole away, resigned to her subordinate role, and told Sean all was well. Then she went to the telephone.

"Aunt Molly? It is Hilda. Can you come? I must talk to you, and I cannot leave here."

Molly wasted no words. "I'll be there in a wink," she said, and hung up the phone.

Of all the animals, the boy is the most unmanageable.

—Plato, *The Republic*
4th century B.C.

6

S O YOU SEE," said Hilda, "I do not know what to do. Sean can tell me nothing—except that he did not steal any money. I believe him. He is too *förvirrad* to tell a lie." She leaned forward from her seat on the settee and waved her hands in the air in frustration. "I do not know the word in English! Thinking badly, anxious—"

"'Befuddled' is the word you want, perhaps," said Molly, smiling. "And just what one would expect from a young man about to become a father for the first time, let alone his other troubles. I'm glad you believe him innocent. That's my own thinking, too. I don't suppose Patrick has had time to find out anything from the police."

"He left just a little time ago. He is going to talk to firemen, too. But I want to know—how did you get Sean out of the jail so quickly?"

Molly laughed. "'Twasn't me did it. Patrick phoned us early to say the baby was on the way, so Mr. Malloy phoned the mayor. Got him out of bed, too. He phoned a friendly judge, and Mr. Malloy paid the bail, and there we are. Where is he, by the way?"

"In the kitchen, I think. They will not allow him upstairs, and he will not sit still. I am glad he is free, but it has not helped very much," said Hilda with a frown. "They will not let him see Norah, and he will not talk to me."

"But Norah knows he's here, and that does her good. Now, what is it you need of me?"

"I do not know what to do next! I promised Norah I would

help her, but I have done nothing, and I must stay here in the house because Norah might need me."

"My dear child! What Norah needs now is women experienced in childbirth, and she has them. Bridget O'Rourke is an excellent woman, and so is Norah's mother, even if she is distracted with worry. You could help Norah far more by going out and looking into Sean's dilemma."

Hilda tucked that new word away in her head, resolving to look it up when she had the chance.

"What about your plan of talking to the boys?" Molly went on. "The snow has stopped. It's beginning to melt, in fact. You should be able to get about." She raised a hand as Hilda opened her mouth. "And if you're still worried about Norah, I can stay here if you like. She's in capable hands, but I could look in on her from time to time, and fetch the doctor when he's needed. And calm Sean down a bit—if I can."

Hilda thought about that. "You might have to cook a meal. I think Mrs. O'Rourke will not leave Norah."

"I've cooked many a meal in my time, child. I've not forgotten how, nor have I got so grand I can't turn a hand to help when it's needed."

"Then I can—or wait. I have forgotten what day it is. So much has happened."

"Friday. December second."

"Then Erik will be in school. But he will be free at dinnertime—what you call lunch-time—and I can talk to him then. He will know which boys might be talking about this. And meanwhile I can go and talk to the boys at the Oliver Hotel. They hear people talk. Thank you, Aunt Molly!"

Hilda hugged Molly and went to put on some old clothes, a cloak her mother had made for her years ago, and her rubber overshoes. For it would never do to call on bellboys in fine clothes and riding in a carriage. She would dress like Hilda Johansson, the servant, and she would walk on her own two feet.

The weather was changing. There was a softness in the air, a heaviness that meant rain soon. The snow had changed to slush underfoot, and dirty gray slush at that, and dead brown oak leaves, pulled off the trees by the weight of the snow, lay in sodden piles. One fell off as Hilda passed under a tree and slid down her neck.

New snow, Hilda had always thought, was beautiful. Old snow, especially in a city, was nothing but a nuisance. As she started to cross Colfax Avenue (named after the South Bend resident and one-time Vice President of the United States, the late Schuyler Colfax), a carriage passed close by her. The horses' hooves splashed slush, and worse, up onto her skirt. Hilda pursed her lips in disgust, but she hadn't been wet through, and the grime would contribute to the impression she wished to convey.

Hilda knew several of the bellboys well. One named Andy—Hilda had never heard his surname—was a special friend of Erik's. Andy was often to be found outside the hotel sweeping the sidewalk or shoveling a path or helping a guest into or out of a carriage. Today, though, he was nowhere to be seen.

Hilda paused. Her old clothes suddenly seemed like not such a good idea, particularly now that they were splashed with muck. She had no wish to go into South Bend's most elegant hotel smelling like a stable-hand. She approached the front door and stopped to peer through the glass panes.

The door opened. "Yes, miss?" said a uniformed doorman. He was new since the last time Hilda had called at the hotel, and he obviously didn't know her. His tone was just this side of rude. He reminded Hilda of every condescending butler she had ever known. She drew herself up and glared at the man.

"I am Mrs. Cavanaugh," she said, her accent as American as she could make it. "I wish to speak to one of your bellboys—Andy, I believe is his name. I would rather not come inside, since a bad-mannered coachman allowed his horses to ruin my skirt a moment ago."

Her manner caused the doorman to thaw a degree or two. "I'm sorry, miss—madam. We could have it cleaned for you if you are a guest of the hotel."

"It is no matter. I wore my oldest clothes because of the weather. And I am not a guest of the hotel. I live only a few blocks away." She nodded her head toward the west, in the direction of the best neighborhood in town, at which the doorman's eyebrows rose. "I will come in only as far as the bellboys' office, if you will be good enough to send for Andy."

If the doorman shook his head at this eccentric young woman, he did it out of her sight. She looked like a beggar, but talked like a lady. Why a lady would want to talk privately to a bellboy he couldn't imagine, but if she lived in that neighborhood, she was a person to be treated courteously. He nodded gravely and showed Hilda into the tiny room the bellboys called their office.

It was lined with hooks where the boys hung their jackets and caps. They were not allowed to wear the jackets over their uniforms, even when they were assisting guests outside, because the jackets were often shabby. The boys made little money, unless guests were uncommonly generous with tips, and even then almost all the earnings went to help their families. From the looks of the garments hanging on the hooks, Hilda thought the families must be in need of a good deal of help. The poor, lately, were even poorer than usual—and with Christmas coming.

"Oh," said Andy in surprise when he skidded into the room after a few minutes, natty in his uniform with its round hat. "It's you, Miss Hilda. His Nibs said as there was a lady to see me, name of Cavanaugh."

"My name is Cavanaugh now, Andy," Hilda reminded him with a smile. "Surely Erik told you I am married."

"Oh. Yes, miss—madam. Sorry, madam. I forgot."

"'Miss' will be best, Andy. I am—I am in *disguise*." She whispered the last word conspiratorially.

Andy opened his eyes wide. "Are you on somebody's trail, miss?"

"In a way. It is difficult, because I do not know very much yet. Do you remember the barn fire a few weeks ago, Andy? In early November, it was, south of town."

The boy screwed up his face in concentration. "I don't think so, miss. Only—was that the one where somebody burned to death?"

"It was. A hired man named Jenkins."

"Burned alive! That'd be a terrible way to die," said Andy soberly. "Almost anything'd be better'n that."

"He maybe did not know what was happening to him," said Hilda gently. "Patrick says when people die in a fire, they breathe in the smoke first and it makes them unconscious. So do not worry too much. But have you heard anyone talking about the fire or the man who was killed?"

"Just the newsboys. They say—I mean the paper says—it was maybe a murder. Miss Hilda! Is that what you're tryin' to find out about?"

"Yes, but do not talk so loud!"

"Sorry, miss. But nobody can't hardly hear what we say in here. So you want me to ask around, like I did before?"

Andy and the other bellboys had gathered information for Hilda once before, very successfully.

Hilda smiled. "You can read, can you not?"

Andy drew himself up. " 'Course I can read! I'm not stupid!"

"I know that you are smart," said Hilda a shade reprovingly. "But you went to school for only a little time, before your father—had his troubles." Hilda had heard from Erik about Andy's father. Out of work, the man had a year or two ago taken to drink and gambling, nearly destroying the family before a job pulled him out of his despondency. Andy's wages, meager as they were, had helped keep the family afloat. Hilda had a good deal of respect for Andy. "Is he doing better now?"

"Yes, miss." Andy didn't sound too sure. "Papa's got a pretty good job, but there's a lot of men losin' their jobs these days, so we never know... but anyway, see, I *like* to read. So I taught myself, sort of. People leave magazines around, see, and newspapers, and when things are slow I read 'em. And there's a dictionary in the lounge, so if I don't know a word I look it up. I can read 'most anything!"

"Have you ever read stories about a man, a detective, named Sherlock Holmes?"

"Oh, *yes*, miss! They're really good. Kind of hard to read, some of them, and maybe not as good as Sexton Blake, but real exciting! I reckon I could figger things out just as good as them if I really tried."

"I think you could, too, Andy. That is why I want you and your friends to be my Baker Street Irregulars."

Andy's face lit up. "Just like in the stories! Yes, *ma'am*! Are you going to pay us a shilling each for an errand? What's a shilling, anyway?"

"Money in England. I do not know how much. Yes, I will give you money. Five cents every time you tell me something useful, and ten cents if you must run an errand."

"Ooh! I can maybe buy some stuff for my little brothers and my sisters, for Christmas! I'm your man, all right. Whatcha want us to do?"

"Listen and look. Report back everything you hear about the fire. I want to know when it started, how it started, who was there at the time—everything you can learn. And if someone seems to know something, see if you can ask them a few questions. But you must not—"

"I know, miss. Not make 'em suspicious, not give anything away—"

"And especially do not put yourself in danger, yourself or the other boys."

"I know, miss," Andy repeated. "And I've got an idea. We all know some of the boys workin' in the big houses. Is it okay if we ask them to be on the lookout, too?"

"If you think they can be trusted not to—" Hilda tried to remember a phrase she had learned recently "—to release the cat from the sack."

Andy giggled. "Let the cat out o' the bag, I reckon you mean, miss. Don't worry. We'll be careful."

"Good."

A bell rang shrilly in the small room. Andy jumped up. "I gotta go, miss."

"Just one other thing, Andy." She glanced again at the thin, patched jackets hanging on the wall and made up her mind.

"How would you and the other boys like to go to a party? A Christmas party, with presents?"

"For real, miss?" The boy looked skeptical.

"For real. I promise."

"I reckon we'd like that fine. I ain't never been to a party."

"I *have* never been, Andy." The bell shrilled again. "Go, then, and I will be back soon to tell you all about it, and to collect your information."

Andy saluted and ran off, and Hilda was left to wonder what she had gotten herself into. A Christmas party! For she did not know how many boys! And she had promised Andy, who had known far too many broken promises in his short life.

Oh! She could make it a project for the Boys' Club!

Of course the Boys' Club did not yet exist, but Hilda refused to worry about that. She would go to—no, she would telephone to Mrs. Elbel and agree to work with her, and then mention a Christmas party. It was the kind of thing wealthy ladies liked to do, give things to the poor. Especially at Christmas time, the wealthy began to think about charity. It was a pity, in Hilda's opinion, that they did not think more about the poor at other times of the year. Of course, it wasn't nice to think about starving children, about women dying of overwork, about men driven to drink, to crime, even to suicide by sheer despair. No. Much more pleasant to plan a party and play Lady Bountiful and then go back to one's own comfortable home. Well, she, Hilda, would see to it that the club was not allowed to die once Christmas was over.

Boys like Andy and hundreds of others shouldn't have to work. They should go to school. Many of them, like Andy, were smart and hard-working. They deserved a chance to make something of themselves, and she, Hilda Johansson Cavanaugh, intended to help see that they got it. There was little she could do by herself, even now that she had some money at her disposal, but with the help of the wealthy and influential ladies of the town, who knew what they might accomplish?

She had read through the years in those forbidden newspapers about boys' clubs in other cities, and of a place in Chicago called Hull House, where poor women and their children were helped, but not with handouts. The women were taught to make the most of what they had, were taught useful trades, how to look after their children properly, how to help themselves. And the women who ran Hull House were mostly wealthy, but they lived there, in a terrible neighborhood, helping to make it better for everyone.

And, Hilda thought she remembered, they had founded a boys' club. If she could find out how they had done it, she might be able to use some of the ideas.

Full of plans, she hurried home to change her filthy skirt and go about her next duties.

7

A baby is an inestimable blessing and bother.

—Mark Twain
letter to Annie Webster, 1876

W HEN SHE WALKED in the door, Hilda encountered
first a heart-rending scream and then a pale,
trembling, desperate young man who rushed to
her and clutched at her arm.

"Hilda!" Sean cried. "Do somethin'! She's dyin', Norah's
dyin', and they won't let me go to her."

"Do not be silly!" Hilda snapped, unnerved herself. "She is
not dying. She is having a baby. Here." She reached in her pocket
for her purse. "Here is a dollar. Go out and buy Norah the most
flowers you can get for that. It will be a gift for her when the baby
is born. Go!"

She pushed him out the door, closed it on his protests, and
sighed with relief. That disposed of Sean, for a time at least. The
nearest florist was only a few blocks away, but they didn't have a
big selection. Sean would probably have to go all the way to the
best florist in town, South Bend Floral, which was at least two
miles south. If the snow had still been falling, Hilda would have
taken pity on him and sent him in the carriage. On this warmish
day, though, the walk would do him good and keep him out of
the house for hours.

There had been no more screams from upstairs. Hilda ran
up the stairs and tapped at the bedroom door. "Aunt Molly? Mrs.
O'Rourke? It is me, Hilda. How is Norah?"

The door opened and Molly slipped out. "Norah's doing well
enough. She's a bit run down, I think, but she'll be fine. Don't
worry too much about the screams. She's suffering more from
fear than pain at this stage. A person doesn't know what to expect
with the first one. After that—well, I wouldn't say you get used

to it, but at least you *know*. It looks like the baby may take its own sweet time. Not in any rush to greet the world, this one. We'll send for the doctor when things start hurrying up a bit. Sean's been at us to send for him right away. Driving us all distracted, he is, scared Norah's going to die. Silly boy."

Hilda nodded. "I have sent him away. To buy flowers for Norah, I said, but really only to make him leave."

"Good for you. Men are nothing but a nuisance at a time like this. Can't stand knowing the result of what they've done," Molly added tartly. "Take their own pleasure and never think of the pain later for their poor wives."

Hilda felt herself blush. She wasn't yet used to frank talk about the marriage bed. "May I go in and see her?"

"Of course, my dear. It'll do her good. Take her mind off the pain and all her other worries, poor child."

Norah was lying in bed, flushed, her hair disordered, but reasonably comfortable for the moment. Mrs. O'Rourke rather grudgingly gave up the chair next to the bed. Hilda sat down and asked, "It is not too bad, *ja*? Aunt Molly says it may be a long time yet."

"That's what they say," Norah said with a grimace. "Some of the pains are bad, but not comin' real often yet. Hilda, is Sean all right? He was in an awful state earlier."

"I have sent him on an errand to give him something to do. He is worried about you, but Aunt Molly says there is no need. She says you are doing well."

"It's not her that's hurtin', is it?" Norah's face changed. She grabbed Hilda's hand and squeezed hard, her lips compressed and eyes tight shut. "That one wasn't so awful," she said, panting, when it was over.

Mrs. O'Rourke bustled over and wiped Norah's forehead. "Now, dearie, I've said over and over, you're not to hold your breath when the pains come. Breathe hard, scream if you want to, but holdin' your breath don't do no good."

"I'll try to remember. Hilda, what are you doing to get Sean out of trouble?"

"You should not think about that now."

"Hilda!" Norah's voice made it clear she would not put up with being soothed.

"Oh, very well. I talked to one of the boys. He has heard nothing useful about the fire, but he will ask the other boys, and they will all listen and report back."

"Boys! What good will they do?"

"Norah, you know they are good for hearing things. They are like servants. No one heeds them. People talk in front of them and forget they are there. They will hear useful things and report back to me."

"And how do they know what's useful and what isn't?" Norah tossed restlessly on the bed.

"Maybe they will not, but I will. I will take what they tell me and put it together and make a picture. I can do that, Norah. You know I can. I have done it before."

"Things were different before."

"Yes. It is maybe harder now. But easier, too, because I have more time, and no butler telling me what to do."

Norah pursed her lips. "Regular queen bee you are, now." She might have pursued that theme had she not been seized with another contraction, a bad one this time.

When it was over, Hilda stood up, flexing her hand behind her back to make sure Norah hadn't broken a bone with her grip. "I will go now, Norah, to talk to other people. Do not worry. It is not good for the baby. Sean will be all right."

That was, she thought as she left the room, the second rash promise she had made in one morning.

She found Molly in the kitchen preparing a meal, assisted by Eileen. "Yer aunt's teachin' me to cook, ma'am," said the maid with a shy smile. "She says a good cook's worth her weight in gold, an' I could get a job anywhere."

"What? You want to leave me so soon?" said Hilda mildly, and then, as Eileen looked distressed, "I was making a joke. I am perhaps not very good at jokes in English. I want you to do whatever will be best for you, Eileen. I hope you will learn as much as you can, but of books also." For in the evenings Hilda usually sat down with Eileen and helped her improve her reading and writing. "I hope maybe you will not have to be a servant all your life."

"It's not so bad, miss, not workin' for you it isn't. And Mrs. Malloy's that nice a lady, she might be me own mother."

"She is a wonderful woman," said Hilda warmly. "And she must be a good cook, for something smells delicious."

"It's only potato soup," said Molly. "Quick to make, and simple, but warming on a winter day. And there's ham, and cabbage, and some beans Mrs. O'Rourke put up. I haven't time to make a cake, but there's preserved peaches and cream, and I found some ginger cookies in the jar. It'll all be ready when Patrick comes home for his lunch."

"And I'm to cook the cabbage," said Eileen. "Mrs. Malloy told me just how to cut it up and cook it, and all. And I helped with the soup."

"Oh, Aunt Molly, I am so glad you are here! This I could never, never do!"

"Then it's time you learned," said Molly firmly. "Every woman should know how to put together a simple meal, no matter how many servants she has. When this crisis is over, dear, I shall teach you to cook, along with Eileen."

Hilda laughed for the first time that day. "Mistress and maid learning together! America is a peculiar country, but very interesting. Aunt Molly, I came to find you because I wonder, do you know if Mrs. Elbel is on the telephone? Because I need to talk to her. I have decided to do as she has asked and help with the Boys' Club."

Molly looked slightly startled. "I'm very glad, dear, but surely it will wait for a little until things are more settled?"

"No, it cannot wait because I—I have done something foolish. I have promised the boys a Christmas party. And there will be many of them, maybe, and I will need much help—and so you see—"

Molly saw. "Child, you do have a talent for getting yourself in a pickle." She glanced at the kitchen clock. "This isn't a usual time for making telephone calls."

"I know, but I will be busy the rest of the day. I must go and see Erik when he is at lunch, and talk to him, and then this afternoon there are other people to see. Oh, and I may be late for dinner—lunch, I mean."

"Don't worry about that, but with everything else on your list for today, would you like me to call Mrs. Elbel for you?"

"No." Hilda set her chin. "I must learn to do these things myself."

"You're right about that, child. Very well. The number at the Elbels' is six-three-four. They're on the Bell system. Mind you don't let that butler of theirs intimidate you."

Hilda quailed inwardly at the word *butler*, but her Swedish stubbornness prevailed. "I will not. I do not have to obey butlers ever again!"

She went to the front hall, lifted the earpiece of the instrument on the wall, and firmly turned the crank. "Bell six-three-four, please," she told the operator, and waited while crackles and pops sounded in her ear. Finally a male voice with an English accent said, "Bell six-three-four, the Elbel residence."

"This is Mrs. Cavanaugh calling. I wish to speak to Mrs. Elbel."

There was a moment of silence, or rather telephone noise. Then the butler, having registered his disapproval of a call at that hour, spoke the usual formula in somewhat acid tones: "I shall ascertain whether she is at home, madam."

Madam. A butler, however reluctantly, had called her madam. And he undoubtedly knew who Mrs. Cavanaugh used to be. Hilda was conscious of a little thrill of pleasure.

There was a long wait, during which the operator inquired whether the call was completed. Hilda had time to get nervous again before Mrs. Elbel came on the line. "Mrs. Cavanaugh!" She, too, registered surprise. "I hope nothing is wrong."

Hilda took a deep breath. "No, Mrs. Elbel. I am sorry to telephone so early, but I will be out the rest of the day, and I did not want to wait to tell you that I think your idea for the Boys' Club is a very good one, and I would like to help you form it."

"Oh! Oh, good. I don't know that there's all that much of a hurry about it, but I'm delighted that you—"

"And I wondered," Hilda interrupted, "if you had thought of anything we might do for the boys for Christmas. It will be here so soon, and so many of these boys are from very poor families. Do you think it would be possible to do something to make the season happier for them?"

"I do hope you're not thinking of giving them money! They would have no idea of how to spend it."

Hilda gritted her teeth, thinking of Andy's wish to buy presents for his family. Not know how to spend it, indeed! Did she think they were all selfish louts? "No, that was not my idea. I do not really know—you have more experience in arranging these things—yoost something festive we might do..." The Swedish accent this time was not an accident. She wanted to make Mrs. Elbel feel superior. She emphasized her almost-lost sing-song cadences as she said, "In our village in Sweden there used to be a gathering, at the church, for all the children. But I do not know what would be the custom here." Had the hint been broad enough? Too broad?

"Hmm. Let me see. Perhaps—yes, a party would be just the thing! Nothing elaborate, of course, we don't have time to organize such a thing, but a simple gathering, with some small gifts and a bit of food—it will take a great deal of work, of course..."

"Oh, Mrs. Elbel, that would be yoost the t'ing. What a beautiful idea! I will be pleased to do much of the work. But we will need money. How will we buy presents and food?"

"That's no problem. I know many women who will be happy to contribute. But this is a busy time of year. I'm very glad you agreed to do some of the work. Now, Mrs. Cavanaugh, I can send word to several women to have a planning meeting. It had better be early next week; we haven't any too much time. Can you meet with us on Monday at three o'clock?"

"I will be happy to do that. At your house?" Hilda knew

she should, at this point, offer her own house, but with a mother and probably, by that time, a baby upstairs and an accused man downstairs—no, not a good idea.

"Yes—no, that won't do. I'm having a dinner party that night and the florists will be here. I'm sure Mrs. Studebaker won't mind having us, for I know she wants to be a part of this. We'll meet at Tippecanoe Place, unless I let you know otherwise."

It was the last thing Hilda wanted. Going back to the house where she had been a servant and where her sister Elsa worked even now, back to the butler who had tyrannized her, the family she had served in cap and apron. She was very fond of the wid-owed Mrs. Clement Studebaker, now usually called Mrs. Clem, but her daughter-in-law, Mrs. George Studebaker, was another story. Hilda swallowed and said the only possible thing. "That will be very nice. Thank you, Mrs. Elbel. Your Christmas party is a very good idea."

"Our Christmas party, my dear," said Mrs. Elbel graciously. "We will all work together, I'm sure. I will see you on Monday. Good-bye."

Hilda's knees were shaking as she hung the receiver back on the hook. But she had done it—and Mrs. Elbel was convinced it was her own idea.

We frisk away like school-boys…
to joy an' play.

—Robert Burns
Epistle to James Smith, 1786

8

ILDA HAD TO HURRY to Erik's school if she was to see him before he went off who-knew-where with his friends. They sometimes went downtown to buy candy, if one of them was in funds, and were late getting back in the afternoon. Erik liked school, but he also liked playing with his friends, and was sadly apt to lose track of time.

Hilda wanted, if possible, to talk to his friends, too. Many of them were children of comfortable homes, since most of the boys Erik's age who came from poor families had already left school, or had never started. Had everyone else in Mama's household not been working, and had Mama not set such great store by education, Erik would not be in school still, either. At any rate, Hilda decided it was safe to use the carriage. Erik wouldn't mind either way, and very few of his friends would be intimidated. And Colfax School was far to walk, especially in slush.

In cold weather the children ate their lunches inside the schoolrooms, if they wished, before going outside to work off a little steam before afternoon classes. Hilda was relieved, when Mr. O'Rourke drew the carriage to a stop, to find no one yet in the schoolyard. She jumped down and strode through the impressive stone archway into the school.

Though she would never have admitted it to Erik, Hilda was a little in awe of his school. It was so big, rising three stories above the spacious basement, which was also used for various activities. The twelve classrooms were large and well lit with tall windows, and the entire third floor was a beautiful auditorium used for concerts and pageants. Erik was excited about the Christmas pageant that was to be presented in three weeks, in which he and two other Swedish boys were to sing a special Swedish *jul* song.

Hilda thought about her schooling in Sweden. There was a small school in the village, but it was too far away for farm children, and too expensive, so Hilda had learned at home with Mama and the other children. They were taught to read out of the family Bible, to do simple arithmetic, painstakingly to write Swedish in a clear, legible hand. Everything else she had taught herself, from the very few books the family owned—a history of Sweden, a book of sermons, an atlas—and in America from newspapers and the vast resources of the Public Library, once she had learned English. How differently Erik was being educated, and Birgit, the youngest girl, now in the High School. This magnificent building, built just for the purpose of helping children learn, was to Hilda one of the miracles of America.

The classrooms were noisy with talk and the pent-up energy of a morning of enforced quiet. Hilda stood for a moment in the square central hall, listening to the shrill voices of the youngest children. The kindergartners and the lower two grades were housed on the first floor, since short legs found the long flight of stairs wearisome. Older children were upstairs, and the oldest of all, the seventh graders, were privileged to use the finest classroom, the one at the front of the school with the fine oriel window. Erik had been quite boringly proud of that window when he first entered seventh grade in September. Hilda smiled, remembering, and climbed the stairs.

Just as she reached the second floor, the big bell in the schoolyard started ringing loudly, and pandemonium erupted as classroom doors opened and children flooded out. Catching up jackets and hats from the hooks arrayed around the hall, the stream of young humanity poured toward the stairs on either side of the hall, paying scant attention to the stranger as they flowed around her.

"Hilda!" Erik and three of his friends stopped in front of her, momentarily damming the torrent. "What are you doing here?"

"Looking for you. And why else would I be here?"

"What's the matter?"

"Nothing is the matter. I want to talk to you—and your friends. Where can we sit quietly?"

Sitting quietly was the last thing the boys wanted to do. They were politely silent, but Hilda read their faces. "I know! We will take my carriage downtown, and I will buy you all ice cream, or hot chocolate, or whatever you want."

That was a much more popular idea. Their school manners in force, they were reasonably decorous until they were outside, when they let out a whoop and ran for the carriage. Erik stayed with Hilda. "You're investigating something, aren't you? I can tell by the way you look. And you'd never want to talk to my friends for anything else."

"Erik! I like to talk to your friends, you know that. And I have something important to tell you."

"Uh-huh. And to ask us, I bet."

"We-ell…"

Erik giggled. "I knew it, I knew it! Say, Tom!" he called, running to the carriage.

"Erik! Do not shout," Hilda shouted, running after him. "This is *private*," she hissed when she caught up with him. "Get in, and we will talk about it on the way to the Philadelphia."

"Ooh! They have the best sundaes!" said one of the boys as the carriage started off.

"I do not know your friends," said Hilda. Erik sometimes needed to be reminded of his manners.

"Oh. Well, this is Tom Reed. He lives almost next door to the school. This is George Kirkham and this is Ed Lindsey. They live down the street a ways. George has a big old house and we play baseball in his backyard sometimes."

"Broke a window last time," said George casually. "Papa says we can't play ball there no more."

Hilda was a stickler for good grammar, but she didn't correct him. Instead she seized on the opportunity. "I have something else for you to do. I am Erik's sister Hilda—Mrs. Cavanaugh. I need your help."

All except Erik looked suspicious. Helping grownups usually meant things like raking leaves or painting fences or beating the parlor rugs. Erik knew better. "What do you want to know?" he asked eagerly.

"Have any of you heard about the man who died in the barn fire last month?"

Tom and George looked blank, but Ed spoke up. "My papa read about it in the paper. He said he'd heard of the man who died, and he was nothin' but a common drunkard, and then Mama told him to hush up 'cause I was around and I ain't supposed to know about things like gettin' drunk. That's how come I remember, 'cause they had an argument about it and made me leave the room and I went in the pantry and ate up the rest of the chocolate cake and had a belly-ache all night."

The boy patted that portion of his anatomy, which was somewhat prominent, and Tom said, "Musta been an awful lot of cake. I never knew anybody could eat as much as you."

"Ah. That is interesting," said Hilda. "Not the cake, I mean, or your stomach-ache, but that the man drank too much. How did your father know that?"

Ed shrugged. "Dunno. Guess he heard talk somewheres. Don't drink himself; Mama's real strict Temperance, and Papa mostly goes along with what Mama wants."

Hilda pondered that. "Drunkard," to a Temperance household, might mean that the man took an occasional drink, or that he was regularly to be found in the gutter. "Hmm. And have none of the rest of you heard anything?"

They all shook their heads. "Say, Hilda, why do you want to know?" asked Erik. "There's nothin' int'resting about some man gettin' drunk and settin' a barn on fire."

She hesitated, looking the boys over. She liked what she saw. There was intelligence in those faces, and honesty. Mischief, too, of course. She had no use for a boy with no spark of mischief. Erik had more than his share, perhaps, but the trouble he got into was never malicious. She leaned forward. "Can you keep a secret?" she whispered.

All four nodded solemnly.

"The police are not sure that the man died accidentally. They think perhaps he was killed, and I want to try to find out the truth."

George slapped his knee in sudden comprehension. "You're that one! The woman who goes around finding out things! But I thought you were a servant." Then he looked abashed. "I'm sorry, miss—ma'am. I musta been wrong."

Hilda smiled. "No, you were right. I *was* a servant. I worked for the Studebakers. But now my life is different, and it is maybe harder for me to 'go around finding out things.' That is why I need your help, but you must not say a word about it to anyone. You must promise."

"But miss—ma'am—how are we going to help if we can't talk to people about it?" asked George.

"You will keep your eyes and ears open, especially your ears. If you see or hear anything you think I should know, tell Erik—in private—and he will tell me. But you must say nothing, nothing—do you understand? We do not know who might be a wicked person involved in this man's death, and you could be in danger if someone thinks you are curious. Will you promise me?"

They all promised earnestly, and sealed the bargain with enormous chocolate sundaes at the Philadelphia.

*Two big corporations operating in South Bend
have made presentations to the South Bend
Fire Department as a mark of recognition for
efficient services rendered at recent fires.*

—South Bend *Tribune*
    December 1904

9

A FINE DRIZZLE WAS falling by the time Hilda took the boys back to school. She was indeed late for lunch, but Patrick was still there, enjoying a pipe in front of the parlor fire. Aunt Molly had kept food hot for her, so Hilda brought a tray and joined her husband. "Now, Patrick," she demanded after she had taken a sip of excellent soup, "tell me what you have learned this morning."

"For one thing," he said, jerking his head toward the ceiling, "there's goin' to be a baby in the house any time now." Muffled cries came from upstairs, along with voices and footsteps. "The doctor's come," Patrick went on, "and Sean's pacin' up and down in the hall. No, stay and eat your dinner," as Hilda jumped out of her chair. "There'll be time enough to admire the babe when it's in its ma's arms. You'd only be in the way now. And do you want to hear what I have to say, or don't you?"

"I want to know. But are you sure Norah is all right?"

"Blessed saints, she's got a passel o' women around her, her ma and all, *and* the doctor. She'll do fine. Stop worryin' and eat, and listen, because I need to get back to the store and do some work this afternoon. Uncle Dan's a patient man, but he can't manage everything himself."

Hilda obediently sat down and began to spoon up her soup.

"I didn't have time to talk to the police this mornin'. I stopped at the station, but Sergeant Lefkowicz wasn't there, and I didn't know most of the ones who were. They've got a lot of new men on the force these days. Don't know if that police chief is as good at his job as he ought to be. Anyway, I found out Lefkowicz will be on duty tomorrow. Saturday's a busy day at the store, but I can maybe get away for an hour or two and talk to him."

"So did you go to the fire station?"

"I did. Out to House Five, there on Sample close to the river. They were the nearest to the farm, so they got there first, but it was way too late. By the time somebody in town saw the smoke and pulled the alarm, the fire had a good hold, and there wasn't much they could do except keep it from spreadin' to the house. We need more fire stations in this town, the way it's growin', 'specially to the south. The firemen can't put out fires if they can't get there in time!"

It was a familiar refrain. Although South Bend was putting up more and more buildings of stone and brick, most of the houses and businesses and factories were still constructed of wood, which made fire a constant, deadly hazard, even with the high-pressure water system provided by the standpipe of which the city was so proud. Of course, out in the country where the hoses had to be filled with water pumped from wells, the firefighters had an even harder job. Hilda knew all the arguments for more fire stations, for new and better equipment. Right now she didn't want to hear them.

"Yes, yes, but what did they *say?*"

"They say the fire was started with kerosene. There was a lamp turned over, right near the door, and they reckon the kerosene leaked out and the heat of the lamp set it on fire. They could tell that part burned fast and hard, so they figure there was somethin' there, a pile of straw maybe, or a rick of firewood, that caught fire directly and set off the rest."

Hilda put down her spoon. She had once had a narrow escape from a fire started by a kerosene lamp. The memory was a terrible one. "That poor man," she said soberly. "I heard this morning that he—the man who died, I mean, Mr. Jenkins—maybe drank too much. If he was drunk, he might have dropped the lantern, and then not been able to get away fast enough. Oh, Patrick, it is horrible!"

"Oh, he was drunk, all right. One of the firemen knew him a

little, and some of his friends, and he—the fireman—said Jenkins
spent most of the morning in a saloon out on Miami Street. His
boss was away for a day or two buying supplies and machinery,
and Jenkins wasn't all that dependable about stickin' to his job
when the farmer wasn't there. His friends told the fireman that
Jenkins didn't even eat any lunch, just went home in the early
afternoon in such a state they weren't sure he wouldn't end up in
a ditch."

"He was walking?"

"Yes, the farmer—Miller, his name is—had taken the wagon
and both the horses. Jenkins wasn't supposed to take the buggy
out anyway, I guess, but his friends think he would have if there'd
been a horse to pull it. There wasn't, so he walked. But Hilda,
you don't have to worry about him bein' caught in the flames that
way. That's the funny thing."

"Funny? Patrick, nothing about this is funny!"

"Peculiar, then. The firemen who saw the barn, when it was
burning and afterwards, swear that fire must have blazed up in a
snap of your fingers. But the dead man wasn't found there by the
door. He was up in the hayloft, in the far corner away from the
door, layin' down nice and peaceful-like. He was hardly burned
at all. They figure he died from breathin' in the smoke when he
was dead to the world from the drink. They say he likely didn't
know anything about it atall."

"But then—Patrick, you are right. It *is* peculiar. He could not
have dropped the lantern?"

"Not and get away from the fire in time, they say."

"And there were no horses on the farm. Were there cows?
Dogs? Other animals?"

"Jenkins should have brought the cows home to be milked,
but he didn't. They were in a fine state when a neighbor rounded
them up next day, I hear, achin' with too much milk and bellerin'
like anything. The hogs have their own pen, the chickens were in
the yard, and Mr. Miller took the two dogs with him."

"Then—the wind knocked over the lantern, maybe."

"No wind that day. It was dead calm. That's the only reason

the brigade could save the house and the other buildings. Wind from the wrong direction and it all would've gone up."

"Then, Patrick—*how did the lantern fall?*"

Patrick opened his mouth to reply, when a loud and prolonged shriek came from upstairs. It was followed by silence, and then an unmistakable wail.

Patrick and Hilda looked at each other. A delighted smile slowly spread across Hilda's face.

Brisk footsteps came down the stairs, and Aunt Molly entered the parlor, a broad smile on *her* face as well. "Hilda, my dear, when she's had a bath and been dressed, you'll have to come upstairs and meet your namesake, Fiona."

∾

Patrick, after a quick handshake for the jubilant Sean, headed back to work, and Hilda found she had recovered her appetite. She was joined by Norah's mother, who was exhausted but serene. Sean was too excited to eat. He had been allowed one glimpse of his daughter, just before the doctor left, and could only babble about her. "Beautiful, she is! Head full of black hair, just like me! And strong! Just listen to her!"

"It is hard to do anything else," said Hilda with a grin. Indeed the baby upstairs was howling lustily, protesting against every detail of her new environment.

"She wants her mother," said Aunt Molly. "As soon as she's allowed to suckle she'll be quiet enough. But you're right, Sean, she's a good healthy baby. It's a fine granddaughter you have, Mrs. Murphy."

"Me first one," said Mrs. Murphy, glowing. "Grandsons, five of them, but this is the first little girl." Her face clouded. "Well, there was one—me oldest son's—but she died after two days. Weak and puny she was, we all knew she couldn't live. This one, she's a hearty wee thing."

"And beautiful!" said Sean. "Such hair! And her hands, so tiny, but perfect…"

Hilda and the others listened patiently. A man's first child comes along but once.

As soon as Hilda and Mrs. Murphy had finished eating, they helped Aunt Molly clear away. Eileen was still helping Mrs. O'Rourke with Norah and the baby, so Molly and Mrs. Murphy set about washing the dishes and getting dinner started. "Babies come, and the world goes on, and people have to eat," said Molly, when Hilda protested about Molly continuing to do menial work. "You're no use in the kitchen, child. Away upstairs with you and take a look at the young lady. But don't tire Norah. She lost a good deal of blood, and she needs her rest."

Hilda tapped on the bedroom door and went in. The room was transformed. Huge bouquets of roses stood on the dresser, Sean's roses he'd bought with Hilda's money. Mother and child had been washed and dressed, the bed had been freshly made, and Fiona lay contentedly in her sleepy mother's arms, nuzzling at a breast. "Such a smart girl she is," Norah murmured. "Found what she wanted the minute they gave her to me. Isn't she the prettiest little thing, Hilda?"

Hilda privately thought Fiona looked like every other newborn baby, red, wrinkled, and ancient. Of course she didn't say so. "I think she will look exactly like you," she lied. "Her eyes are just the same color blue."

"All babies have blue eyes," said Norah with the authority of an hour's motherhood. "She will be much more beautiful than me. Look at all that lovely black hair."

Many of the babies Hilda had known had been born with lots of black hair, and lost it in a month or so. Hilda didn't say that either. "Sean thinks her hair is like his."

"But nicer," said Norah with a yawn. "And her hands—just look at her hands."

Hilda obediently looked. People were so silly about babies' hands, but really, it was a bit amazing that anything so small could be so perfectly made, right down to the minute fingernails. Hilda gently touched one tiny palm, and the baby's hand immediately curled around her finger and grasped it tightly.

Hilda was instantly enslaved. This was, after all, a beautiful baby! "Look, Norah! Look, she likes me! She is holding my hand!"

"Mmm." Norah was almost asleep. "Smart little girl."

Sean knocked and came in, carrying a wooden basketwork cradle. "Me brother brought this from home," he told Norah. "He thought we'd need it before long. I told him about our angel girl!" He set the cradle tenderly on the floor beside the bed.

The miniature bed had obviously been prepared with much love. It wore deep, ribboned flounces on the hood and sides, and was fitted inside with a white pillow and a soft white blanket of finest wool.

Fiona had fallen asleep, still grasping Hilda's finger. Carefully Hilda moved the baby's hand and lifted her away from Norah, also asleep. "Do you know how to carry a baby?" she whispered to Sean.

"Eight younger brothers and sisters," he whispered back.

Reluctantly Hilda handed the small warm bundle to its father. "Here is your daughter, then. She will sleep in her cradle for a little now, and Norah must sleep, too. She is a wonderful little girl, Sean. You must be very proud."

Sean cuddled the baby and beamed. Hilda planted a kiss on the baby's forehead and stole out of the room. This was a time for the little family to be alone together.

Heaven holds all for which you sigh —
There! little girl; don't cry!

—James Whitcomb Riley
A Life-Lesson, 1890

10

HILDA WANDERED downstairs to the parlor and dropped into a chair, still in something of a pink haze. What a wonderful baby! Named after her, Hilda. Well, in a way. And so adorable, to hold her finger so tightly. Almost as if she knew whose namesake she was.

Aunt Molly came into the room. "I'm going home, child. Mrs. O'Rourke's reclaimed her kitchen, and she's in no sweet temper, I must say. Worn out, and not pleased about other women in her domain. What you'll have for dinner, I'm sure I don't know, but I'm tired, too. I'm an old woman, and now all the excitement's over, I need to put my feet up. Mrs. Murphy's gone home, too. I gave her one of the umbrellas in the hall. I knew you wouldn't mind. She'll be back this evening, she said, with some things for the baby. I think she plans to take them both, Norah and the wee one, to her house until Norah's on her feet again. For a week or so, though, I think she'd be glad—Mrs. Murphy would, I mean—of an invitation to stay here and cosset Norah and the baby."

Hilda wasn't paying attention. "She held my hand, Aunt Molly," she said dreamily. "Well, my finger. Her hand is so little that was all she could get it around, but she held on so tight!"

"Yes, dear. All babies do that. Don't you remember your young sisters and brother, when they were born?"

"Oh. Well—I suppose—"

"She's a dear little thing, I admit. And she's going to be pretty. I'll wager that hair will turn red like her mother's. She has a redhead's skin."

Hilda giggled. "She has a redskin's skin!"

"That will pass in a few days. It will be very fair, just you wait. Now, dear, you need some rest, too. You've had little sleep and a busy morning. Time enough to worry yourself with other things when you're fresh."

Other things. Hilda came down to earth with a bump. "Oh! I had forgotten! Sean—the dead man—the billfold—Aunt Molly, the firemen say they don't see how the fire could have been an accident."

"Tell me."

Hilda explained.

Molly frowned. "Then it sounds like arson. But I can't see for what purpose."

"Robbery? Someone stole Mr. Jenkins's billfold and then set the barn on fire so he could not accuse the thief?"

"You're tired, my dear, and not thinking properly. They say Mr. Jenkins was inebriated, probably to the point of unconsciousness. It would have been easy for anyone to take his billfold and simply leave. Mr. Jenkins would wake in the morning with an aching head and no money. There was no need to burn down the barn, and no apparent purpose."

Hilda thought about it and then shook her head. "You are right, Aunt Molly. There is no sense in it. But there is one thing certain. Sean could not have set the barn on fire. He was working with the other men until they all saw the smoke."

"True. That's important. But, child—he still could have stolen the money."

Hilda bowed her head. To that argument she still had no rebuttal. She sighed and stood. "We need rest, all of us. Mrs. O'Rourke and Eileen, too. They were up nearly all night. I will go to the kitchen and tell them that a cold meal will do for tonight, and that they must take a nap."

"You'll need to be very firm. Cook's on the rampage."

"I will be firm." Hilda tossed her head. "Good-bye, Aunt Molly, and thank you. You have been so good. I do not think I could have managed about Norah and the baby without you. I will ask Mr. O'Rourke to bring the carriage for you."

Molly kissed her on the cheek. "You're learning, my dear, learning to deal with servants, and to deal with household crises. You've always had sense, and that's mostly what's needed. Good luck with Mrs. O'Rourke." She hesitated in the act of putting on her hat. "You'll be all right, will you? With no one to help? Norah and the baby are perfectly all right, but Norah is very tired, and will not be able…"

"I have three younger sisters, and Erik. I was nearly ten when Erik was born. I know how to look after babies. And there is Sean. He has younger brothers and sisters, too. Do not worry." Hilda pulled the bell rope and Eileen hurried into the room, looking a bit limp. "Eileen, dear, please tell Mr. O'Rourke I need the carriage to take Mrs. Malloy home. And ask Mrs. O'Rourke to come here. I need to talk to her. And then, Eileen, go up to your room and take a nap. I will not need you anymore today."

"But Mrs. O'Rourke—"

"Mrs. O'Rourke will not need you, either. Quickly, Eileen."

Molly exchanged smiles with Hilda and then whirled away home.

∾

It was the wailing of a baby that woke Hilda, in the late afternoon. The room was dim and the steady sound of rain pattering on the roof made Hilda want to stay asleep. She sat up, wondering for a moment why she was fully dressed and lying on top of her bed. But as the baby's cries were succeeded by low murmurs and then by silence, she remembered. Norah and Fiona.

She smiled as she remembered the baby's tight grasp of her finger. Even if it was a common thing, it had felt very sweet. Babies were more lovable than Hilda had ever realized. And the feel of the warm, tiny bundle in her arms as she had picked up Fiona and handed her to Sean…perhaps one day…

Sean. Hilda abandoned her daydreams. She had to talk to Sean seriously. Now that the baby had safely made her appearance in the world, and Norah was doing well, Hilda intended to get some sense out of the blissful father if she had to shake him.

Nobody's bliss would last long if Sean was returned to jail for stealing.

Or even for murder. Hilda was convinced by the evidence of the firemen that Sean could have had nothing to do with the fire, and could therefore not be charged with arson or murder. But did the police knew what the firemen found? Would they believe them? There was a certain amount of rivalry between the two services, each thinking it deserved more public recognition, more civic resources, and better wages than the other. The firemen, after all, were offering what amounted to their opinions about how the fire started and where. What if the police rejected their opinions?

Still—how could it have been Sean when he was working hard at the next farm, a quarter of a mile away?

It wouldn't have taken long to set the fire. A healthy man could easily run the distance, there and back, in less than ten minutes. If one allowed five for finding a lantern, lighting it, and tipping it over…would anyone have noticed if Sean had been away for fifteen minutes?

But why would he do such a thing? It made no sense, whoever had done it. Robbery from a man so much the worse for drink that he didn't even know the barn was on fire?

The police didn't always worry about why. If a person could have done a crime, that was often enough to convince the police that he *had* done it. In Hilda's experience, the police were often lazy at best, incompetent at worst.

She got off the bed, tidied her hair, put on her shoes, and went to find Sean.

He was at Norah's bedside, of course. Norah was feeding the baby while Sean looked on adoringly.

"Norah, when is the last time you had something to eat?" asked Hilda.

"Eat? I don't know." She sounded dreamy.

Hilda made scolding noises with her tongue. "You must eat, or you will be unable to feed Fiona. I will go down to the kitchen. I have told Eileen and Mrs. O'Rourke that they must rest, but there will be cold food for everyone. I will bring you a tray. Sean, come with me to help, and to get some food for yourself. I think you have not eaten for a long time, either."

"Oh, I'm not hungry—I'll stay here with Norah—"

"I need your help, Sean. It will not take long." It would take, thought Hilda grimly as she led him from the room, as long as was necessary to get a coherent story out of him.

The cook had set out cold ham, cheese, pickled beets, and applesauce. There was a fresh loaf of bread, and the kettle of potato soup from lunch was sitting on the stove, needing only a match touched to the gas burner to reheat it. "Now, Sean," said Hilda as she busied herself with finding matches and trays, "sit down. Mrs. O'Rourke has left everything in good order. I can do the work myself, but I must talk to you. I want you to tell me exactly what happened the day of the fire."

"The fire?" Sean sounded as if he had never heard of such a thing as a fire.

"The barn fire," said Hilda with as much patience as she could muster. "The day you were working with your friends to build the barn on the next farm. The day you found the billfold." He still looked dazed, and Hilda realized she had to harden her heart. "The billfold with the money the police think you stole."

"Oh." All the happiness faded out of Sean's face as he sat down, heavily, on a wooden chair. "There wasn't no money in it, Hilda. They don't believe me, but it's God's own truth. The blessed saints know we could have used money. With Norah not workin', and my job maybe shaky, and now the baby...I don't know what we're goin' to do, Hilda, and that's the truth. But I never stole nothin' in me life. That wallet was empty when I found it, and if it hadn't of been, I'd've taken it to the police first thing."

"Where did you find it, exactly? And when?" She stirred the soup and got out plates, napkins, cutlery.

"It was after the fire wagons got there. We could see there was nothin' we could do—us as was workin' next door, I mean. We was just in the way, without no animals to get out or nothin'.

The barn was pretty well gone by that time, anyway. They was just worryin' about savin' the house and the pigpen and that. So we walked back to our suppers, and on the way I kicked some-thin'. I couldn't hardly see what it was, it was that dark—"

"So it was not close to the barn?" Hilda interrupted.

"No, it was near to the fence, by the drive up to the place. I'd forgot that part. How did *you* know?"

"If it had been near the burning barn, there would have been enough light for you to see what it was. Go on."

He scratched his head at Hilda's perspicacity and contin-ued his story. "So I picked it up, and when we got to where they was givin' us supper, there were lanterns and I could see it was a man's billfold, and a fine one. Good leather, only a little worn on the folds. It was pretty dirty, though, so I cleaned it off a bit and asked if anybody there had dropped it. And later, I went back and asked the firemen. And nobody knew nothin' about it, so I kept it. Musta been one of them told the police I had it. But where the harm is in that, to make the police come after me, the good Lord alone knows."

Hilda handed him a knife. "Slice some ham and put it on this plate," she directed. "I have only one more question for you. Were you with the rest of the men, building the new barn, the whole day?"

"What would ye think, I'd go off and leave the rest of 'em workin'?" Sean was beginning to be annoyed. " 'Course I was there all day."

Hilda cut some bread and cheese while she considered how to ask the next question delicately. "I mean—you must have had to—to go off by yourself sometimes. Were you ever gone longer than a few minutes?"

Her cheeks were burning, and Sean's turned fiery red. "I don't know what a decent woman is doin' askin' me such a ques-tion, but the answer is no."

Hilda started filling plates and soup bowls and putting them on trays. She added a tall glass of cool, creamy milk to Norah's tray. "I am sorry, Sean. I had to know if you had enough time to go over to the next farm without anyone noticing and set the fire."

"Nobody noticin'! There wasn't enough of us to do the job as it was, and we was working that hard, we noticed when anybody stopped for a drink o' water. If you think I could've sneaked off, you've lost your mind. The whole gang of 'em would've lost their Irish tempers, and you know that's no comic thing."

"Not for most Irishmen," Hilda said with the hint of a smile. "For you—I wonder what would make you angry?"

Sean took it as a serious question. "I never had much of a temper, but now—well, if somebody hurt Norah or the baby—I don't know what I'd do to 'em, but for sure they wouldn't like it."

"No, but you have showed me you do not anger easily, or you would have become angry with me for my questions, instead of just being annoyed and embarrassed. And you have showed that you would not be good at lying. Me, I can lie if I have to, but I am sure that you would give yourself away. Your face shows what you are thinking. So I believe that you did not steal any money, and I believe that you did not start the fire, and I will do everything I can to prove that you are innocent. Now, will you carry up this tray while I take the other?"

LADIES LISTEN TO A POEM
Meeting of Women's Missionary Society
of First Presbyterian Church [There follows
an account of the meeting, including a nine-
stanza poem by one of the members]

—South Bend *Tribune*
December 3, 1904

HALF AN HOUR LATER, Hilda carried both trays downstairs again. Sean had eaten a good meal, but they
had been unable to persuade Norah to eat much.
She had drunk the glass of milk, reluctantly—"I've
always hated milk"—but had pushed away the food after a few
bites. "I'm so tired! I wish you'd all go away and let me sleep."
Fiona had wakened in her cradle and whimpered, so Hilda had
changed her diaper and given her to Norah, but the baby nursed
for only a minute or two before falling asleep.

"Sean, will you stay here with them? I must prepare supper
for Patrick. He will be home soon."

Sean was delighted to stay with his wife and child, so Hilda
went back down to the kitchen and put together a substantial as-
sortment of food for Patrick. She also made a fresh pot of coffee,
and pouring herself a large cup, sat down with him at the kitchen
table. They both found it more inviting than the dining room,
though they dared enjoy it only when Mrs. O'Rourke wasn't
around. Patrick ate and Hilda drank in companionable silence.

Her nap had refreshed her somewhat, but she was still tired,
and her mind refused to function in its usual clear manner. She
hoped she wasn't getting one of her headaches. They had been
less frequent since her marriage, but now her head felt as if it
were stuffed with damp cotton, and there was a threatening tension behind her right eye.

"So," said Patrick, when he had polished off all the food
and fetched a bottle of beer from the cool larder, "how's the wee
spalpeen?"

Hilda frowned. "What is a spalpeen?"

"A mischievous young one. A rascal." And when Hilda still looked puzzled, he grinned. "The baby, I'm meanin'."

"Patrick! It is not nice to call that lovely baby a—whatever you called her. She is an angel!"

"Ah, it's easy to see she's got round you, then. Norah all right?"

"She is very tired, and does not want to eat. I hope she will wake soon. The baby will need food." Hilda yawned. "And I am tired, too." She went to the range and turned on the burner under the coffeepot. "I think maybe I might have a headache later. I hope the coffee will help."

Patrick looked around the kitchen and then back at Hilda. "Where's Mrs. O'Rourke? And Eileen? Tending to Norah and the babe?"

"No, I left them with Sean. I told the servants to take a nap. They were busy all night." Hilda was a little embarrassed. The word *servants*, applied to their employees rather than their colleagues, still felt strange.

Patrick didn't notice. He stood up. "That was a kindly thought, darlin', but you need them. You can't run a household and look after a baby and a new mother and chase down a murderer, all at the same time."

Reluctantly Hilda put down her coffee cup. "Yes, you are right. I will go and wake them."

"You will not. You've been runnin' all day. Leave it to me."

"You will be polite? You will not make Mrs. O'Rourke angry?"

"And when did ye ever know an Irishman couldn't wind any woman round his little finger when he wanted to?" said Patrick, a twinkle in his eye and an exaggerated brogue on his tongue.

"Me you could not wind. Not always."

"And that's true enough, darlin' girl, but you're different to the rest, aren't you? Sit still, I'll be back before ye know I'm gone."

Alone and quiet, Hilda drank coffee and felt her headache

recede a little. She looked around the kitchen. It was a peaceful, comfortable room, at least when the volatile cook wasn't there. Not as warm, true, as the Tippecanoe Place kitchen with its massive coal-fired range, kept alight even in summer. Oh, how she had roasted when errands took her to that kitchen in summer! But in winter it had been a haven, first thing in the morning, from her cold bedroom at the top of the house.

This kitchen wasn't as grand, but it was well appointed. Patrick's aunt and uncle, who had given them the house as a wedding present, had redone the kitchen completely. The very latest in Hoosier Kitchens stood against one wall, with its flour bin and sifter, compartments for spices, canisters, many doors and drawers, and a lovely big, tinned work surface that pulled out for convenience. The ice box was the finest available, the gas range and the coal heating stove shone with polish, the sink gleamed with white enamel. Everything from the white walls to the blue wainscoting to the blue-and-white checked linoleum was fresh and new and bright. And hanging from one wall was a prized possession, the coffee mill Hilda's brother Sven had made for her and painted with a gay Swedish design of birds and flowers.

Yes, it was a good kitchen. Perhaps, thought Hilda somewhat guiltily, the best thing about it was that she didn't have to cook in it.

But she'd better clear away the dishes Patrick had used, or Mrs. O'Rourke would be angry. Hilda knew it was foolish to let the cook bully her. She had served under a bullying butler for years and had had quite enough of it. On the other hand, if Mrs. O'Rourke got angry enough to leave, Hilda simply did not know what she would do. She could clean, oh, yes, she could clean anything, but cook—especially with a new mother and a baby in the house—she shuddered and hastened to rinse the dishes and stack them neatly in the sink. Then she poured out the last cup of coffee and retreated to the parlor.

Patrick joined her there in a few minutes. "Well, they're up, and downstairs, and cheerful about it, so that's off your mind. Is your head feelin' better?"

"Yes. The coffee is good. Thank you, Patrick, for talking to Mrs. O'Rourke."

"You ought to stand up to her, darlin'. She'd be the better for a good talkin' to."

"I was yoost—just thinking that. I do not think I can do it. I am afraid she would lose her temper and leave us, and I do not know how to cook. Aunt Molly has said she would teach me, but I cannot take the time now. There is Sean's trouble, and the baby, and—oh! I forgot to tell you. I am starting a club for the poor boys in South Bend, and there is to be a Christmas party for them, and there will be much to do."

Patrick made a face. "When I married you I thought I was givin' you a life of leisure. Do ye not want to be a lady and—do whatever they do all day?"

Hilda laughed. "No, Patrick, I do not! It is boring, that life. They do nothing except call on each other and go to silly meetings and change clothes all day long. A dress for morning, a dress for afternoon, a dress for calling, a dress for staying at home for tea, a dress for dinner—it is foolishness. And with every fancy dress one must wear stays, and I do not like them." She shivered a little with sudden pleasure. To be able to talk of stays with a man, a man who had, moreover, seen one's stays, had seen…

Patrick's thoughts were traveling along much the same line. "You've a neat little waist, and no need to cage it up." He put out a hand and pulled her up into his arms. "Mmm, yes, a neat little waist indeed…and a neat, soft little—"

The doorbell rang. Hilda sprang away and smoothed her dress.

"Who's callin' at this time of night?" said Patrick, displeased.

"I do not know. Oh, I hope it is not a policeman for Sean!"

They listened anxiously while Eileen went to the door. There was a murmur of feminine voices.

"Oh!" Hilda's hand went to her mouth. "It is Mrs. Murphy. I forgot! I think Aunt Molly told me she might want to stay here for a few days, and there is not a bedroom ready for her."

Patrick rose to the emergency. "You talk to Eileen while I entertain Mrs. Murphy. We'll have her off to bed and settled in no time." And then, Patrick's look said, we can also be off to bed....

"Yes," Hilda whispered, "and be sure to invite her to stay as long as she wishes. And tell her—"

"I'll say the right things. You can trust me, my girl."

Eileen showed Norah's mother into the parlor, and Patrick stepped forward to charm her, while Hilda beckoned Eileen out of the room. Twenty minutes later Hilda returned to the parlor, where Mrs. Murphy was sitting comfortably with a cup of tea, chatting with Patrick.

"How are Norah and the baby?" Mrs. Murphy asked as soon as courtesies had been exchanged.

"Norah is very tired and wishes mostly to sleep. The baby woke a few minutes ago and Norah is feeding her now. Would you wish to go up and see her? And I hope Patrick asked you to stay with us as long as Norah needs you." Hilda bit her lip. That sounded as if Norah's mother was welcome only as a nurse, and was not what Hilda had meant to say, but it was too late to take it back now.

"Yes, I'll go up," said Mrs. Murphy briefly. "You don't need to bother about me. I'm used to doing for myself."

Worse and worse. "It is a pleasure to have you here," said Hilda, but it sounded stiff even to her, and Mrs. Murphy did not reply as she started up the stairs, Patrick following with her bag.

After a moment of indecision, Hilda went into the kitchen. Mrs. O'Rourke was fussing, rearranging things that intruders had evidently moved a few inches from their appointed positions. "Yes, madam?" she said in her most formal voice.

"I came to thank you, Mrs. O'Rourke, for all you have done. The baby arriving has made you much extra work, but I am so grateful you were here, because I would not have known what to do." There was art as well as truth in Hilda's remark. It would, she thought, be good to make the cook feel superior. Not that she didn't feel that way already, of course.

The cook unbent a little. "I was glad to do what I could, madam. Has Norah been eating well?"

"No, and that is the other reason I wanted to talk to you. She is very tired and does not want to eat, but I know she must. What can we give her that will tempt her?"

"Well, now. I can make her a little custard, that goes down easy, and some rice pudding. And maybe for right now, some good rich eggnog. And then soup for tomorrow, rich broth with noodles—oh, there's lots I can give her that she'll like. You leave it to me, madam. I've cooked for many a new mother in my time. I'll send up the eggnog directly. Where's that Eileen?"

Hilda explained and left the kitchen feeling that at least one burden was off her shoulders. With luck it would not be very long before she and Patrick could forget all their burdens for a few hours in sleep and other joys.

*Tears, idle tears, I know not
what they mean...*

—Alfred, Lord Tennyson
The Princess, 1847

12

THE STORM BROKE very early the next morning. Eileen knocked at their bedroom door and came in, looking scared.

"Ma'am, it's sorry I am to wake you so early," she whispered, "and on a Saturday, too, but Mrs. Murphy's that upset. She says Miss Norah—I mean, Mrs.—Mrs. O'Neill—she says she's real sick!"

Hilda got up at once, hastily put on a robe and slippers, and flew down the hall to Norah's room, where Sean and Norah's mother stood by the bed, the baby wailing in its grandmother's arms. Norah sat up in bed, panting, her face white as chalk.

"What is wrong with Norah?" asked Hilda.

"We don't hardly know!" It was Sean who answered. "She can't breathe right, and she's got such a pain she can't eat, or even hardly drink, so she doesn't have enough milk for the babe! And she's been cryin' and saying she feels terrible, and she seems so weak. And listen to this poor little mite—she's hungry, bless her. Oh, don't cry so, my darlin'! It breaks my heart."

Sean stroked the baby's head as if it were a kitten. Fiona, red-faced, arms and legs pumping, paid no attention. She wanted food and she wanted it now.

Hilda looked helplessly from the screaming baby to the distraught father to the worried grandmother. Then she turned to the bed. Norah's hand was pressed to her chest.

"Norah, what *is* it!"

"Scared," Norah whispered. "My heart—dying—can't breathe—"

"Hush, then, do not try to talk." Hilda turned again to the family. "Has anyone called the doctor?"

"No—we just found her. We didn't know what to do!"

Hilda pulled the bell cord, not once but several times, hard. She could hear bells jangling on the third floor and in the kitchen. Then she began giving orders. "Sean, there is brandy in the pantry. Bring it here, quick, with a glass. Mrs. Murphy, let me take the baby. Get a cloth, wet it with cold water, and put it on the back of Norah's neck. Eileen, call the doctor at once. Tell him Norah is in bad trouble. Her heart, maybe. And then—no, go, Mrs. O'Rourke is here, *Gud ske lov*—thank God. Mrs. O'Rourke, Norah is ill and cannot feed the baby. We do not have a nursing bottle, but please find a way to feed her."

Mrs. O'Rourke, in her nightdress and robe, her gray hair in braids and a scowl on her face, looked like a Teutonic deity. Hilda would have quailed, but the situation was too desperate for her to worry about angry servants. She handed the frantic baby over to the cook, whose expression softened at once.

"Ah, poor little colleen, hungry, are you?" she murmured. "We'll have to do somethin' about that, won't we now?" She took the baby away and quiet reigned once more, broken by Norah's sobs.

"She'll die," said Norah weakly. "She'll die without me."

"Nobody is going to die," said Hilda fiercely. "Not you, not little Fiona. The doctor is on his way, and your mother is here. Oh, and here is Sean. Now, then, sit up a bit more—that's it—and drink some of this."

Norah sputtered as the brandy went down, but her breathing became more regular. "Now, Sean, go back to the kitchen. Mrs. O'Rourke will be warming some milk for the baby. Bring some of it here in a cup. Norah will have it with more brandy."

"Is that—do you think she should have brandy when she is feeding the baby?"

Hilda lost her temper. "I do not know! She is *not* feeding the baby, for she cannot. I am not a doctor. I do the best I know. You sent for me, now do as I say!"

Hilda looked at Mrs. Murphy to see how she was taking all this. She might very well resent someone else giving orders about her own daughter and granddaughter. But she was occupied sponging the back of Norah's neck, a remedy Hilda thought would cure the hysterics she suspected were a large part of the problem.

Hilda turned to Eileen, who had returned from her phone call. "Eileen, please go back downstairs and let the doctor in when he comes. I must go and dress, and then you can get dressed yourself. I wish I could let you sleep, but I think there will be little sleep for anyone in this house for a few days."

She patted Eileen on the shoulder and then went back to her own room, where Patrick was sitting on the edge of the bed. "It is very early, Patrick. Why are you getting up?"

"Couldn't sleep for the hullabaloo. What's goin' on?"

Hilda explained briefly while she dressed. "And I said they would be well, but Patrick, I am frightened. It is maybe just worry that makes Norah feel so ill, but Aunt Molly said she lost much blood in childbirth, and what if she *does* die?"

She struggled with the hooks at her back and Patrick came over to fasten them. "Where's Eileen?" he asked, his hands clumsy at the task.

"She waits for the doctor, to let him in."

"Then I'll light the gas," said Patrick. "Brrr!" He pattered across the floor in his bare feet and touched a match to the gas fixture on the wall. "Got to have some light if I'm to fiddle with tiny hooks. Don't know why they make women's clothes so hard to get into. And out of," he added, aiming a little smack at the petticoat as he finished fastening it. "And why are you dressing, anyway?"

"I cannot see the doctor in my nightdress, Patrick! And this is not the time to be foolish."

"But d'you have to see the doctor yourself? There's Mrs. Murphy, and Sean—"

"Norah is my friend, and a guest in my house, and she is seriously ill! I must not neglect her."

The doorbell rang and Hilda rushed out of the room to greet the doctor. Patrick looked at the cold, dark fireplace, at the clock whose hands stood at four-thirty, and then back at his bed with the warm comforter. With a fatalistic sigh he pushed his feet into slippers and his arms into a robe and picked up the coal scuttle. There was nothing useful he could do in this medical crisis, but as long as his Hilda believed she must help, then he must be ready to serve if she needed him. He started downstairs for coal.

He had made a fire and dressed and was about to go forage for some breakfast when Hilda came in and sat down on the bed. "Norah is better," she said in response to his cocked eyebrow. "Doctor Clark says she did not have a heart attack. He is not happy about her, though. He says she is very weak and that is what made her chest hurt, and that she needs building up. He asked many questions about what she had been eating, and said she must have much meat, and milk, and eggs. And Sean tried to hide it, but he is troubled because he does not know how he can pay for such things. They have not much money, even when he is working every day."

Patrick took her hand. "You know she can stay here with the baby as long as she needs to. We can see she gets the food she needs, if that's what the trouble is."

Hilda nodded and went on. "And he says she must not try to feed the baby until she is stronger. She must nurse a little, or she will not be able to later, but Fiona will have to have most of her milk from bottles. He told Mrs. Murphy just how to mix the milk, and how much Fiona should have. Eileen will go out for nursing bottles as soon as Vanderhoof's opens. Norah is to take a tonic he gave us, and must be made to eat. He says she will soon be hungry and want her baby in her arms again. I hope he is right, but I am fearful." She yawned hugely. "And Patrick, I am so tired I could sleep for a week."

"There's no reason you can't sleep today, darlin'. With two capable women in the house to look after Norah and the baby, there's no sense talkin' about neglect. You can rest. And if that baby screams again, I'll give her a little good Irish whisky. She'll sleep after that, I'll wager."

Hilda suffered herself to be undressed and tucked in, and fell into an exhausted sleep that ten crying babies could not have disturbed.

When she woke the weather had changed. The rain had stopped, the sun was shining brightly, and Patrick was not there. She sat up, not able for a moment to remember the reason for her feeling of unease.

There was a tap at the door and Eileen entered. "Here, ma'am. Mr. Cavanaugh thought you might be glad of some coffee. And the fire needs tending. It's bitter cold out, ma'am, for all it's so bright. And the baby's been sleepin' like a little lamb now she's gettin' her food, but Miss Norah, she's still feelin' bad. Her ma's made her eat her food and take that tonic, but she didn't like the taste of it, and she's cryin', and she still thinks she's goin' to die."

"She is not," said Hilda, sipping the hot, fragrant brew. "I will go and talk to her."

"Yes, ma'am. Only, Cook says as how she's known other women like that, just too tired and weak to want to live, even, and sometimes they just pine away and die, and maybe their poor babes, too. She says—"

"Eileen, you must not believe what Mrs. O'Rourke says, and you must not, either of you, say it where Norah can hear you. Norah is weak, but she will become strong if she does everything the doctor tells her. We must help her do that."

By that evening, everyone in the house was exhausted. Hilda had spent most of the day coaxing Norah to eat food for which she had no appetite and to take tonic she detested. She kept whispering she only wanted to be allowed to die in peace, she was too tired to eat. Hilda tried not to lose her temper, for she knew the weariness was real. The doctor had warned her that her friend was so weak, even opening her eyes was an effort, but it was hard to see Norah lying there, nearly as pale as the sheets on which she lay, able to do nothing for herself and without even the strength to argue with Hilda. Sean had been banished, for his presence kept Norah awake and worrying. With no more spare beds in the house, Sean had retired to a bed in the carriage house, where the coachman would have slept if he had been unmarried.

Mrs. Murphy, who also kept Norah fretting, had refused to leave her side except to harass the cook in the kitchen. Patrick, who had put in an extremely long, busy day at the store without even a moment to talk to the police, had escaped to his den and fallen asleep behind a newspaper.

The doctor returned after supper and came out of Norah's room shaking his head. "She has lost so much blood," he told Mrs. Murphy, "and she was not strong even before the baby was born."

Norah's mother struggled against tears. "I've heard as there's a way to give a person someone else's blood," she said in a frightened whisper. "I'll do it! If it kills me, I'll do it!"

"It wouldn't kill you," said Dr. Clark gently, "but it might kill Norah. Blood given to a patient must match the patient's own. The wrong kind of blood is worse than none."

"But I'm her mother. She's blood of my blood, bone of my bone. Certain sure, my blood—"

"It isn't that simple. There's a lot about blood we don't know, but we do know that sometimes fresh blood saves a person's life—and sometimes it kills. I can't risk it. The best we can do is give her good food and lots of rest, and don't let her worry about anything. The tonic will help. You must see that she takes it every day."

"And since when," said Mrs. Murphy in something nearer to her usual manner, "did Norah Murphy ever do as I told her? She hates that tonic, if that's what you call it. Smells like cod liver oil to me, and I don't wonder it's hard to get down her."

"She must take it," said the doctor sharply. It had been a long day and he hadn't had his dinner yet. "I tell you frankly, good nursing will make all the difference to your daughter."

Dr. Clark found Hilda in the parlor before he left the house.

"You're a sensible sort of woman," he said. "I can be more blunt with you than with the girl's mother. Mrs. O'Neill's in a bad way. I'll wager she wasn't getting the right kind of food through her pregnancy, and she's thoroughly run down. That, with the blood she lost, means she'll have a struggle to recover, and I can't see any signs she cares to struggle. She seems to think there's no point in living, even for her baby. Do you know why she feels that way?"

Hilda had to swallow hard before she could reply. The doctor was saying Norah might die! "Yes," she said at last. "She worries that her husband might lose his job. Also—the worst thing—she worries that he might—Dr. Clark, he is suspected of robbery, at the best, maybe even of arson and murder. He did not do it, Doctor! But she fears that the police will not believe him, and he might—might be hanged."

The doctor abandoned his need for rest and food. "You say he didn't do it. You sound very sure."

"Yes, I—oh, please sit down. You would like some coffee?"

"I would." He sat down heavily in the nearest chair, letting his bag drop to the floor beside him. "And if there's such a thing as a sandwich—"

Hilda pulled the bell cord, forgetting for the moment her embarrassment over summoning servants. "You have had no supper?" she asked anxiously.

"Not yet. It doesn't matter. Tell me about Mr. O'Neill. He has a job?"

"He works for Black's Bicycle Works, but he fears for his job. The company is not doing well, and even before—oh, Eileen, please bring us coffee. And Dr. Clark has not had supper. Can you bring him something to eat, please?"

"There's still soup, ma'am. I could heat it up in a minute."

"Thank you. And some bread, and pie if any is left over."

"Plenty, ma'am." Eileen vanished.

"Go on," said the doctor. "Even before what?"

"Before the trouble. They have not had very much money, I think. Norah could not work—she is a maid like me, Doctor."

He raised his eyebrows.

"Like I was, I mean. We worked together at Tippecanoe Place and she is my best friend. But when she married Sean things were different. We did not see each other so much. And then I married Patrick, and it was worse. She thought I..." Hilda ran down.

"Yes, yes, but what about Mr. O'Neill?"

"Besides worry about money, there is the fire, and the trouble."

Eileen came in with food and coffee, and as he ate, the doctor extracted the whole story from Hilda, the events of the fire, Sean's arrest and release on bail, Norah's request of Hilda. "So it comes down to this," Dr. Clark said, sipping coffee, "Norah O'Neill thinks you can get Sean off. You're sure he's innocent."

"Yes."

"What about the police? Seems to me this is their job."

"The police are not always kind to immigrants, Dr. Clark. Even though many of them are Irish, even the chief, they have forgotten, I guess, what it is like to be poor and despised. And they are lazy, I think. They will arrest one person and not look for others. I know Sean did not set that fire or steal any money, but the police believe he did, or pretend they believe it, and they will not give up their beliefs easily."

"Well, then, it seems you're Norah's last hope. See here, young woman. If Norah goes on worrying about finances and her husband, if she worries about anything at all, she's not going to sleep well or eat well, and she may well die. Forgive me for speaking plainly, but you'd best bestir yourself and go about proving Sean's innocence. Think you can do that?"

He looked at her over the top of his glasses, his bushy eyebrows drawn in a frown.

Hilda drew herself up and looked straight back at him. "I think I can. I have done such things before. I will try."

"Good girl. And look after yourself as well. You look tired. I don't need two patients in this house."

"There is much to do, Doctor. The Boys' Club—that will help me to find out what really happened to Mr. Jenkins. And

I must help look after Norah. And Mrs. Murphy is staying here, too, and she does not like me. And there is the house, and of course Patrick, and—"

"Enough." The doctor held up his hand. "We're talking about saving a life here. If you say this Boys' Club will be some use, very well. But you can let the servants run the house for the time being. Your husband won't starve, I'm sure. And as for Mrs. Murphy, surely she can see that you're helping her daughter. I'll send in a nurse for Norah; I'm none too sure her mother's good for her just now."

"She is too sad," said Hilda in a whisper, looking around to make sure Mrs. Murphy wasn't there. "She weeps over Norah, and I think it is better to be cheerful. And she will not make Norah eat or take the tonic, and becomes angry with me when I try. She will not like a nurse coming to take over, but…" Hilda took a deep breath. "Send the nurse, Dr. Clark. We must have help."

As Hilda went to bed that night, tired and worried as she was, she suddenly burst into a fit of giggles. Patrick stared at her.

"Oh, Patrick, it is nothing—yoost that I had a thought. It is only two days ago I thought I might die of boredom!"

O what their joy and their glory must be,
Those endless Sabbaths the blessed
ones see...

— O Quanta Qualia
Peter Abelard, c. 1129

13

S UNDAY WAS ALWAYS a difficult day. Hilda and Patrick
separated, Hilda to the Swedish Lutheran Church with
her family, and Patrick to—where else?—St. Patrick's
Catholic Church with his. Patrick usually walked, as his
church was nearby. Hilda, who had walked over a mile to her
church from Tippecanoe Place every Sunday for more than six
years, now took the carriage. She found it pleasant to arrive with
clean, dry skirts and shoes, no matter what the weather, although
some of her family tended to look askance at what they viewed as
an unseemly display of wealth.

This morning Hilda was especially glad of the carriage, for
it gave her an extra few minutes to look in on Norah. The nurse
had arrived the evening before, starched, cool, and competent.
Norah had eaten a little late supper, taken her tonic, and was sitting up in bed eating breakfast when Hilda came into the bedroom.

"Good morning, Norah. You look much better today."

Mrs. Murphy, sitting in the corner, sniffed. "Pale as a ghost,
she is."

"*Much* better color, today," said Miss Pickerell firmly. "And
eating her breakfast like a lamb. Just you finish that egg, dear,
and then it's time for your tonic."

"Horrible stuff," said Mrs. Murphy. "It'd make *me* sick, I can
tell you that."

"I don't want it," said Norah weakly.

"Ah, we'll follow it up with some good rich milk to take the
taste away. Open up, now."

Norah opened her mouth for another protest, and the nurse deftly inserted the spoon. Norah swallowed, then gagged and coughed.

"Just you hurry and get well and there'll be no more need for the tonic," said the nurse. "Now the milk, dear."

"Norah, I am going to my church," said Hilda, eager to escape the conflict between Mrs. Murphy and Miss Pickerell, "and Patrick is going to his. I thought he might ask Father Faherty to come and visit you."

"Glory be to God," cried Mrs. Murphy, falling to her knees and crossing herself, "and are you sayin' my Norah's dyin', that she needs a priest?"

"No! I thought you both might like to see him, and Sean when he comes to see you, and perhaps the good Father could baptize little Fiona. I do not know what you do in your church, but in mine babies are baptized when they are tiny, and you have been tired and ill, I thought you might have forgotten."

At that Mrs. Murphy set up a complicated wailing, invoking the saints, rebuking Norah for putting her baby in danger of hell, praying for mercy, expressing amazement that a heathen should remember duty a good Catholic forgot. Hilda fled before the storm. Let them solve their own religious problems!

∾

Hilda usually enjoyed church with her family, enjoyed the opportunity to hear and speak Swedish, enjoyed the beautiful new church and the hymns. Sometimes she even enjoyed the sermon, though their new Pastor Borg, inclined to be gloomy, didn't preach as well as had Pastor Forsberg. But after church came the time of trial. For Sunday afternoon was family time, spent with Hilda's family or Patrick's, alternately. And since neither family entirely approved of the marriage, the time together was always something of an ordeal.

Today they were all going to Sven's house, two blocks from the church. Mr. O'Rourke had picked up Patrick, whose service let out before Hilda's, and brought him to the Swedish Church. There Hilda got into the carriage. On days when the weather was bad, Mama and the two eldest sisters joined them in the carriage. Otherwise Hilda and Patrick were driven in solitary splendor, which to Hilda's discomfort emphasized her new wealth and the family's relative poverty.

Mama, this time, chose to walk. Patrick raised one eyebrow as Hilda settled herself on the cushioned seat. "How's Mama's temper this mornin'?"

Hilda shook her head. "As usual. She has said nothing except good morning, and she kissed me, but she has *looked*."

Patrick grinned. "I know those looks, darlin'. Never mind. Looks won't kill us, and I'll talk them around in time. Be patient."

"I am *not* patient! They should not treat us this way. It was your family who brought Mama and the young ones to America. It was your family who gave you a job and gave us a house, and you do everything for my family that they will let you do. It was you who helped find Erik when he was in such danger. They should be grateful!"

"Ah, but folks don't like bein' grateful, ye see. It's like bein' in debt, and your people'd sooner starve than be in debt to the no-good Irish. They've got this idea that the Irish are all idle lay-abouts, and knowin' me uncle's rich and respectable upsets 'em."

"It is foolish. They should know better."

"Ah, well, it isn't all of 'em. The younger ones like me fine, and Sven never says a word agin me. Anyway, there's nothin' they can do to us. And here we are, so put on your best Sunday face and together we'll charm 'em all."

He handed her down with tender care, winked at her, and escorted her into the small house.

Hilda immediately put on an apron over the traditional Swedish clothes she liked to wear on Sunday, and went to the linen chest for the old, embroidered tablecloth used on Sundays and special occasions. Hilda's grandmother, whom she could barely remember as a very old lady, had made it for her wedding chest when she was younger than Hilda. Now it was worn fine as a handkerchief, and neatly darned in places, but the embroidery was still bright and beautiful.

Meanwhile Patrick was helping Sven and Erik put up the trestle table and arrange chairs. Nine people made a tight squeeze in the tiny living/dining room, but the young ones didn't mind being crowded and the older ones coped.

When Birgit and Elsa had set the table and Gudrun and the older girls had set out the food, Sven took his place at the head of the table and Mama at the foot, and they all stood while Sven solemnly pronounced a long Swedish grace. Patrick bowed his head as devoutly as any of them, and chimed in on the *Amen*. He had no idea what Sven was saying, but he doubted God cared much one way or the other. The idea of gratitude was enough. Truth to tell, Patrick didn't understand much of the Latin in his own church, either, and he took the same attitude toward that. God presumably knew what was being said and what was intended; that was what mattered.

Dinner, as usual, was delicious. Gudrun and Mama were superb cooks, and the little gifts of special, expensive foods that Hilda slipped them from time to time didn't hurt. There wasn't much talk until everyone had satisfied their first hunger, and then Erik swallowed a mouthful of potato sausage and dropped a bombshell.

"Have you found out any more about that murder, Hilda?" he demanded.

Several pairs of eyes swiveled in Hilda's direction. Mama and Gudrun laid down their forks. Patrick, under the table, reached for Hilda's hand and squeezed it.

Hilda raised her chin. "I do not think it is a thing to talk about at dinner," she said sternly, aiming a kick at Erik.

"Oof!" said Birgit, and then put a hand to her mouth. Hilda grimaced. Evidently the kick had missed.

"Hilda, we will speak of this later," said Sven in his head-of-the-family voice. "Have you had a pleasant week?"

The change of subject was not entirely welcome. Hilda rapidly reviewed her week, but all she could think of was the murder, the police suspicion of Sean, the baby, and Norah's illness. She chose the least controversial. "Norah—you remember my friend

Norah—had her baby on Friday. At our house. She was visiting when—" she glanced at the younger children "—when the stork arrived. She will be staying with us for a little while, she and her mother and the baby."

There was a chorus of exclamations and questions, to which Hilda replied as seemed prudent. A little girl, very pretty, with lots of dark hair. Named after me, but in Irish—Fiona, which means fair. Because *my* hair is fair, Erik, and we do not yet know what color the baby's will be when she is older. Yes, her husband is very pleased. Well, Norah is very tired, of course, but getting lots of rest. (Hilda crossed her fingers under the table at that one. It was not really a lie, just not all the truth. And Norah *was* going to be better soon—she *was*.)

"And yes, there is one other interesting thing to tell. Mrs. Elbel and I, and some other ladies, are to form a club for boys." The sour look on Mama's face made Hilda realize she should have said *women* rather than *ladies*. Again a reminder of the elevation of Hilda's station in life. Hilda hesitated, then mentally shrugged. The change was real. Her family was going to have to get used to it. "The club will be for the children of immigrants, mostly—"

"Hilda! You never told me! What'll the club do? Where's it going to meet? Can I bring—"

"Erik, you interrupted your sister." It was Sven's authority-voice once more. Erik subsided, but he reminded Hilda of a jack-in-the-box, ready to pop up again at any moment.

Hilda smiled. "I will tell you everything I know, but I do not know very much yet. I am to meet with the other ladies tomorrow to make plans. We must work quickly, because the first thing we will do is give a Christmas party—"

"Ooh!" said Erik, but he said it quietly, with a glance at his brother.

"—and Christmas is only three weeks away. Yes, Erik, before you burst from wanting to ask, there will be presents for everyone. Not big things, you know. We will ask people for donations, and I think they will give, but there are many boys who—who will want a gift." She had almost said *need*. It was tiresome being so careful of her speech, she who had said exactly what she thought all her life, but she didn't want to hurt any feelings.

"I will give," said Sven. "I have little money to give, but I can make good toys. And Mama and the girls can maybe make scarves and hats and mittens."

"Thank you!" Hilda was truly grateful. "I am not so good at knitting and sewing—"

There was a roar of laughter, in which even Patrick joined, for Hilda's total lack of needlework skills was a joke in the family.

"Well, I said I am not! I am not good at making anything with my hands, even cooking."

"I can teach you to cook," said Gudrun eagerly, at the same moment that Mama made a sour face and said, "But you have a cook to do that for you."

Hilda could not let that awkwardness continue. "Yes, we have a cook, and Patrick is fortunate that we do, for if he had to eat my cooking he would starve." Patrick looked so bland that sister Elsa stifled a giggle. "But we may not always be so lucky," Hilda pursued, "so I think it would be better for me to learn a little. I would be happy, Mama, if you would teach me, too. You and Gudrun are the best cooks I know."

Mama looked slightly mollified, and nodded, but Sven frowned. "Do you mean that Patrick may lose his job, so you cannot afford a cook? That would be very serious. You are working hard, *ja,* Patrick?"

Patrick nodded. "Yes, my uncle seems happy with me. I admit that times are bad and folks aren't buying as much at the store as they sometimes do, but there's no chance I'll lose me job. I wish I could say as much for everybody in town. I'm worried by these bank failures all over the state."

"I meant only," put in Hilda, "that Mrs. O'Rourke, our cook, has a very bad temper and threatens every week to leave us."

"Yoost like the Irish. Undependable," muttered Mama.

"If she ever does," said Hilda, ignoring her mother, "it will not be easy to find another cook. So I must learn. Mama, Gudrun,

I know you are busy with Christmas baking now. May I come and help one day, and learn?"

"On me knees, ma'am!" said Patrick. He pushed his chair back and fell to his knees, looking up at Mrs. Johansson in the attitude of a begging dog.

Everyone roared except Mama, who said, "Get up, Patrick," with would-be severity. But Hilda was sure her mother was hiding a smile.

When the afternoon was finally over and Hilda and Patrick were heading home in the carriage, Hilda had one more touchy subject to discuss. They always took Elsa back with them to Tippecanoe Place, where she now worked and lived. She was required to be in by twilight, and the carriage ride meant she could spend a few more minutes with her family.

"Elsa," said Hilda, and then stopped.

"*Ja?*" said Elsa dreamily. She was thinking about Kris Olsson, who had smiled at her three times in church that morning. He was a very handsome boy...

"Elsa, I will be at Tippecanoe Place tomorrow afternoon."

"Why? It is not my afternoon out, and I will not have time to talk. Some ladies are coming and I will have to help with the tea. Hilda, there is a new waitress again, and she is no use at all! She—"

"I am one of the ladies."

Elsa sat with her mouth open as she worked out the implications. Then she laughed. "I hope I am in the room when you come. I want to see Mr. Williams have to welcome you as a guest!"

Hilda was taken aback. She saw nothing funny in the situation. Awkward, humiliating perhaps, but not funny. But then, Elsa had always had the least imagination of the younger children. She couldn't see Hilda's deep embarrassment, only the ridiculous side of things.

Hilda wished she were gifted with such a matter-of-fact outlook on life, but she could always see where pitfalls lay. Walking around them was becoming exhausting.

Once Elsa had said good-bye and gone into the magnificent house, Hilda could speak her mind.

"It is like walking in the chickens' nests!" she exploded.

"Walkin' on eggs, I suppose you mean," said Patrick lazily. He loved teasing her about her English.

"Hah! You have maybe never tried to find eggs that the chickens have hidden, climbing over beams in the hay barn, wondering if you will fall off or crush the eggs. And I *know* you have never done that in skirts that twist around your ankles and trip you up. I said what I meant to say, so there!"

Patrick kissed the tip of her nose. "And what is like walkin' in the nests, then?"

"Talking to my family today! I cannot say this, I must not say that, I must be careful always not to remind them we are richer than they are. And you may not show you are angry when they say bad things about the Irish or hint that you are idle and shiftless."

"But I'm not angry, darlin' girl. I like them all, even your mama. She's just repeatin' what she's heard everybody else say about the Irish, not really meanin' it. And Sven wasn't hintin'. He's your big brother. He wants life to be good for you, and so do I. And Elsa, o' course—she sees about as far as the end of her own nose. She wouldn't hurt a fly unless it landed on that nose."

Hilda smiled, but went back to her grievance. "They do not like it when people talk about dumb Swedes. Why can they not see talking badly about the Irish is the same thing?"

"Dunno, but lots are like them. Don't want to be insulted themselves, but don't care if they insult other folks."

"That is not Christian," said Hilda firmly. "The Golden Rule—"

"Don't reckon they think about it that way. Don't reckon they think about it atall. Do ye know nobody else whose mouth gets goin' ahead of their mind?"

"Mmm." Hilda quieted. She could remember all too many times when her own tongue had hurried ahead of her better judgment.

"And it's gettin' better. Your ma was laughin' inside when

I played the fool, I'll swear, for all she sounded so stern. Don't worry about it so much, me girl. Just be yourself and love them, and things will come right in the end."

"The end is a long time coming," said Hilda tartly, but she pulled up his hand and laid it against her cheek.

Their house was utterly quiet when they entered. The servants had Sundays off, and Hilda, more lenient than a butler, did not ask them to be back until eight o'clock. There was no sound from upstairs, either.

"The baby must be asleep," said Hilda, "but what about Norah and the nurse and Mrs. Murphy? Do you think something has—has happened?"

A door opened quietly and soft footsteps sounded. Hilda started up the stairs.

"Quiet, if you please, madam," said a soft but firm voice. A white skirt came into view, crackling as it moved. "Mrs. O'Neill and the baby *and* Mrs. Murphy are all asleep."

"How is Mrs. O'Neill?" asked Hilda in a whisper.

The nurse came around the corner and gestured downstairs. Hilda obeyed. The nurse was as forceful as any butler, if somewhat less heavy-handed in manner. If anyone could get Norah to eat and take her medicine, Hilda thought, it was Miss Pickerell.

"I don't like to talk about a patient where she can hear," said the nurse when they reached the front hall, "even if I think she's asleep. She is somewhat better. Mr. O'Neill went to church and brought the priest back with him. I left them alone, of course, but I believe he said a few prayers with her, and baptized that little lamb of a child. If *she* were my only patient, I'd have nothing to do! Sweetest, quietest baby I've ever seen. But Mrs. O'Neill..." The nurse shook her head. "She ate a good supper and took her tonic, though her mother fussed about it as usual. But she makes no effort, even when her husband talks to her. Just lies there and cries. We'll start doing something about that soon," said Miss Pickerell confidently.

"Yes," said Hilda, hoping it was true. "And Sean? Is he also asleep?"

"Mr. O'Neill has gone home. He must work tomorrow, and Mrs. O'Neill is too tired even to talk to him."

"Miss Pickerell, what is *wrong* with Norah? The doctor says only that she is run down."

"Well, of course I'm not a doctor. But there is something called anemia—something to do with the blood. No one knows much about it, but I've done enough nursing to know that poor people, who don't eat enough meat, seem to have it more than rich ones, and women more than men. And of course Mrs. O'Neill's just had a baby, so it's natural that she's tired. She'll pull out of it in time, if I have anything to say about it. Mrs. Cavanaugh, don't you worry. Keep Mrs. O'Neill cheerful, keep giving her good food, and she'll be fine. She just needs a firm hand."

And Miss Pickerell crackled away, her starched skirts emphasizing the firm treatment Norah was going to receive, whether she liked it or not.

Highest Award is Given to the Starr
Piano Co. at the World's Fair

—Elbel Bros. Music Store ad
South Bend *Tribune*
December 1904

14

THAT EVENING after a little cold supper, Hilda and Patrick sat in the parlor, grateful for a glowing fire and a glass of wine, and most of all for peace and quiet. The past few days had demanded much of them.

"I am glad the nurse is here," said Hilda. "I feel now there is not so much for me to do for Norah and the baby."

"You never did *have* to do anything much," said Patrick. "Been a whole pack o' women about the place to do what was needed."

"I know, but Norah is my friend. I wanted to help. Patrick, I do not know what is to become of them. If Sean loses his job—or if he goes to jail—"

"Between us, darlin', we'll see he doesn't go to jail. As for his job, that's a worry for certain."

"Patrick, did you mean what you said to Sven today? That your job is safe? Or were you only pretending, so we would not worry?"

"I'm a partner in Malloy's, darlin'. Half the business is mine. As long as there is a business, I have a job, and a fine one it is. And Malloy's is sound. Uncle Dan's built the store up gradual-like and kept it runnin' with cash."

Hilda frowned. "I do not understand. Money is what runs every business. Not?"

Patrick smiled. "There's money and money. I've been learnin' a lot about business these past few months. Y'see, a lot of people, startin' out, will borrow money to get things movin'. Say it's dry goods, like Uncle Dan. Well, you have to have money to buy the things you're goin' to sell, and if you start big, sellin' lots o' goods, you have to have lots of money. And that's not all. You rent a building, you hire people to work, you have insurance—oh, there's no end to what you need before you ever earn a penny. So you borrow from a bank. And if everything goes right, you can make enough money to pay your rent and pay the people who work for you and pay back the bank, a bit at a time, and still have enough left over to buy more goods to sell, and even some to live on. If things don't go so well, you don't live so well. If things get really bad, maybe the bank decides it wants its money back. So it calls in the loan, and there you are with no money left to pay anything, and you're ruined."

"But—but that is frightening! Patrick, are you sure—we have this house, and servants, and food, and everything is very expensive—"

"Don't be getting in a stew, Hilda me love. I told you Malloy's is sound. That's because Uncle Dan never borrowed a penny to start the store. He worked for other people for years, and he and Molly saved every cent they could put away. Then when he had enough to go off on his own, he started small. Had a itty-bitty store, sellin' linens an' dress goods. He and Molly did all the work, so they didn't have to pay anybody else, and hard work it was, too. You'll have to get Molly to tell you about it sometime. She's a small woman, but blessed saints, the energy she has! And they didn't live in that fine house, neither. Lived above the store, and happy as a pair o' larks, to hear her tell it. And they saved more, and when they had a bit put by, they built up their stock, little by little, till they had to find a bigger place to put it all. And that's how Dan got where he is now, workin' hard, and doin' it all with his own money. He's got a lot saved, too, so if there's a slump in business, he has enough to keep goin' for a long time, and without anybody losing a job, neither. That's what I meant by doin' business with cash.

"But that's not the way of it with everybody these days, more's the pity. This outfit Sean works for..." Patrick shook his head. "His brothers and his cousins, we all tried to tell him not to leave

Birdsell's. He had a good job there. They maybe don't pay the highest wages in town, but they're dependable, and they make a good product. As long as farmers raise clover for feed, they'll need clover-hullers, and Birdsell makes the best in this part o' the country. But no, Sean said he had a wife now, and a baby comin', and he could get higher wages at the new bicycle factory. Now I'm not sayin' Black's isn't a good place to work, because it is. Sam Black's a decent man, from what I hear, and he treats his men right. But he's thinkin' about gettin' into motorcars, and he's borrowed money left and right, and there's talk he won't be able to pay it back if a bank calls in the loan."

Hilda felt cold. "And it might do that?"

"Farmer's Bank's only been around two, three years, and it's owned by a new man in town, name of Townsend. They don't only lend to farmers, though that's their main business. If Black borrowed money from them—well, the word is, Farmer's isn't doin' too good. If they fail, a lot of people could be in big trouble."

"People like Sean," said Hilda. "The little people. The people who work hard and do not borrow money they cannot pay back, the people who earn their wages. It is always the little people who are hurt!" She stood up and began to stride up and down the room, her sense of peace gone. "You say Mr. Black is a good man. He is not a good man if he is so foolish in business that he lets his workers starve."

"Nobody's right all the time, love. You own a business, you've got to make decisions. Sometimes you've got to take risks. If you guess right, you get rich, and your workers along with you. If you guess wrong, everybody gets hurt."

"Hah! This Mr. Black, he will not get hurt, I bet you. He will sit—what do you say, when someone leaves a wreck without harm?"

"'High and dry,' I guess. Or 'sitting pretty.'"

"Yes. He will be sitting pretty."

"That's where you're wrong. I happen to know his house is mortgaged, because I overheard some men talking about it. He'll lose everything, right along with his men. Come here, darlin'."

He stretched out his arms, and Hilda came and sat next to him on the settee. She leaned back into the curve of his arm, but she was still stiff with indignation.

"It is not right!" she muttered stubbornly.

"No, darlin'. It's not. Lots o' things in this life aren't right. We're all born to trouble, like the Good Book says. But the good Lord made us tough, us Irish, and the Swedes, too. We can stand up to trouble." He stroked her cheek. "You and me, we'll help Sean and Norah if they need it. They'll do well enough."

Hilda was silent. Patrick looked down at her. Her eyes were very bright.

"You—you are a good man, Patrick Cavanaugh," she said in a very low voice.

Upstairs a faint cry sounded. Hilda sat up, sniffed, and touched her handkerchief to her eyes. "Fiona is awake. I will go up and see her. And then let us go to bed. Tomorrow there will be much to do."

Patrick turned off the gas brackets, checked to make sure the doors were locked, and then followed her up the stairs.

Sunday's bright, cold weather was only a memory come Monday morning. Hilda awoke to find Patrick gone and his side of the bed cold, and wondered where he was, since it was still dark outside. The room was warm, though. Why would Eileen have lit the fire in the middle of the night?

When Hilda went to the window she saw. Snow was falling, heavy, thick snow that obscured the light from the sun. She shook her head at the variability of Indiana winter weather. In Sweden, they had known what to expect in winter—snow and more snow. She lit the gas and looked at the bedside clock. Eight-thirty.

She clicked her tongue. A comfortable life was already making her lazy. Never, from her childhood on the farm in Sweden through her years under the butler's authority at Tippecanoe Place, had she risen later than five-thirty except in cases of dire illness. Now she could often sleep as late as she pleased, and as a result, she realized with a grimace, she had a headache. Or perhaps it was that glass of wine last night. She hadn't so much as raised one eyelid when Patrick had risen early for his usual Monday morning meeting with Uncle Dan and the other senior employees at the store.

She rang for Eileen, who brought coffee without being asked and helped Hilda dress. "How is Norah?" was Hilda's first question as soon as the coffee had brought full wakefulness and eased her headache a bit.

"Not so good, ma'am. She's like—like a doll or somethin'. All limp an' floppy."

"A puppet?" suggested Hilda.

Eileen looked doubtful. "Like Punch and Judy? But she's not funny, ma'am, just sad-like. Does as she's told, but don't take no interest in nothin'."

"Does not take interest in anything," Hilda corrected automatically.

"Yes, ma'am. Will you wear the pink velvet dress this mornin', ma'am?"

"No, I am not going out until this afternoon. Just something comfortable. The old black skirt will do, with a plain waist. Is Norah eating well, and taking her tonic?"

"She does what that nurse tells her." Eileen made a face behind Hilda's back, but Hilda was looking in the mirror.

"You do not like Miss Pickerell? She seems good at her job."

"She's bossy."

"A good nurse must be bossy with a patient like Norah," said Hilda firmly. "We must be bossy, too, I think. Norah must begin to—to have some starch, like the nurse's skirts."

"And the nurse's nose," said Eileen, but so quietly that Hilda thought she could ignore it.

"Has Mr. Cavanaugh left for the store?"

"No, ma'am. It's been snowin' that hard, he doesn't think the horses could get through. Hardly anythin's gettin' through, by the look of the streets. Mr. Cavanaugh, he called Mr. Malloy up on the telephone, and Mr. Malloy said he's not openin' the store till the snow stops. He went round himself, Mr. Malloy did, walkin' in all that storm early this mornin', puttin' a sign on the door and stoppin' at houses and boardin' houses to tell the clerks—most of 'em ain't got no telephone."

"Do not have a telephone. That was kind of Mr. Malloy, but very foolish. He is not a young man, and might have fallen in the snow. He should have sent Mr. Cavanaugh."

"That's what Mr. Cavanaugh told him, ma'am. Right sharp with him on the telephone, he was."

Hilda wasn't sure who was sharp with whom, but both, she imagined. Uncle Dan and Patrick were as close as father and son, but like father and son they often shouted at one another.

"There, that's your hair done," said Eileen, pushing the last pin carefully into the coronet braids with a little sigh. "I wish you'd let me do it up in a Gibson Girl. You'd look beautiful with little curls down just here, and here, and the rest piled on top of your head so." She gestured with one hand, building an imaginary mound of hair above Hilda's eyes. "I mean, you look beautiful now, ma'am, but don't you want to be fashionable, now you're rich and all?"

Hilda laughed. "I will wear fashionable clothes when I must, even though it means I must also wear a corset, but I like my hair the way I have always worn it. It suits me, I think. It is the Swedish way, and it means I do not look like everyone else. This afternoon I must wear something 'fashionable,' though. I must go to a meeting at Tippecanoe Place."

"Ooh, ma'am, how excitin'! Goin' back to where you used to be a maid, and goin' as a fine lady!" Then her face clouded. "If you can go. The way it's snowin', ye might not get out."

Eileen, too, was unable to imagine the strain of such a visit, thought Hilda. Perhaps she was making too much of it. Perhaps it would be all right. Or perhaps, if she prayed hard to the old Norse gods (more likely, Hilda thought, to know about winter weather than the temperate Christian God), the snow would continue and she wouldn't have to go.

But capricious Indiana weather paid little heed, apparently, to Thor or Odin or whoever might hurl snow down upon the hapless earth. By midmorning the snow had tapered to a light flurry, by noon it had stopped, and when lunch was over the sun was shining brightly, blindingly, on a world blanketed in white. Mr. O'Rourke was out helping other neighborhood servants clear their drives and the street, and soon carriages and sleighs were moving briskly along Colfax.

"A sleigh. That's the next thing, when we can afford one," said Patrick as he kissed Hilda good-bye. "Quicker and safer than wheels in snow."

"Do not let Mr. O'Rourke drive too fast, Patrick."

"Don't worry. He loves those horses like they were his own. He'll not let them slip. And don't you go fast to your meetin', neither. I might be a bit behind my time for supper, if Uncle Dan keeps the store open late."

He kissed her again and went out the door. Hilda watched as Mr. O'Rourke slapped the reins and urged the horses into a slow, careful walk.

Oh, no, she wouldn't go to her meeting at any faster pace than that. Slower, if possible.

She turned away from the door in time to hear Eileen picking up the telephone in the hall. "Yes, ma'am. She's just here, ma'am. I'll call her."

"It's Mrs. Elbel, ma'am," said Eileen in a stage whisper.

GANG OF BOY BANDITS

*...police believe they have struck the
trail of a gang of boy bandits that
has been operating along the
Lake Shore railroad...*

—South Bend *Tribune*
December 5, 1904

15

"Thank you." Hilda had to swallow twice before she could take the receiver Eileen handed to her. "Mrs. Elbel!" she said in as cordial a tone as she could muster. "How nice of you to phone."

"Hello, Hil—Mrs. Cavanaugh. I just wanted to remind you about the meeting this afternoon. To organize the Boys' Club. You remember?"

"Thank you, I remember. Three o'clock, Tippecanoe Place, yes?"

"Yes. I—um—I wonder if there is anything I can do to help you—that is, if your afternoon gowns are being cleaned or—I would be happy to lend you—"

Hilda's trepidation changed abruptly to fury. "Thank you, Mrs. Elbel," she said in a voice chillier than the December air, "but happily my afternoon gowns are in perfect order. It is so kind of you to make the offer. I will see you at three, then?"

"Er—yes. If you—yes. Good-bye until then."

"She t'inks I do not know how to dress, Eileen! She t'inks I am a servant still! She is such a grand lady and I am a little immigrant without gowns fit to be seen! I will show her I have gowns. I will—"

"Madam, I *must* ask you to be more quiet!" Miss Pickerell's starched skirts crackled down the stairs. "Mrs. O'Neill has been very fretful today, very fretful indeed, and in consequence so has the baby. I've only just got them both to sleep, and they must not be disturbed."

"Yes, of course." Hilda could not imagine how Norah, or

⌒ 109

anyone else, could stand up to this woman. "I am sorry. Is Mrs. Murphy with them?"

"She is not." The nurse's tone made it quite clear what she thought of Mrs. Murphy. "I think it best to keep them apart as much as possible. Mrs. Murphy's manner of dealing with her daughter is not—she is not a help, not just now."

The nurse's voice had lowered almost to a whisper, but it wasn't low enough. Hilda looked up the stairs and saw Mrs. Murphy descending, her bag in her hand and a black expression on her face.

"And I'm leavin'!" she said furiously to Hilda. "As ye've seen fit to bring *her* into the house to look after me own daughter, as I reared and cared for her whole life, and know what's best for her, and then bein' ordered out of her room, like I wasn't workin' me fingers to the bone for her and the babe, as is me own grand-daughter, and the first one, but no, I'm not good enough to take care of her, neither, me what's raised eleven of me own and know all there is to know about babies—"

Mrs. Murphy, having run out of breath and lost the thread of her diatribe, paused and glared at Hilda, ignoring Miss Pickerell completely.

Hilda tried to defuse the situation. "I am sorry," she said calmly. "You know you are welcome—"

"Welcome, am I! Welcome, when you think you need a fancy nurse and a doctor and all, as poor folks like us can't pay for, but you, you're a fine lady, you know best, you can throw away your money! Well, you can throw it in another direction next time, for the Murphys don't need you *or* your money, and I'm bringing' Norah and the baby home as soon as I can get a place ready for her!"

With that she stumped out the door and down the steps.

"Wait, Mrs. Murphy! The carriage will be back—"

"*That* for your carriage!" And Mrs. Murphy made the rudest gesture Hilda had ever seen from a woman, and trudged off down the street.

"Oh, dear," said Hilda, closing the door. "Oh, *dear!*" she

repeated, for from upstairs came the loud wail of a baby and the fretful whine of a woman.

Miss Pickerell muttered something under her breath and went back upstairs. Hilda could have sworn the words were "Good riddance."

Eileen, who had taken in the whole scene, said it aloud. "She's an ungrateful woman, ma'am," she added, "and no mistake. All you've done for Norah and the baby, and her to treat you like that! It's a downright shame, that's what it is."

Hilda sighed. "It is natural, Eileen. She is not exactly *un*grateful. She does not want to have to be grateful. If I was still poor, and Norah was rich, I would not want to take favors from her. I understand."

"Well, I don't, then!" said Eileen, stoutly partisan. "You're a good person, and for all I don't care for that nurse meself, Mrs. Murphy's got no right to talk to you that way."

"Yes, well. I think, Eileen, I will have a bath. That will maybe take my mind off all the bad things that have happened. And then you will help me dress, please, in the finest afternoon gown I own. And I will give you your wish. You may put up my hair."

When Hilda arrived at Tippecanoe Place precisely at three o'clock, Mr. Williams did not at first recognize the tall, fair, beautiful lady. "Who shall I say is calling, madam?" he asked with a bow.

"And do you not know me in my fine feathers?" asked Hilda demurely.

"Hilda! That is, Mrs.—Mrs. Cavanaugh. I beg your pardon, madam. I—it is your hair, madam. Very nice, if I may say so."

"Thank you." She could not bring herself to call him "Williams," and "Mr. Williams" was now inappropriate. She simply smiled and handed him her cloak. The look on his face when he saw her gown was one she hoped she would remember forever.

She wore a pale green velvet gown, made in the latest style with the skirt falling in graceful folds from the natural hip, with no hint of a bustle, but a very slight train. The bodice had lace inserts in rows forming a V, with a lace collar rising almost to her chin. Her matching hat was worn well forward on her piled-high coiffure, giving her the true Gibson Girl look, and the colors of the ensemble set off her pale golden hair admirably.

Williams tried to pull himself together. "You are here to meet with the other ladies, miss—madam? I will show you—that is—"

"The meeting is in the library, yes?" As Hilda well knew, such gatherings at Tippecanoe Place were always held in the library. "Good." She gave a sharp little nod, making her new coiffure wobble slightly. She cleared her throat. "I will go through, then. There is no need to show *me* the way." She glided away, the short train of her gown whispering softly on the polished floor of the great hall.

She didn't let him see her take a deep breath. She'd cleared that hurdle. Williams had actually been more embarrassed than she. Now for the next challenge.

She ducked into a hidden corner to pin her hat more securely, then lifted her head and sailed into the library.

Several women were already assembled around a table there. Hilda knew almost all of them from her servant days. She had taken these women's cloaks, served them tea, opened doors for them, done a thousand little things the women were, in her opinion, perfectly capable of doing for themselves. She doubted they would recognize her. People never really looked at servants, never saw past the cap and apron to the human being inside.

Mrs. Clement Studebaker was one of those rare people who looked beneath the surface. She recognized Hilda instantly and came to greet her. "My dear, you look perfectly lovely," she whispered, taking her gloved hand. Hilda began an automatic curtsey, but Mrs. Clem pulled her hand up in a firm grip, and Hilda was able to turn the movement into a half stoop to rearrange her skirts.

"Ladies," said Mrs. Clem in the sort of quiet voice that somehow manages to command, "this is Mrs. Cavanaugh. Though relatively new to South Bend society, Mrs. Cavanaugh is one of the moving spirits of the effort we have met here to discuss. She is working closely with Mrs. Elbel and Mrs. Malloy."

Hilda was flooded with gratitude. She had always been fond of Mrs. Clem; now she came close to loving her. With that careful and tactful speech, the gracious old lady had left Hilda's options open. She could reveal as much or as little of her background as she chose.

Hilda also saw, with a good deal of pleasure, the shock on Mrs. Elbel's face. She hadn't recognized Hilda in her new persona. Hilda smiled sweetly at her.

"Mrs. Malloy you know, of course." Aunt Molly gave her an encouraging smile and the tiniest wink as Mrs. Clem continued with introductions around the room. "Mrs. Brick, Mrs. Ford, Mrs. Witwer, Mrs. Darby, Mrs. Cushing, Mrs. Townsend, and of course Mrs. Elbel. I realize that's very brief, and you'll forget, but we have a good deal to do today, and I'm sure you will get to know all these ladies well as you work together."

"I believe I can remember the names," Hilda said, striving to make her English sound as American as possible.

She didn't add that she had known for years who most of these women were. Mrs. Brick was the wife of a prominent local politician, Mrs. Ford the wife of an eminent lawyer. Mrs. Witwer's husband worked as private secretary at Studebaker's, and Mrs. Cushing was married to a prominent pharmacist, now retired. Mrs. Darby, recently married to an up-and-coming young businessman, had been Arlene Martin, one of the prettiest brides of the social season. Mrs. Townsend was the only one she did not know, but she'd ask later. She exchanged a private smile with Mrs. Clem.

"Good! Then please take that seat, between Mrs. Malloy and Mrs. Elbel, and I'll turn the meeting over to her."

Mrs. Elbel was obviously still trying to reconcile the radiant creature in velvet with the former housemaid and the somewhat combative young matron she had met only once, but she stood and cleared her throat. "Yes. Good afternoon, ladies. I'm so pleased you could all come on such short notice, and delighted that the weather improved so as to make it possible for you to get here. As most of you know, Mrs. Malloy and I have formed the idea of an organization whose purpose is to help keep some of the boys of this community off the streets." She glanced nervously in Hilda's direction. "We are all aware that there are many—er— many families living in less than ideal circumstances in South Bend. They have few resources to devote to their children, some of whom must work rather than going to school, in order to help support their families."

She cleared her throat again. "Unfortunately, some of these boys have taken other paths. In place of either jobs or education, they spend their time in idleness and worse. Mischief, vandalism, even thievery can be laid at the feet of gangs of roving boys."

She glanced again at Hilda, on whose face an ominous frown was growing, and hurried on. "I spoke some time ago to Mrs. Malloy about what we might do to find some more wholesome outlet for these boys. She suggested that Mrs. Cavanaugh might be able to help us with some ideas. Mrs. Cavanaugh—er—has some background with—er—boys, since she has several broth-ers, and is—that is—has some familiarity with the problems cre-ated by—er—poverty."

"Were you associated with Miss Jane Addams before you came to South Bend, Mrs. Cavanaugh?" asked Mrs. Brick, who had an interest in social reform.

"No, Mrs. Brick." Hilda decided to throw caution to the winds. If she were to accomplish anything, she must be able to educate these women, well meaning but woefully ignorant of the scope of the problem they were trying to deal with. "No, I know only a little of what Miss Addams has tried to do at Hull House, but I believe her way of working is the best. Instead of giving charity to the immigrants she serves, she works with them to make a better life. She teaches them skills and lives among them. I can understand why this is better because, you see, I am an im-migrant myself."

There was a rustle in the room, small movements of shock or disapproval. Hilda lifted her head higher and continued. "I have only recently been married to Mr. Cavanaugh, who can support me very well. Before that I worked, and worked hard, and so does my family still. My youngest brother is a friend to many of the boys you—we—wish to help, and I know them well. I know that they are not idle by choice. They cannot find work in these days when many grown men cannot find work."

"Then they should go to school and learn a good trade," said Mrs. Townsend, the one woman in the room whom Hilda did not know. "There's no excuse for them being on the streets making life miserable for decent folks!"

"They cannot—" began Hilda at the same moment that Molly Malloy said, "I don't know that—"

"I am sorry, Aunt Molly. Please go on."

"I was about to say that I don't know that I'd go quite as far as Mrs. Townsend. I imagine there are some good excuses for these boys. Can you tell us some of them, my dear?"

Hilda was so eager to make her argument that she didn't notice Molly's careful avoidance of the name "Hilda," which would recall to some of the women exactly who she was. "Yes, I can," she went ahead. "The boys cannot go to school, or do not want to go, because they have had little or no education before. They are big boys of twelve, thirteen, fourteen years, and they do not want to start with the babies, learning to read, learning their numbers. The other children would make fun of them, and these boys have been made fun of all their lives. They want to make other people respect them, treat them properly, instead of calling them names and thinking they are stupid."

Her voice grew passionate. "They want to have a better life. That is why they came to America, or their families came—for a better life. But many of them have not found that better life. They have found bitter poverty and poor food and shabby places to live, and then besides, they are treated with contempt because perhaps they cannot speak English well, because they look different, even just because they are poor!"

The ladies were nodding. Two or three touched handkerchiefs to their eyes. Mrs. Townsend sniffed, but not with tears. "Hmph! A good life is for those who earn it. I can't see sympathizing with young hoodlums who can't find anything better to do than break windows and steal and hang around on street corners insulting decent women!"

Aunt Molly laid a gentle hand on Hilda's arm before she could utter her heated reply. "I believe, Mrs. Townsend," said Molly calmly, "that it is to give them something better to do that we have met here today. I find Mrs. Cavanaugh's insights to be persuasive. Of course I, myself, am also an immigrant, though of the generation before my niece's. I, too, have known poverty and near-starvation, have understood the temptation to steal when there was no food in the house, the temptation to scream at those with fine clothes who walked past me holding their skirts away lest they touch my rags.

"When we were first married, Mr. Malloy and I had nothing, but we were fortunate enough to find a place to live where there were jobs to be had. Ladies, I took in washing for some years, and glad to have the work. Mr. Malloy did whatever odd jobs came his way, and we scrimped and saved until there was enough money to start a small business. If we hadn't been able to find work, if our children had been starving—I don't know what we'd have done, but I cannot swear that our children might not have ended up begging on the streets—or worse."

Mrs. Clem nodded. "Most of us are in the same position, or a similar one. After all, we are all only a few generations away from our European forebears. I have never known real poverty, but my dear late husband certainly did. His father was deeply in debt when the family left Ohio. Indeed, when Mr. Studebaker and I were first married, we were in much the same position as the Malloys. Working hard, living frugally, raising two children in a very small house. But Mr. Studebaker was always able to work. I think if we remember that many of these boys have no living father, and that their mothers often fall ill under the burden of their circumstances, we can begin to understand why the boys need a guiding hand."

"With a switch in it! Spare the rod, spoil the child." It was, of course, Mrs. Townsend again, but before she could expand on her theme, Mrs. Brick spoke.

"I believe, Mrs. Elbel, that *most* of us are in favor of your idea of a boys' club. Have you any concrete proposal to make?"

"I hope that we can formulate some plans in the next month or two. However, as Christmas is coming, I did think that a modest party for the boys would be a good start. We could find a hall, perhaps in a church or club, give the boys punch and cookies and perhaps small gifts, and explain to them what we would like to do for activities later in the winter and in the spring. What would you ladies think about that?"

"Excellent idea!" said Mrs. Ford, and the others nodded. Mrs. Townsend, seeing that her opinions did not prevail, said nothing.

"There's a good deal of work to be done, and this is a busy time," said Mrs. Cushing. "We would need to organize a committee immediately."

Mrs. Elbel smiled. "Mrs. Cavanaugh has discussed the party idea with me, and has already promised to do much of the work. Now, I have made a list of what needs to be done, with copies for all of you. You've all run similar affairs before. Let me pass these out, and then we can set a date and you can tell me which job each of you can take on."

There was a good deal of polite wrangling about who would do what. The pleasant, attractive jobs like decorating the hall and planning refreshments were snapped up at once. All the women promised dozens of cookies, an easy promise to make because of course their cooks would do the work. The women who were mothers of sons agreed, somewhat reluctantly, to purchase gifts, aware that finding large quantities of inexpensive presents for boys from five to fifteen (the agreed-upon age span) was not going to be an easy task. One or two of the culturally minded ladies promised to arrange for entertainment.

By the end of the meeting, Hilda found herself with the thankless jobs, and with less than two weeks to get them done. The party had been set for Saturday, December seventeenth. She would be responsible for finding a location, preferably free, for making all the arrangements about tables and chairs, and most important and hardest of all, for getting the word out to the boys and providing a count for the refreshments and gifts ladies.

There had been some discussion about exactly who should be invited, but Aunt Molly, wise as always, had come up with the best solution. "Invite *every* boy of that age in the city, and make it clear that the poor are especially welcome. There will be well-to-do parents who don't wish their children hobnobbing with poor children. Very well, those privileged boys will not come. The wealthy parents who do allow their boys to attend will be asked to help, and to contribute money. It will be very good for rich boys, at least those with enlightened parents, to mingle with those who have less. It will teach them compassion. And the two groups can teach each other a great deal in the way of new games, new ways to live."

"Glad I don't have children," muttered Mrs. Townsend, but the others ignored her and concentrated on the excellent tea served by Elsa and the new waitress.

Hilda was exhausted by the time the meeting was over, but she stayed on after all the others had left. Mrs. Clem had given her a discreet signal, so she pretended she had lost a handkerchief.

When the last guest had been seen out the door, the last hat vanished into a carriage, the last high-pitched voice died out, Mrs. Clem returned to the library. Hilda, who had been drooping in a chair, sprang to her feet. The older woman smiled.

"Sit down, my dear. You must be worn out. I thought you carried out your role splendidly." She sat down herself, and propped her tiny feet up on a footstool.

Hilda stared. She had not expected the wealthiest woman in South Bend to see what her own sisters could not. "It was not easy, madam—Mrs.—Mrs. Studebaker," she said, stumbling over the words.

"Old habits die hard, don't they? Just call me Mrs. Clem. Everyone does. And don't think I don't know the courage it took for you to come here this afternoon. Your new life is a bit hard to get used to, isn't it?"

"Oh, madam—Mrs. Clem—you do understand! It is very hard. I do not even know how to talk to people, my own kind of people or your kind, either one. Always I must watch my words, my manner, even my gestures. You know I nearly curtseyed to you."

"Yes, but I don't think anyone else noticed. You recovered very well. You must care a great deal about boys to involve yourself in this cause."

"I do. There is my youngest brother, Erik. He has friends among these boys, and he could so easily get into trouble. He is like me, you see," said Hilda confidingly, and wondered why her hostess burst into laughter.

"Oh, Hilda—do you mind if I call you Hilda? That's an old habit of *mine*, and not at all proper in your new position."

"I would like you to call me Hilda. You are my friend, I think. But why did you laugh?"

"My dear child, do you think I was unaware of all the trouble you got yourself into when you worked here? I was very careful not to notice unless I absolutely had to, but your—er—extracurricular activities did not escape me. And if your brother is like you, then indeed he needs some restraining influence."

She smoothed her skirts and then looked seriously at Hilda. "My dear, I'm sure you noticed that one of the ladies in the group seemed not to be of quite the same mind as most of us."

"Mrs. Townsend." Hilda said the name as if it tasted bad in her mouth, and her cheeks flamed. "Aunt Molly would not let me say what I thought, and it is good that I did not, but oh, I wanted to tell her many things!"

"I can just imagine, but I'm very glad you didn't. Mrs. Townsend is—she can be a bitter woman, and she is, I'm afraid, not well liked in South Bend society. That's one reason I urged Mrs. Elbel to invite her to join in this effort, but it was a mistake, I fear. I don't quite understand why she can't fit in, for she entertains a great deal, and very lavishly at that. I do have the feeling she is worried about something, but she never hints at what it might be. However—I thought I should warn you to watch your step with her if she continues with the Boys' Club."

"What do you mean? What could she do?"

"I don't know that I mean anything very particular, and I can't predict what she might do. That's just the point. She's unpredictable, sweet as pie one minute and sour as vinegar the next. As I say, perhaps a worry that nags at her from time to time. You'd do well to walk on eggs with her."

Hilda sighed. She knew all about egg-walking.

Mrs. Clem stood. "You look tired, Hilda. I had hoped your marriage would ease some of your burdens."

"Oh, it has, but now there are others. It is not only finding the place where I belong now. There are other things, serious things. Norah—you remember Norah Murphy?"

"Of course. Norah O'Neill now, isn't it?"

Hilda marveled again. She had underestimated her employer, all those years. "Well, Norah has had a baby. In my house, on Friday. She came there to tell me Sean—that is her husband—that Sean was in trouble, arrested. There has been a murder, and Sean is suspected. And now Norah is very ill with something called a-neem—something, and her worry is making it worse. And so…"

"And so Hilda is going to the rescue. Again. Well, see you take care of yourself while you're taking care of everyone else. Don't work too hard on the party arrangements, dear. You have enough to do."

"Yes, but the party is part of what I have to do for Norah. The boys, you see, they know things others do not. I hope to learn many things from them at the party."

"And I wouldn't be a bit surprised if you do. Take care, child. Please tell Norah I'm terribly sorry to hear she's ill. I'll send over a little gift for her and the baby. And be sure to let me know if you need anything from me."

Hilda thanked her profusely, collected her cloak from a bemused butler, and swept out the door to the porte-cochère and into her carriage.

DECEMBER MEETING OF

THE ORPHANS' HOME BOARD

Many Donations Reported—

Need of a New Home is Greatly Felt

—South Bend *Tribune*
December 1904

16

NO SOONER HAD Hilda driven away than she regretted her grand exit. She should have stayed to consult with the butler. She was, now, charged with several duties for the boys' Christmas party, and she had no idea how to go about some of them. How did one procure a hall? How large did it need to be? Where was one to find tables and chairs? She was sure Mr. Williams—no, Williams, she must remember—would know about tables and chairs, anyway. The Studebakers often hosted dinners on a scale large enough to require that furniture be brought in.

Having acted the grand lady in front of her old boss, however, Hilda was reluctant to go back to him with hat figuratively in hand. Why, she berated herself, had she volunteered to do so much work, when she already had more than enough to do? She needed desperately to free Sean O'Neill from suspicion, and at the moment she had only the vaguest idea how she was to go about that task. She hoped Patrick would have had time today to talk to Sergeant Lefkowicz. Perhaps a report from the police would give her a path to follow.

Meanwhile there were the party problems to solve. Hilda called to her driver. "Mr. O'Rourke, I have changed my mind. Please take me to Mrs. Malloy's house."

Aunt Molly was a very present help in time of trouble—any kind of trouble. She had become Hilda's counselor in almost every situation.

Aunt Molly, however, was not at home. Hilda was met at the door by the frozen-faced butler who had so intimidated her when she had first become acquainted with the Malloys some years ago. His manner today was quite different. Plainly he didn't recognize Hilda in her finery.

"I am sorry, madam. If you would care to wait, I expect Mrs. Malloy soon. She attended a meeting this afternoon and was to be home before five o'clock."

"I attended the same meeting. It ended some time ago. She must have made another stop." Hilda consulted the lovely little watch pinned to her gown. Patrick would be home very soon, and she was pining to talk to him. "Oh, dear," she said, unsure of what to do. "I cannot wait. Perhaps I can return later."

"May I give her a message, madam?"

She made up her mind. "Yes, please tell her Mrs. Cavanaugh called."

The butler's mouth dropped open, but his training held. He shut it again and resumed his deferential look.

"Tell Mrs. Malloy that I need some advice about planning the Christmas party, and I would like to speak with her very soon about a hall and other matters. It is urgent."

"Madam, if I may make a suggestion: since the matter is urgent, I might be of some assistance. I have some experience in arranging large parties. I take it this is to be a large party, if you need a hall?"

"Yes, I think so. It is all to be done in a great hurry. The party is planned for Saturday, the seventeenth, at two o'clock, and we do not know yet how many are to come. It is for boys, you see— poor boys, and others, if they wish to come. We will not know for certain until they arrive. It is difficult!" She was beginning to see just how difficult it was.

"I see," said the butler thoughtfully. "This would have to do with the Boys' Club that is being planned?"

Hilda nodded, not questioning how he knew. No one was more aware than she that servants always knew everything that was going on.

"Madam, if you will allow me to make some inquiries, I believe I might be able to solve your problem. There are several

halls that are often available for charitable events without charge.
Some of them are able to accommodate large crowds and have
sufficient tables and so on. Is there to be food?" He checked himself. "Of course. The party is for boys."

Hilda gave a great sigh of relief. "Oh, if you could help! It cannot be a church, you know. Some of the boys will be Catholic and
some Protestant, so they could not all go to the same church."

"Yes, I see." The butler nodded. "I'm sure it can be arranged
without too much difficulty, madam. The Odd Fellows Hall will
be best, I think. They have a large meeting-place."

"Thank you—I am sorry, I do not remember your name."

"Riggs, madam."

"I am very grateful—er—Riggs—very grateful for your
help."

"Thank you, madam. I am happy to be of assistance." A
strange expression crossed his face. "I am fond of boys, madam."

That was unexpected. "You have a son, maybe?"

"I had a son, madam." The mask was back on his face. He
bowed. "Was there anything else, madam?"

"No, thank you, Riggs, but tell Aunt Molly I called."
Thoughtfully she went down the steps and back to her carriage.
How odd that she had never really thought of a butler as a human being with troubles of his own. *"I had a son."* Was the boy
dead, then? Did Riggs have a wife living? If so, where? She certainly didn't live at the Malloys'.

It was a mystery, but a minor one compared to the huge question of who killed Mr. Jenkins.

The Cavanaugh home was only a block from the Malloys'.
Hilda rushed inside, hoping Patrick would be home, but he was
not. Hilda was greeted by Eileen, who took her cloak and whispered, "The doctor's come, ma'am. He's upstairs."

"Norah isn't worse?" Hilda whispered in return. There was
no real need for quiet, but whispers are contagious.

"I don't think so, ma'am. The nurse seems well enough
pleased. Doctor's just checking her."

"I'll go up."

Norah's bedroom door was still shut, so Hilda took a moment to step into her bedroom and remove her hat. She wished fervently that she could also remove her stays, but that meant a complete change of clothes and Eileen's help. Hilda couldn't imagine why they couldn't make sensible clothing that was also pretty, clothing a woman could get into and out of by herself. When she had been a maid—but the sound of a door opening put an end to her musings. She rushed into the hall.

"How is she, Doctor?"

The doctor blinked. "Er—Mrs. Cavanaugh?"

"Yes, yes!" She was getting a little impatient with the reaction to her new appearance. "How is Norah?"

"Feeling somewhat better. Good food and rest are doing her some good, and the tonic's put some roses in her cheeks. It may be months, mind, before she's back to normal. She's been run down for a long time. And you, young woman. What have you been doing on her behalf? Found out anything yet?"

"No. This morning I could not go out, and this afternoon I was busy about the Boys' Club. But tomorrow I will go and talk to many boys, and see what I can learn."

"Mind you do. What your friend needs more than anything I can give her is a quiet mind. If you think you can give her that, you'd best be about it." He glared at her over the top of his glasses and stumped off down the stairs.

Hilda knocked on Norah's door. The nurse opened it, looked Hilda up and down, and smiled. "Come in. The sight of you would do anyone good. Mrs. O'Neill, here's a visitor for you."

"I don't want—who—Hilda?" The last was said on a rising note of astonishment.

"It is me," said Hilda, twirling to give Norah the full effect. "I should have left my hat on, but it is heavy and uncomfortable."

"Go and get it!" commanded Norah.

When Hilda returned, hat in place, Norah shook her head. "It's that grand you look, I'd scarce have believed me eyes. You're as pretty as the roses. Prettier—they're fadin' a bit. And your hair!"

"Eileen wanted me to wear it like this. I do not think it looks like me, and nobody recognized me. Except Mrs. Clem. Norah, she has a sharper eye than we ever knew."

And Hilda took her hat off again and sat down to tell Norah all about the afternoon. "And she said she will send something for you and the baby. She is a good woman, Norah."

"We always knew that. Many's the time I wish I was still working there. Though Mrs. George..." She left the sentence unfinished.

"Yes, she is not as kind sometimes, but I think it must be hard for her, living in the same house as her mother-in-law. Even a big house like that. And Norah, if you still worked there, you could not have Sean. Or Fiona." She smiled over at the sleeping baby in her cradle.

"No. And Fiona is such a darlin' wee thing. And Sean..." Tears started in her eyes, and Hilda could have kicked herself. She had not intended to remind Norah of her troubles.

"Do you know, Norah," she said, reverting to the earlier subject, "I think Mrs. George is still looking for a good waitress. Elsa says there is another new one who does not do her job well. I wonder if, when you feel better, she would hire you to come in by the day."

"And who would look after me babe?" said Norah, still weepy.

"I would," said Hilda, who had not until that moment thought of such a thing.

Norah sighed. "Maybe. It is a long way off. I am so tired."

Hilda stood. "I should not have stayed so long. I have tired you. But I am happy that you feel a little better, and I want you to know that you must not worry. Everything will be good. I promise."

Yet another promise, she thought as she gently closed the door. And she was not at all sure she would be able to keep this one.

She heard the front door open and close. Patrick! She paused at a hall mirror and put her hat on again, then glided down the stairs.

"Hilda! Me darlin' girl, ye look like the Queen of the World! Turn round and let me see all your glory."

Hilda rotated before him while Eileen giggled behind her hand. "Do you like my hair this way?"

"It's beautiful and no mistake. Makes me feel shy, though. Doesn't look like you, somehow."

"That is what I think. I will wear it sometimes this way, when I want to look like a grand lady. But I like my braids. And I do not like this corset!"

Patrick put a practiced arm around her waist. "And no more do I. Feels like a cage around my darlin'. Go and take it off and put on somethin' ordinary, so I can tell you what I found out today."

"Patrick! You have learned something?"

"Not much, but a little. Go on, now. I want you beside me lookin' like yourself."

When she was settled with him in front of the fire, his arm around her and his pipe lit, he told her. "Uncle Dan closed the store just past the regular time. The snow's begun again—don't know if you noticed. Fallin' thick, it is, just like this mornin', and nobody out on the streets. Dan wanted our people home before it got too bad. Well, I reckoned I had time to go round to the police station, so I walked over there and phoned O'Rourke to come pick me up. And while I waited, I had a nice little chat with Sergeant Lefkowicz." He took a few puffs on his pipe.

Hilda's nerves tightened, but she had learned in the few months she had been married that there was no point in trying to rush Patrick. He would tell his story in his own good time.

"Well, as I suspected, the police aren't looking very hard for a murderer, and they're convinced Sean is the thief. They reckon the fire was an accident—"

"But the firemen say it couldn't be!" said Hilda, interrupting. "The lantern, so far from the hired man—"

"I know, darlin', but there's a bit of a feud between the police and the firemen, y'know. The police claim it was the wind knocked over the lantern, and never mind there was no wind that afternoon. And they think Sean's tellin' the truth about findin' the billfold on the ground, but that there was money in it and he took it. They're just bidin' their time before they take him back in and charge him with theft."

"But they have no proof! Who says that there was money in the billfold at all? I do not believe it! Sean did not lie to me. I can tell when people are lying."

"Because you're so good at it yourself, most like. You know there doesn't have to be proof when they take the likes of us up before a judge. The police tell their story, the accused man tells his, and who does the judge believe?"

"It depends on the judge," said Hilda sagely. "There are some who will believe the one who tells the story that is sensible."

"There's that," Patrick admitted. "And there's this, too. Sergeant Lefkowicz doesn't believe any of what the rest of the police do. He has nothin' to do with the case; a man named Applegate's in charge. Don't think Lefkowicz has much use for Applegate. He didn't exactly say anything against him, but he said he's heard enough talk to know Applegate's not dealin' with the case right. He's workin' long hours these days—Lefkowicz is, I mean—'cause he's savin' up to get married, but he's tryin' to find out what he can in his hours off."

Patrick puffed on his pipe, then said, in a lower tone, "And I'll tell you this, girl, but you're to keep it to yourself. Lefkowicz reckons the farmer burned down his own barn, not knowin' the hired man was sleepin' there."

"But why would Mr. Miller burn down his own barn? A barn costs very much to build, and what would he do with his horses and cows and hay?"

"Well, you know there's trouble with a lot of banks, and Lefkowicz has found out Miller has a mortgage on the farm, and not a lot of cash. He has insurance, too."

Patrick let that sink in.

"Oh!" said Hilda. "He would burn down the barn to collect the insurance, and then he could make the mortgage payment." Hilda thought about that for a moment. "But then he would have no barn. I do not understand."

"He's keepin' his stock with a cousin near Lakeville for the time bein'. Maybe he plans to sell his own farm and move in with the cousin for good. Both of 'em bachelors—it'd make sense. And when he collects the insurance, he'll be well off for cash."

Hilda mused. "Sergeant Lefkowicz has done a lot in just a few days."

"That he has. And he's goin' to follow up on it, too. His next day off's Wednesday, and he says he's goin' out to Miller's farm and talk to him a bit. Meanwhile, darlin', there's no court session till after Christmas, so there's time."

"Yes," said Hilda slowly. "But there is maybe not time for Norah. She is a little better, Patrick, but every time someone says something about Sean she cries. She will worry herself into more illness until he is cleared."

"And you'll worry until she stops worryin'. I know you, dar- lin' girl."

The doorbell rang and Hilda heard Sean's voice as Eileen an- swered the bell. "And here is Sean to visit his wife and daughter. I hope he is cheerful."

But Sean was anything but cheerful. His head drooped and his shoulders slumped as he walked into the house.

"What is the matter?" Hilda cried.

"They're shuttin' down the bicycle factory. Somethin' about the bank loan. We're all of us out of work after Friday. And with Christmas comin', and me with a new baby!"

17

THE NEWS OF Sean's loss of employment was a shock, even though it was not entirely unexpected. Hilda had been giving some thought to the possibility. After she had sympathized with Sean, and Patrick had offered him a drink (which he refused), Hilda asked, "Can you go back to work for Birdsell's?"

"First thing I thought of," he replied despondently. "They're not hirin' now."

"What about Oliver's, then? Or Studebaker's?"

"Haven't tried them. Don't know much about plows or wagons."

Hilda could have shaken him. "You didn't know anything about bicycles until you went to work for Black's! You know how to use your hands. You can learn. I will talk to—" She came to a stop. Clement Studebaker, co-founder and first president of Studebaker's, had been a kind man who would almost certainly have hired Sean if Hilda asked him to. But Mr. Clem was dead. His son, Colonel George, took no active part in the company. Hilda didn't know J. M. Studebaker, Mr. Clem's brother and current president, at all well. There was, really, no one she could talk to on Sean's behalf.

Patrick thought it was time to intervene. "Ye'll find somethin' soon, me boy. Meantime we can tide ye over. Ye can move in here, if ye want. Norah's like to be here for a while yet, anyway, and the baby. Why not stay yerself and save the rent on yer house?"

Patrick always became more pointedly Irish when he was

talking to his cousins, who, as far as Hilda could tell, were numbered in the hundreds. Usually the thick accent and the charm laid on with a trowel helped him win his point. Not this time.

"I'm thankin' ye kindly, but we're not wantin' to be beholden to anybody," Sean said stiffly. "I'd move Norah home if she weren't so sick, and I'll pay the bills for the doctorin' as soon as I can. Tomorrow I'll go out and find work. And now I'll be goin' up to see me wife and daughter."

"Sean," said Hilda. Patrick shook his head at her, but she ignored him. "Sean, you must not go to Norah with that look on your face. She must not know anything is wrong."

Sean's face as he looked at her was expressionless, but as he left the room he straightened his shoulders, and they heard him greet Norah with a cheerful "How's me girl, then?"

"If ever there was a stubborn mule of an Irishman," Patrick began, but Hilda interrupted him.

"He is proud. I can understand that. I am proud, too."

"And stubborn."

"And stubborn, yes. I stay up for what I believe—is that right?"

"Stick up." Patrick began to smile.

"Stick up for what I believe. Sean is right to be independent. But if he does not get a job soon, you must try to make him accept help. You could lend him money, *ja?*"

"I don't like lendin' money to kinfolk. It makes for bad blood with 'em. If I pretend it's a real loan, Sean'll worry about payin' it back, and start bein' scared to talk to me. If I tell him not to pay it back, he'll resent bein' helped behind his back as ye might say. No, there has to be another way, but blest if I see what. It's a pickle."

Sean refused to stay for dinner, and though Hilda and Patrick spent most of the evening trying to find a solution to the O'Neill family's problems, they came up with nothing. Uncle Dan needed no one with Sean's skills at Malloy's, especially with business slow, and Sean would be quick to detect and resent a make-work job offered to him out of charity. Hilda stayed awake for hours worrying about him and Norah. She got up early Tuesday morning, though, so she could talk to Patrick about her job for the day.

"It is the boys, you see. I must invite them all to the Christmas party, but I do not know how. Most of the poor boys do not go to school, so a notice in the schools will not work. Many of them cannot read, so a notice pinned up on the streets will not work. I cannot go to all the places where they might work. I do not know how to find all the boys!"

"Churches," said Patrick, putting down the South Bend *Tribune*. "Write up a notice and have them print up a lot of copies at the *Tribune* or the *Times*. Go round to as many churches as you can, and ask the priests—the pastors—whatever you Protestants call them—to tell any others they know."

"Patrick, you are so clever! Yes. That is the way to do it. And I will say in the notice—no, I will ask the pastors to write to me, saying how many boys they know will come to the party. Then I can tell Mr.—can tell Riggs, and he will tell them at the hall."

"Aunt Molly's butler? What's he got to do with this?" asked Patrick, bewildered.

"I forgot to tell you. I went to ask Aunt Molly for help, and she was not at home, but Riggs—he told me to call him that, but it is hard for me—he said he could help find a hall for the party. He was *nice*, Patrick!"

"He'd be interested in anything for boys," said Patrick, nodding. "He lost his own son when the *Maine* blew up in 1898."

"When Maine blew up? I do not understand."

"THE *Maine*. The ship. Beginning of the Spanish-American War. Riggs's son was a navy man. Only about our age when he was killed."

Hilda said nothing, but she thought a great deal. Thought about her own ingrained prejudices, her failure to see beneath the surface. Was that at the heart of all prejudice, the inability to see anything but what one expected to see? She looked at Mr. Riggs or Mr. Williams and saw "tyrannical butler." Other people looked at her and saw "dumb Swede," or at Patrick and saw "drunken Irish."

"I am as bad as they are," she murmured to herself.

"Mmm?" said Patrick, absorbed again in the newspaper.

Hilda wrote out the notice immediately after breakfast, very careful about her English. Then, after checking on Norah and kissing little Fiona, she was ready to set about her many calls. She decided to use the carriage. The gray skies threatened nasty weather, and with a choice, why should she walk and risk a soaking or worse?

She was about to climb into her seat, with the coachman's assistance, when she suddenly turned around and looked at him. Really looked at him, for the first time. "Mr. O'Rourke," she said, "are you warm enough when you drive in the snow or the rain?"

He was affronted. "I've never complained, ma'am."

"I know you have not. That is not what I asked."

He frowned. "Gets a bit cold now and then, doesn't it? And wet when the rain's drivin' in me face, or the snow."

"That is what I thought. It is not fair, Mr. O'Rourke, that you should sit in front where it is wet and cold while I sit in back wrapped in a warm carriage robe."

"Somebody's got to drive, ma'am."

"Yes. And I am not a very good driver."

"A lady doesn't drive herself, ma'am!" He sounded scandalized.

Hilda smiled. "But I am not really a lady, you know, only a Swedish maid who was lucky enough to marry a fine man. And I am happy to have you drive me, but you must have a warmer coat. After you leave me at the library, please go and buy one, and tell them to send the bill to me. Buy anything else that will keep you warmer, as well. I am sorry, Mr. O'Rourke, that I did not notice before."

"Anything you say, ma'am." O'Rourke sounded grumpy as he handed Hilda into the carriage, but then he nearly always sounded grumpy. Perhaps, thought Hilda, to whom a new world was opening, perhaps one day he will be able to see me as a real person.

Hilda dropped her notice off at the *Tribune*. Although the office was separated from the compositing room, the noise from several linotype machines being operated at once, and the heat they emitted, made Hilda slightly dizzy. The office girl promised Hilda she could pick up a hundred copies in two hours, and she was glad to escape to the quiet of the Public Library.

It was a beautiful building, donated by the Studebakers and the Olivers and other wealthy families in the city. Hilda was proud every time she walked into it, proud that all those books belonged just as much to her as to anyone else who entered. Today as she asked to see the City Directory she had the sudden thought that she could buy a copy for herself. She could buy any books she wanted! It was such a glorious idea it nearly diverted her from her mission.

Nearly, but not quite. Today was December 6. Only a week and a half before the party. She had to get the word out quickly, especially so she could concentrate on her other, more important task of solving the murder of the hired man.

She was daunted by the number of churches listed, nearly fifty. Many of them were Catholic, of course. She would need to visit only a few of those; they would pass the word. Then there were the many Protestant denominations, including some Hilda had never heard of. Well, she would just have to visit the ones downtown and trust they would get the word out to others.

She made a list of the churches she needed to call on. It took quite a while; the list was still very long. She looked out the window. At least nothing was yet falling, neither rain nor snow nor sleet. She hoped that respite would continue. For she had decided that she positively would not ask Mr. O'Rourke to drive her if the weather turned really nasty. New coat or not, she refused to let him get soaking wet in her service.

He was waiting when she came out of the library, resplendent in a black coat with a shoulder cape and a new black fur cap.

He jumped down to help Hilda up. "The new coat is fine, Mr. O'Rourke."

"You don't need to call me Mister, ma'am," he said. "Thanks for the coat. It's warm, right enough. And waterproof, s'posed to be, anyway."

"You are welcome. And I prefer to call you Mr. O'Rourke. It is more polite."

He shook his head. Hilda's new attitudes made him extremely uncomfortable. "If you say so, ma'am. I got your notices from the *Tribune*."

"Good. Now, I do not need you to drive me to the first few churches. They are very near. I will go to the First Christian Church, and then the First Baptist. You can pick me up there."

Her errands took Hilda longer than she expected. Some of the churches had adjacent parsonages where she could speak to pastors, but many did not, and on a Tuesday morning church doors were locked up tight. Hilda pushed several notices under those doors, with scant hope that any attention would be paid to them, until she got a better idea.

"Take me to the factories, please, Mr. O'Rourke. First the ones on the river, because they are near, and then Studebaker's and Oliver's."

The coachman was shocked. "No place for a lady, ma'am, if you don't mind me sayin' so. Dirty places, factories, and some of those men are none too polite."

"I am not a lady," Hilda said for the second time that day, as patiently as she could. "I worked hard for many years, farm work and housecleaning. Dirt will not kill me. And I can deal with rudeness. Birdsell's first, please."

At each factory she asked to speak to the owner or president. Many of the factories in town were run by men like Clement Studebaker, men who took a benevolent interest in their employees and in the community. "Fine idea, a club for the boys," said Joseph Birdsell when the idea was presented to him. "I'll see to it that the men know about it."

"And please, if we could know how many will attend the party?"

"Hard to throw a party when you don't know how many guests you'll have, eh? My secretary can give you a count. Just give her your address."

"Thank you, sir—Mr. Birdsell."

Mr. Birdsell grinned, and Hilda had a feeling he knew very well she was the same woman who had often taken his hat at Studebaker dinner parties, but he bowed as he showed her out.

She met with the same reception almost everywhere she went, until the noon whistle sounded and she was swept out of Oliver's on a tide of workmen seeking their dinners.

"Home, ma'am?"

"Yes, please. No!" she corrected herself. "No, I must go and talk to the boys at the Oliver Hotel."

O'Rourke sighed. He had been a boot boy when he was young, then a gardener, and of recent years a coachman for many wealthy families. He and his wife had thought this new situation would suit them, because they could be together and had a pleasant little set of rooms on the top floor of the Cavanaugh house. Nor was the work onerous. But never had he had a mistress who insisted on visiting factories and talking to bellboys. She meant well, he supposed—the new coat and hat were welcome—but she didn't understand the way gentry were supposed to behave. Mrs. O'Rourke said she turned up in the kitchen at all hours, even serving food on the kitchen table when the cook was busy elsewhere!

If Mrs. Cavanaugh didn't become more conventional, they might have to rethink their employment. Scowling, he clucked to the horses and turned the carriage in the direction of the Oliver Hotel.

"Shall I wait, ma'am?" he asked sourly when they arrived.

"No, thank you, Mr. O'Rourke. Go home and tell Mrs. O'Rourke that I will have my dinner here, and I will make my own way home. If the weather becomes unpleasant I will telephone for you."

O'Rourke didn't hold with telephones. Grumbling to himself, he made off.

Hilda shook her head. Clearly the O'Rourkes did not understand the way a former-servant-turned-lady behaved. If they couldn't be trained in her ways, she might have to try to find a more adaptable couple.

Dear Santa, please bring me a train
of cars a toy steam engin. A little barn
with toy anemals in it... Some nuts
and candy. I go to school when I can.

—Earl A. Carr, 9 years old
South Bend *Tribune*
December 1904

18

NDY WAS ON duty in the front lobby. He saluted when he saw Hilda and rushed to her side. "Help you, ma'am?" he asked, and winked at her.

"Yes, please. Will you show me where the restaurant is?" She waited until they were climbing the grand staircase to the dining room and had escaped the oversight of the doorman, and then whispered to Andy, "Are you allowed to eat with me?"

The eager light faded out of his face. "No, ma'am. It's my dinnertime in a half hour, but we have to eat in our office. Can't never eat in the dining room."

"Cannot *ever*. Not even if a guest asks for you?"

"Don't think so, ma'am. I got things to tell you but—we're in uniform, y'see."

Hilda saw. She thought it grossly unfair, but the boy couldn't afford to lose his job. "Then I will eat my dinner, for I am very hungry, and will meet you in your office when you have yours. What would you like me to bring you as a treat?"

"Ooh, a Hershey bar, please, miss—ma'am. I don't know if they sell 'em in the dining room, but the newsstand does."

Hilda smiled indulgently. It was pleasant to have money for treats. "And what is a Hershey bar?"

"Chocklit, miss! A big slab of nothing but chocklit! Ain't you never had one?"

"*Have* I never had one, Andy. And no, but it sounds very good. I will buy one for myself, too. I will eat my meal quickly and meet you soon."

Luncheon in the big hotel was intended to be a leisurely affair, eaten in courses and accompanied by cigars or pipes for the
gentlemen. Hilda, who felt somewhat conspicuous as the only
woman eating alone, chose to have a quick meal of chicken cro-
quettes and a salad. She refused coffee, knowing it would not be
made to her exacting standards, and left as soon as she had paid
her bill, stopping at the newsstand for three Hershey bars.

Andy was just unwrapping his lunch when Hilda came into
the "office." Hilda saw that he had only bread and an apple. He
flushed when he saw her look of dismay.

"Mama's been sick, miss. She hasn't had no time—*any* time to
cook. So me and my big sister Ellie've been tryin' to help, but we
don't cook so good. So this mornin' all there was, was some bread
and a piece of meat from last night's supper, and Papa needed
that for his own dinner. I'm not really hungry, anyway."

Hilda looked at Andy's thin face and made a mental note to
speak to the chairman of the Christmas party refreshments committee. Whatever was being planned, Hilda thought it should
probably be doubled. "Yes, well, before you tell me what you
have learned, I want to give you this." She reached into her capa-
cious pocket and pulled out one of the notices. "I promised you a
party. Here it is."

Andy's meager lunch was forgotten as he read the notice. She
watched his lips move as he worked out difficult words, watched
his pale face take on animation as he grasped the facts.

"It's really gonna happen, then, miss!"

"Yes, Andy. I promised."

"Can I tell everybody?"

"Yes, every boy in town is welcome, especially boys whose
families have not much money. I want you to tell every boy you
know, and ask them to tell others. And have them report back
to you, and you report to me, so that we will know how many to
expect. We must have enough food and enough gifts."

"Yes, *ma'am*! And speakin' of reports, miss, I found out some
stuff. Good stuff, miss."

Hilda handed over one of the chocolate bars, unwrapped another, and settled herself to listen.

"Well, see, I talked to everybody I could think of, but care-less-like, see? Made out I didn't believe there was anything int'restin' about that fire, and said I'd give a nickel to the first boy who could show me the police wasn't—weren't—just makin' a fuss about nothin'." He looked anxiously at Hilda. "Cost me three nickels, miss."

Without a word Hilda reached in her pocket, pulled out a small purse, and counted out three nickels.

"So the first thing is, that farmer, that Mr. Miller, he said he was buyin' supplies that day, right?"

Hilda nodded. "That is what Patrick—Mr. Cavanaugh told me. Supplies and machinery."

"Well, if he was, it wasn't around here. Some of the boys asked around. He wasn't at none—any—of the feed stores, nor anyplace where they sell stuff for farms. Hay rakes and stuff, I guess. I dunno. Never lived on a farm."

"I did," said Hilda. "Yes, rakes and hoes and shovels and plowshares and fencing and—oh, there are hundreds of things a farm needs."

"Well, Mr. Miller didn't buy none—any—of that sort of stuff. And I know that for a fact, because one o' the boys knows him, or knows what he looks like anyway, and he saw him goin' back to his farm the next day, when he heard about the fire. Drivin' hell for leather, he was—beg pardon, miss, but that's what Tom said—and there wasn't nothin' in his wagon 'cept the two dogs, and they was whinin'—scared, y'see, cause they was goin' so fast and bein' jounced all over the place."

Hilda was thinking so hard she forgot to correct Andy's grammar. "Machinery—he might have bought it to be delivered."

"Yes, miss. But why'd he take the wagon for supplies, if he wasn't goin' to bring back no supplies?"

"That is very interesting, Andy. Very interesting. You have done well."

"That ain't all, miss. There's this one boy who knows a girl who knows a kid—well, anyway, somebody works at the bank, emptyin' out the trash cans and that, the bank where Mr. Miller does his business. And he heard somebody say—I wrote it down, 'cause it didn't mean nothin' to me—" Andy searched his pockets and finally found a grubby piece of paper. "Somebody said, 'If he doesn't pay up soon they'll call in his more-gage.' I don't know what a more-gage is, miss, or how they call it in, but that's what this person said, and they was talking about Mr. Miller."

"I think maybe I know. Who was the person who said that, Andy?"

"Dunno. I had it down the line, you might say. But I reckon I can find out."

"Do that, if you can without—"

"I know, without makin' nobody suspicious. I can do that easy. And I gotta go back to work in a minute or two, but there's one more thing, miss."

"Andy, you are worth any three policemen. What else?"

"Well, you know that billfold somebody found at the fire?"

Every muscle in Hilda's body tensed. "Yes?" she said in a voice that didn't sound like her own.

Andy was too interested in his tale to notice. "Well, your brother was really the one who found this out, so you should maybe ask him. But he told me, so I'm tellin' you. Erik was in the stables at the fire department, and he heard some of the firemen talkin', and they said one of 'em at another station seen that billfold earlier, and threw it down when he saw it didn't have money in it. Figured it was an old one somebody dropped out there a long time ago. But see, it had letters on it."

"Letters in it, you mean?"

"No, *on* it. In gold, only they'd been wore off and you could hardly see 'em."

"Oh, initials! What were they?"

"Dunno. Just that there were some. Guess you'll have to find out from whoever's got it now."

"Andy!" The call from the doorman was peremptory. Andy jumped up and looked expectantly at Hilda.

"Yes. You have earned your pay and more. You told me four important things, not just three—no, you must go, I do not have time to explain. And they were so important you deserve a little more than I promised. So here is a quarter, and here is another bar of chocolate, and you may have the rest of mine—and thank you, Andy!"

She embarrassed him by giving him a hug and a hearty kiss, and fairly danced out of the hotel.

*The love of wealth is therefore to be
traced, as either a principal or accessory
motive, at the bottom of all that the
Americans do....*

—Alexis de Tocqueville
Democracy in America,
Part II, 1840

19

I**T WAS SNOWING** hard when Hilda came out onto Washington Street. She didn't notice until her foot slipped on the slick sidewalk and she nearly fell. "Careful, ma'am!" said the man who caught her by the elbow. "May I get you a taxi?"

"Thank you, but I have only a short distance to go. I will walk."

"But, ma'am—the snow is very wet—"

Hilda didn't hear. She was already on her way again, though a little more carefully. She couldn't wait to get home and talk to Norah.

She was wet through, and shivering, by the time she reached her front door. Eileen brushed off the snow and fussed over her.

"Yes, I will take a hot bath, but not just now. You may fill the tub for me. First I must see Norah."

However, she was not permitted to do that. "Mrs. O'Neill is asleep, madam," said Miss Pickerell firmly. "She is feeling somewhat better today, and has a little more color. I cannot allow her to be disturbed. I will let you know when she is awake."

Hilda, perforce, had to bide her time. "Say that I have something to tell her, something good," she told the nurse, and then went away to submit to Eileen's ministrations.

Hilda had her bath, and changed her clothes, and drank a cup of hot tea she didn't want, and then paced her bedroom floor and fumed. Here she was with good news, excellent news, and was barred from telling Norah. Sean was innocent, and it could be proved! The fireman had seen no money in the billfold. Sean had said it was empty, and he was telling the truth.

142 ❧

Sean was on the scene before the firemen got there, said a nasty, cold voice in Hilda's mind.

He was not fussing with billfolds! He was with the other men, trying to find a way to help put out the fire.

How do you know that?

Hilda sat down. She didn't know. She knew only what she had been told.

She stood up and began to pace again. She did not know enough. She needed to talk to the firemen herself. If, she reasoned, if the billfold had been very close to the barn, the fireman might have picked it up to save it, and then thrown it away. And Sean and the other men would not have dared go that close to the fire, not without protective clothing and hoses full of water.

Sean said he found it by the fence. The fireman could not have thrown it that far.

Hilda pushed the curtains aside and stared out the window at the snow, falling ever more thickly. She could not go out at all now, not even in the carriage. She would not ask Mr. O'Rourke to drive in such weather. Even if she had no concern for the coachman, the horses could easily slip in heavy, wet snow, especially on paved streets, and a broken leg meant death for a horse. It was a day to stay in by the fire, not go out investigating a crime.

Sean's life might be in danger. What did it matter if she, Hilda Johansson Cavanaugh, got a little wet?

She looked out the window again. Twilight came early in December, even when the sky was clear. Now, with the snow, midafternoon looked almost as dark as evening. And the snow was getting deeper by the minute. It would be hard to tell where curbs were, or bumps in the sidewalk or the street. Patrick would have something to say if she fell and did herself some damage. And the fire station where she wanted to talk to the men was a long way from West Colfax, probably two miles.

There was no help for it. She would have to wait until the weather was better. Patience, she reminded herself with gritted teeth, is a virtue.

Meanwhile, she could think about the other information

Andy had given her. Really, Andy was a precious resource. She should have given him more than a quarter. Two quarters, at least. Fifty cents would buy a very nice toy, or something pretty for his mother. Next time she saw him she would make amends.

The farm owner, Mr. Miller, had not been where he said he was, according to Andy. She and Patrick had talked about him—was it yesterday, or the day before? So much had happened in the past few days that she couldn't remember, but she recalled that she had not seen then, nor did she see now, any reason why the farmer would burn down his own barn. Even though the animals were safe, he must have lost equipment and tack. The buggy, for instance. Someone had said the hired man would have taken the buggy into town if there had been a horse to pull it. Surely the buggy was kept in the barn, and buggies weren't cheap.

And yet—Mr. Miller had lied. He had told Jenkins, the hired man, that he was going to town for supplies and machinery. At least that was what Jenkins's drinking friends had said, and even if one didn't believe them, Mr. Miller himself, after the fire, had told the police that was where he had been. And it was not true.

What did the lie mean? Where had Mr. Miller been? What had he been doing, that he didn't want to tell?

If the bank was indeed going to call in the mortgage on Mr. Miller's farm, that was a reason for the farmer needing money badly—and quickly. But burning down the barn wouldn't get him money. Any insurance money would have to go to replace his losses. Unless—Patrick had suggested that he might move in with his cousin in Lakeville.

But Mr. Miller would have nothing to bring to a combined farm. He would have to sell everything to pay the mortgage, unless it was a small one. The insurance on just the barn wouldn't pay the whole debt.

Hilda's head was spinning. She was not stupid about money—years of poverty had taught her to be watchful of every penny—but she knew little about finance. She wished Patrick would come home. He could help her straighten out the tangle.

A discreet knock on the door. The nurse put her head in and

said, smiling, "Mrs. O'Neill is awake now, and eager to hear what you have to tell her."

Herre Gud! Hilda took a deep breath. Why had she said anything to the nurse? Now she had to pretend that the news about Sean and the billfold was good, when she knew—now—that it might mean nothing at all.

Well, she could lie convincingly in a good cause. In the few seconds it took to walk from her bedroom to Norah's, she had put together what she hoped was a believable story.

Norah was in fact looking somewhat better, and she was cuddling little Fiona to her breast, which was definitely a good sign. "Look, Hilda, how sweet she is! She's hungry, the little darlin', but Miss Pickerell says I'm still not strong enough yet to let her nurse very long. So I'll give her only enough that my milk doesn't dry up, and then she'll have a bottle for the rest."

"She is beautiful," said Hilda with perfect truth. The baby had, in fact, improved a great deal in the—was it only four days since her birth? She had lost the red, wrinkled look and seemed to have rounded out a bit. Hilda touched the soft little cheek with one finger. Fiona turned her head and regarded Hilda with incredibly blue eyes for a long moment.

"She knows me!" said Hilda, delighted.

The nurse coughed. "Probably not, Mrs. Cavanaugh. A newborn baby can see very little, you know. She may simply like the light color of your hair."

Hilda looked at Norah and rolled her eyes to the ceiling. Norah's look in response agreed. *That nurse doesn't know everything, even if she thinks she does.*

"But Nurse said you had something to tell me. Something good, she said."

"Yes. And Miss Pickerell, I must ask you to leave the room for a moment, because what I have to say is private."

"A nurse is trained to keep private matters to herself. But as you wish." The nurse left the room with a few extra rustles of her starched skirts, her head high. Hilda had the feeling that she had observed the exchange of unspoken comment.

"What?" asked Norah when the door was shut, jiggling the baby who had begun to whimper when Norah took her from the breast.

"Would you like me to hold her?" asked Hilda, putting the moment off as long as possible.

"No, she's just a little fussy. She'll start howlin' in a few minutes when she gets really hungry. Tell me!"

"Norah, it is this. I have learned something about that billfold—about someone else who saw it and saw that it had no money in it!"

"Oh, but that *is* good news! Who found it? Where? When? Do the police know? Have you told Sean?"

Hilda laughed. "Which question shall I answer first?"

"Do the police know?"

"Not unless someone else has told them. I have not. I wanted to tell you first."

"So Sean doesn't know, either?"

"No, and Norah, you must not tell him!"

Norah frowned, and the baby yelped. "Sorry, darlin'. Mama didn't mean to pinch. Hilda, Sean has to know! He's that worried, and scared, you don't know. He tried to keep it from me, but I know he's frettin'. He deserves to know."

"Norah, listen to me." The admonition was necessary. Fiona was wriggling in her blanket and her face was getting red. She was going to scream her displeasure in a moment, and she was stealing her mother's attention. "Give her to me for a moment, and listen."

Hilda picked up the baby competently, but the change from her mother's arms to unfamiliar ones was too much for the hungry baby. She began to wail. Hilda went to the door.

"Miss Pickerell, will you take her for a moment?"

"She needs to be fed, and Mrs. O'Neill wanted to feed her."

"And she shall, but in a moment!" Hilda handed the baby over to the nurse and closed the door on her cries.

"Norah, forget about the baby for one moment. This is important." Norah looked mutinous.

"Sean must not know that there is someone who can confirm his story. If he knows, he will go to the person and talk to him. And if the police then learn the story, they will be able to say that Sean made the person lie for him. Do you not see? Until all is known, it is better that no one except the police learn about this new fact. I told you only because I wanted you not to worry so much."

"And you're not even goin' to tell me who the person is, are ye?"

"No." Hilda closed her mouth firmly.

Norah glared at her for a long minute and then lay back on her pillows, suddenly weary. "All right. I've not got the strength now to worm it out of ye. But I'm tellin' Sean, when he comes by, that there's good news, and he's nearly out of trouble. And you can't stop me, Hilda Johansson!"

"I will not try, Norah Murphy! For you are as stubborn as I, and well I know it. And here," as the door opened on ear-splitting screams, "is your sweet little daughter. Enjoy her!"

Never had Hilda been so happy about a baby's cries. Loud as they were, they were far less bothersome than Norah's questions. She had shut them off for the moment, but in case Norah started thinking logically and reached the same conclusions as Hilda, she, Hilda, had a great deal more work to do—and quickly.

Blessed is he who has found his work;
let him ask no other blessedness.

—Thomas Carlyle
Past and Present, 1843

20

PATRICK WAS LATE getting home for supper. He had ridden in Uncle Dan's sleigh, safer than a carriage, but almost as treacherous for the horses. It had been a slow, dangerous ride, and Hilda was very glad to see her husband home and safe.

"Gettin' bad out there," said Patrick when he had been relieved of his snow-covered garments and had sat down in front of a good fire with the hot whiskey-and-water that Mrs. O'Rourke had insisted on making for him.

"Yes," said Hilda dolefully. "I may not be able to go out tomorrow, even, and there is so much I must do."

And she told him the whole story of Andy's revelations, her first reaction, and her frustration when she realized that the information, by itself, was worthless. "I *must* talk to that fireman who found the billfold, and soon, before Norah realizes I have not told her the whole story."

"I won't have ye goin' out in such weather," said Patrick firmly, and Hilda flared up immediately.

"I am not stupid, Patrick. I know I cannot go out in a blizzard! You do not have to give me an order. Do you think a Swede, who knows about the dangers of snow, would do such a foolish thing?"

"You did once," he reminded her. "That time when Erik ran away. Not so long ago, either."

"You were with me, and my brother. And it was an emergency. And the snow was not so bad as it is now. I have never before seen it this bad. But in the morning, somehow I must find a way. The streetcar, perhaps. Does it run to Station House Five?"

"Don't know. But listen, darlin'—"

The doorbell rang. Hilda started to get up and then remembered and sat back while Eileen ran in from the kitchen to answer the bell. "It does not seem right," she said with a little frown, "that Eileen should be taken from her duties in the kitchen to go to the door, when I am nearer."

Patrick, tired from a day's work, was not eager to debate about the work of a servant. "It's her job," he said briefly. "But Hilda, about the fireman. I could—"

Sean's voice was heard in the hall. Hilda put her finger to her lips and rose to greet him. "Sean, it is good to see you," she said warmly as Eileen took his coat. "But you have walked a long way, and you are wet and cold and tired. It is not good that you should catch a chill and maybe pass it on to Norah and the baby. Come and sit by the fire and have something to chase away the cold before you go and see Norah. Eileen, another of the same, please. Very hot."

Sean was, in fact, tired nearly to exhaustion. He had gone to work very early to work extra hours, knowing that the Friday pay packet would have to last a long time. He had left as soon as he possibly could and had gone home to change to cleaner clothes. Then he had made the long trek out to Oliver's, hoping to find work, but he had been too late. The man who did the hiring had already gone home. Studebaker's had been the same. Sean had thought about stopping at home again, to get warm before going to see Norah, but home was a cold and empty place without her, so he slogged on through the blinding snow. Now he stumbled into the Cavanaughs' parlor, nearly fell into the chair Hilda pulled close to the fire for him, and sat, the picture of dejection.

Hilda scarcely knew what to say to the man. He was so obviously in a state of despair and physical near-collapse. "Things did not go well today, perhaps?" she suggested tentatively.

Patrick roared with laughter at that. "Darlin' girl, you'll be the death of me! Here's me cousin, frozen and worn to a frazzle, and you're sayin' it was maybe not a good day. What the man needs is some good food and some good drink—ah, that's the cure, Eileen. Here, me lad, get that into you and the world'll look a lot brighter."

Dully Sean did as he was told. He took a sip from the drink Eileen handed him, and spluttered. "It's boilin'!"

"Good," said Hilda. "Do not burn your tongue."

"Too late," Sean muttered, but he took another cautious sip, and then another.

"I put honey and lemon in," Eileen whispered to Hilda before returning to the kitchen. "It's good against a cold, and makes it go down nice and smooth."

By the time he had finished the drink, he had color back in his face, though his shoulders were as stooped as ever. Hilda and Patrick had kept up a gentle flow of unimportant talk to give him time to recover, but he had taken no notice. He put his mug down and stood. "Time I was seein' my girls," he said. "Though what I'm to say to 'em I don't know."

"I will send up two trays," Hilda said. "Supper is ready, and you can eat yours with Norah. Come, Patrick."

And she swept her husband to the dining room before Sean could protest that he didn't want any supper.

"He hasn't found work," said Hilda as they sat down.

"Doesn't look that way," Patrick agreed. "Never saw a man look so down."

"He will feel better when Norah tells him that there is news," sighed Hilda, "and then maybe it will all come to nothing."

"Listen, me girl. I was about to say, when Sean came in, I can send a note to that fireman tomorrow, if the snow lets up at all. Unless Uncle Dan closes the store, I can send it by one of our messengers who's goin' that way. Then after work I can pick up an answer. It's not as good as you talkin' to him yourself, I know, but seein' as you can't hardly do that in this weather, I thought..."

"It is a very good idea, Patrick," said Hilda with one of her sharp little nods. "Unless the fireman who picked up the billfold is not on duty tomorrow."

"If he's not, it wouldn't do you any good to go traipsin' out there anyway, now would it? And a note can be left for him to answer when he can."

Hilda nodded. "A *very* good idea. I should have thought of it."

Patrick grinned. "Now, what is this other rigmarole you're tellin' me about the farmer?"

"It is complicated, Patrick, but it is true that Mr. Miller was not telling the truth about where he went and what he did when he left the farm that day, the day of the fire. And I do not understand why. And it is true that the bank is going to call in his mortgage. At least I think it is true. Andy is going to try to learn more about that. I cannot work out a way that anything makes sense."

Patrick grunted and attacked his meal. It was one of his favorites, boiled beef and potatoes and winter vegetables. Mrs. O'Rourke, an accomplished cook, would have liked to prepare more elaborate evening meals, but she recognized in Patrick an Irishman who liked plain food and plenty of it.

Hilda was hungry, too, so they ate in thoughtful silence for a time. Finally Patrick put his knife and fork down. "I can't make sense of it, either. Somebody needs to find out where Miller was that day."

"Did you not say Sergeant Lefkowicz planned to go and see him?"

"I did, and he did. Plan to, I mean. But he'll not get there soon in this weather. It's bad enough in town, with workers to clear the snow from the streets, if it ever stops comin' down. It'll be hopeless in the country. Even a sleigh can't get through if it gets too deep for the horses."

"Hmm. At home we skied to town when the snow was deep. I wonder if Sven still has his skis…"

"You're *not*…" He looked at her frown and changed what he had planned to say. "You're not thinkin' of skiin' out to that farm, I hope? There's not much in the way of mountains around South Bend, ye know."

"Do not be foolish. This is a different kind of skiing. It is meant for traveling, not flying downhill. But I have not done it for a long time, and probably I am out of practice. No, it was Sergeant Lefkowicz I was thinking of. Poland has snow in winter. If he knows how to ski…"

"Darlin' girl, you forget he's a policeman. He has to do what he's told, when he's on duty. It was in his spare time he was goin' out there, because he wasn't—he isn't—happy about the way the police are thinkin'." Patrick shook his head. "There's some talk about that Applegate, Uncle Dan tells me. Seems he lives a little higher than you'd think a man could on what they pay a policeman in this town. Nothin' you can put your finger on, mind, but Dan could see why Lefkowicz wanted to do a little investigatin' on his own. Now this blizzard changes everything. Yes, we need to know, or anyway the police need to know what Miller was doin' that day. But right now there's just flat no way to find that out. So you'll have to content yourself with whatever you can learn from that fireman, and whatever you can work out with your own clever mind, without leavin' home."

Hilda sighed. "You are right, I suppose. But I do not like to sit and do nothing."

Patrick snorted. "That'll be the day. One thing you can do is tell Eileen to make up a bed for Sean, for he's not goin' home tonight. It'll help nobody if he freezes to death in a snowdrift, and so I'm tellin' him, the minute he comes down."

"He will be happier than he was last night," said Hilda with a grimace, "so maybe he will accept."

"There's no question of acceptin' or not. He's stayin'." And Patrick stood and picked up the apple pie Eileen had left on the sideboard. "Ah. A big piece for me. What about you?"

"A small one, please. And coffee. I must think hard tonight, so I must stay awake."

"And you've got to write that note I'm to take to the fireman tomorrow. If there's any gettin' anywhere tomorrow."

Hilda wrote the note, and Sean, after one look out the window into the frenzied swirl of whiteness, borrowed a nightshirt from Patrick and went up to bed. But Hilda's good intentions to stay awake and think were overcome by a weariness not even strong coffee could combat. She nodded in her chair one, twice, and the third time Patrick put a hand on her shoulder. "Come up and do your thinkin' in bed where it's comfortable and you won't get a crick in your neck," he said with a grin.

She was yawning on her way up the stairs, and asleep before Patrick was undressed.

*The first genuine snow storm of the
season visited South Bend and...
trains on all of the railroads
entering the city were delayed...*

—South Bend *Tribune*
December 1904

21

I T WAS APPARENT, in the morning, that no one was going
anywhere. And no one was happy about it.

"Eggs we need, and ham, and flour, and we're near out of
coffee and sugar," grumbled Mrs. O'Rourke. "And how am
I to cook with nothin' in the cupboard, will you tell me that?"

"There's beef and chicken," said Eileen. "And potatoes and
carrots and turnips and beets. And all the fruits and vegetables
you put up in the fall. There's food enough for an army, but today's my afternoon off, and I was goin' home to help me mother
with the little ones."

"Hmph! Not my idea of a day off. And she'll know why you
can't come. There's nothin' movin' out there. Look at it!"

The world outside, what could be seen of it through the still-
falling snow, had lost its definition. There were no corners anywhere. Bushes were rounded humps, roofs were weird shapes
with peaks here and valleys there where the wind had sculpted
the snow into drifts or scraped the roof tiles bare.

"And how are my horses supposed to get any exercise?" demanded O'Rourke, stamping snow off his boots as he came into
the kitchen. "They're restless with all this wind, and need a good
run. Not to mention they'll need hay in a day or two. I was expec-
tin' a delivery today. Is there tea, Mrs. O'Rourke?"

"There is, Mr. O'Rourke, as you should know after thirty
years. No storm stops me havin' me mornin' tea. At least we've
tea in the caddy, still, though for how long I don't know. Worst
storm I've ever seen, and I've seen some miserable weather in my
time. Might as well be livin' at the North Pole."

There was consternation in the rest of the house as well. Nurse Pickerell, stopping in the kitchen to get trays for herself and Norah and a bottle for the baby, needed clean uniforms and fresh milk. Sean fretted about losing a day's work. Patrick worried about the effect on the store of losing at least a full day's business, for there was no hope now of having the streets clear enough for even a sleigh before tomorrow at the earliest. And Hilda stewed about her investigation—stewed silently, for with Sean there she could say nothing.

All morning as Hilda paced irritably around the house, helping here and there with household duties, visiting Norah and the baby, she kept glancing out the window at the snow. The sky grew brighter as the morning progressed, the snow fell more slowly, and finally blue sky began to show. By noon, when everyone sat down to a dinner of fried chicken and applesauce, the sun was blindingly bright.

Patrick, nearly as restless as Hilda, went out with Sean when they had finished eating to help Mr. O'Rourke clear the sidewalk and the drive. Hilda watched them for a few minutes from the bay window in the parlor. They all wore tall boots and warm coats, Sean's borrowed from Patrick, and the snow flew as they threw shovelfuls high above their heads. The path they were creating more nearly resembled a tunnel, nearly shoulder-high in places.

Hilda sighed deeply. She had still cherished hopes of going to Firehouse Five, but she saw that it was impossible. With skis she would have tried it. She had been good on them back in Sweden. But the only skis that had traveled to America with her and her siblings were Sven's, and Sven's house was nearly as far away as the firehouse.

She tried to read but gave it up after looking at the same page for five minutes. She went to her desk and tried to make lists of things to be purchased for the Christmas party. Toys, of course. But for how many boys, of what ages? And would the older ones prefer practical things like warm clothing? Then there was food. Mrs. Brick was in charge of that part, but Hilda hoped she understood about different kinds of food. There would be

boys of so many different nationalities, and they all ate different things. Polish, Hungarian, German, Irish, Swedish, as well as
plain American. Maybe even Jewish boys, and Hilda had a vague
idea they couldn't eat the same things as the others. She made a
note to call Mrs. Brick about it. Potatoes, for certain. Everyone
ate potatoes.

It was hopeless. She couldn't keep her mind on the problem.
Thoughts of all she should be doing to find a murderer kept wiping away every other consideration. She threw down her pencil
and went upstairs.

Norah was awake, her west-facing room bright with the sun-
light on the snow, and warm from the roaring fire. Hilda hoped
they had enough coal, but if they didn't, it was Norah's room that
mattered. The rest of them would come to no harm if they were
chilly for a few days.

The baby was cradled in Norah's arms, drinking hungrily
from a bottle while Nurse Pickerell kept careful watch. The look
on Norah's face brought a lump to Hilda's throat.

The doting mother looked up at Hilda. "I'm wishin' I could
feed her more meself, but Nurse keeps saying I'm not strong
enough yet. As if a tiny babe could take enough from me to make
a difference."

"You must do as the nurse says," Hilda pronounced. "You
are getting better, but you are not well yet."

"Knowin' Sean's out of danger is the best medicine," said
Norah. She shifted her position in bed and the bottle fell out of
Fiona's mouth. The baby began to wail immediately. "There,
hush now, darlin', here's your milk, and here's your mama, and
all's well." The last few words were sung to a lullaby tune. Hilda
didn't recognize it, but the soft lilt could be nothing else.

She restrained a sigh. The scene in the room was blissful, but
the world without was not. Oh, it looked like a Christmas card, but
out there in the cold men were tramping through the snow, looking for work—or sitting in front of a cold hearth, perhaps drinking to keep warm and forget, for a while, their poverty and despair.
Children with ragged clothes and pinched, old faces shivered as

they tried to hope there would be something to eat for supper. Young women in gaudy dresses looked from their bedroom windows and lamented that this was a bad day for their sordid trade, and no business today might mean no food tomorrow. Worst of all, somewhere out there the murderer of James Jenkins walked free. And though she would never say so to Norah, Hilda knew that until the real murderer was apprehended, Sean was in danger.

Fiona, full of milk and nearly asleep, made a tiny noise between a sigh and a gurgle. Nurse Pickerell came to Norah's bedside and picked up the baby. "She needs a nice pat-down now, so she won't get a tummy-ache, don't you, darling? And then a clean diaper and a nice nap. And you need a nap, too, Mrs. O'Neill, as soon as you've had your tonic."

Norah made a face.

"None of that, now," said the nurse briskly. "It's doing you good, you know. You've a much better color than a day or two ago. I'll mix a little syrup into it, shall I?"

Norah shuddered. "No! Horrid as it is by itself, 'tis much worse mixed with sweet. Here, give it me quick, and then a peppermint to take the taste away."

When the nurse had taken Fiona out of the room, Norah settled back in her bed and looked at Hilda, who had moved to the window and was staring out at the snowy world. "You've not come in just to see me, I'll wager. You're as restless as a cat in a room full of rockin' chairs. You've somethin' on your mind."

Hilda turned back to Norah and said, "Yes, many things. There is much I should be doing today, and I can do nothing, nothing, with all this snow!"

"Ought to be used to it by now, livin' around here for—what is it now, eight years?"

"Nearly. We came to America in the spring of 'ninety-seven, and here to South Bend soon afterward. And yes, I am used to snow. At home in Sweden we had much more than this, but we had skis and sleds, and when it was very bad we had no need to leave the farm. Here in a city it is different. I want to go out, but I cannot. How I wish I had my skis!"

"And where would you be goin' if you could?"

To the fire station, but Hilda didn't want to tell her that. "I must find Christmas presents for the boys," she improvised. "And oh, Norah, I want to talk to Mr. Miller. The farmer whose barn burned?"

Norah rolled her eyes. "I'm maybe not feelin' quite so well, but I've not lost the use of me brain. I know who Mr. Miller is."

"Well, then, I found out yesterday that Mr. Miller was lying when he said he was away buying supplies on the day of the fire. Andy's friends saw him driving back to the farm the next day, with nothing in his wagon. And no one had seen him at any of the places where he might have bought supplies or equipment. So what had he been doing? And why did he lie about it?"

"Hmm. Don't know, but most times when a man lies it's because he's up to somethin'. Maybe he has a lady friend."

"Oh!" That was one thought that had never entered Hilda's mind. "Yes—he could have gone calling—but why in the wagon instead of taking the buggy? And why wouldn't he just say what he was doing?"

"Maybe he has a wife someplace!" Norah pushed herself up on one elbow and looked excited. "Maybe he left her, but he's still married, and he wants to marry someone else—his lady friend—but he can't unless he can get rid of his wife somehow. So he has to call on the lady in secret. Or maybe—ooh, I've got it! He was out doin' away with his wife, and he started the barn fire himself to burn up her body!"

Norah's reading tended toward the sensational. Hilda was skeptical. "Well—perhaps. Perhaps he has a wife, I mean. Or there is a woman involved somehow. But if there is one thing we do know, it is that Mr. Miller and the wagon were not around the farm when the fire started. And no one burned in the fire except the hired man."

Norah lay back on the bed. "Well, if you don't want my ideas, don't ask. And I don't know why you care, anyway. Me, I don't give two hoots where the man was that day or any other day, now that the police have stopped chasin' after Sean."

"But Norah, I want to *know*. Someone started that fire and killed poor Mr. Jenkins. If the police never find out—"

"Now we'll have none of that kind of talk here, Mrs. Cavanaugh." The nurse rustled in, frowning. "Mrs. O'Neill should be thinking of pleasant things, not crimes and police and I don't know what all. Let me brush your hair, dear, so you'll look pretty and your husband can come in and see you for a moment before you have a nice sleep." She gave Hilda a sharp look and Hilda understood she was dismissed.

She paced. Down the stairs, through the hall, into the parlor, back to the hall, the library, the dining room, Patrick's den, back to the hall to gaze out the door. Outside, the men had finished clearing paths from houses to the street and were now working on the street itself. City workers would come around eventually, but there were too few of them and far too much snow. If the people of Colfax Avenue were to be freed from their snowy prisons, their own men would have to do the work. Merchants and bankers worked alongside their servants. At the end of the block, Hilda thought she saw Schuyler Colfax, Junior, son of the vice president after whom the street had been named, taking off his hat and wiping his brow before lifting another shovelful.

Hilda resumed her pacing. Norah had given her something to think about. If a woman were involved, Mr. Miller's absence was easily explained. Hilda didn't accept Norah's melodramatic embroidery of the situation, however. The simplest explanation was also, unfortunately, the most likely. If Mr. Miller was carrying on an affair with a married woman, he would certainly do it with discretion. Take the wagon, which implied business, rather than the more comfortable and conspicuous buggy. A buggy sitting in front of a house meant a caller. A wagon meant a tradesman of some sort. And if he, Miller, cared at all about the reputation of the lady in question, he would continue to lie about the matter, even when asked by the police. As long as he was demonstrably not at the farm when the fire started, it mattered little to the police where he actually was or with whom.

Unless—unless somehow James Jenkins had found out what

his employer was doing on other occasions when he was absent from the farm. Suppose he had threatened to tell the woman's husband unless—unless what? Unless Mr. Miller raised his salary, lightened his duties, paid him a sum of money?

Blackmail. Blackmailers have been killed before now, thought Hilda. And Mr. Miller *could* have hired someone to set his barn on fire when Jenkins was in it, drunk. It was possible, but it was thin. And, she reminded herself with a sigh, it was a creation of her own mind, without a single fact to support it.

Tomorrow she would go out and find some evidence, learn some facts, if she had to walk all the way to Sven's and borrow his skis.

*The Studebaker Bros. Manufacturing
…will erect a large and modern
plant upon [its] property for the
manufacture of automobiles.*

—South Bend *Tribune*
December 8, 1904

22

HILDA WOKE ON Thursday morning with big plans. She would go out to Firehouse Five, on foot if necessary, and find out about the billfold and the initials that might reveal its owner. Then she intended to set her Baker Street Irregulars to work on the matter of Mr. Miller's activities off the farm. She would have to find time to finish her list of possible Christmas presents for the Boys' Club party, and telephone them to Mrs. Ford, and to see if any of her lists of attendees were ready, and telephone that information to Mrs. Brick or Mrs. Clem. Then she wanted to try to talk to Sergeant Lefkowicz. And somehow she was going to get herself a pair of skis. She would probably have to send away for them—were they in the Sears, Roebuck catalogue?—but she did not mean ever again to be stuck at home on a snowy day.

Sean also had plans. "Today I'm workin' through me lunch hour, so I can leave early. The sun looks like shinin' all day, so it'll be a better day for findin' work. Hilda, do you really think Studebaker's will hire me?"

She was careful not to be too optimistic. "In Mr. Clem's day I know they would have. He was a kind man and would always give a workman a chance. Now, I do not know for certain. But the *Tribune* said they're building a new plant to make automobiles, and that means they'll need new men. If you will find Sven, he will take you to someone who may help you." Hilda's older brother worked in the finishing department, painting fancy designs on wagons in the familiar Studebaker green and red, and on carriages in gold. "Oh, and ask him if he has made any toys for the Christmas party. He promised he would, and Mama and the others are maybe knitting warm things."

Sean looked worried. "Does he—I mean, I've never met him, and I'm Irish, and there are some…" He trailed off, unwilling to ask openly if Sven cherished the usual prejudice against the Irish.

"He is a fair man," said Hilda crisply. "He will not judge you because you are Irish. Tell him what jobs you have had, and he will know what you might be able to do at Studebaker's."

Sean paid a quick visit to his wife and daughter, Patrick kissed Hilda on the tip of her nose, and both men went off whistling cheerfully.

Hilda dressed carefully for her day, in clothing serviceable enough for riding the streetcar to the firehouse, but respectable enough for the Oliver Hotel. She did not intend to be snubbed again by a doorman uncertain of her social status.

She had adjusted her everyday hat and Eileen was handing her the fur muff that Uncle Dan had so thoughtfully given her, when the doorbell rang.

Hilda frowned. "It is very early for a caller. Barely nine o'clock."

Eileen, looking dubious, opened the door.

Sergeant Lefkowicz stood on the porch.

"Sergeant! I was about to go out, but please come in. I wished to speak to you at some time today, so I am glad you came. I can go on my errands later."

"There's no need to put yourself to any inconvenience, ma'am. I'm looking for Sean O'Neill. I understand he's staying here."

There was no warmth in his manner. Hilda's welcoming smile died on her face. "Yes, he waited out the storm here, but he has gone to work. Is something wrong?"

Lefkowicz hesitated. Strictly speaking, he didn't need to tell Hilda anything, but they were old and friendly acquaintances and had worked together on several occasions. He made up his mind. "Yes, ma'am, I'm sorry to say there is. Sergeant Applegate sent me here with a warrant for O'Neill's arrest."

Hilda took a step backwards. "On what charge?" she asked through stiff lips.

"Arson and murder, ma'am. The murder of James Jenkins."

Hilda's head felt peculiar. She let herself down on the bench seat of the hall rack and tried to take deep breaths. It wasn't easy in a corset, but the effort steadied her. "Sean was not there when the fire was set. He was working with the other men on the next farm. You know that."

Lefkowicz sighed. He should have said nothing. Now he had to explain. "We thought we knew that, Miss Hilda. Mrs. Cavanaugh, I mean. And I believed him when he told us he knew nothing about the fire. But we've found new evidence, and it looks pretty bad for him, I'm afraid."

"What new evidence?" Hilda spoke sharply. The shock was beginning to wear off and she was becoming combative again.

"His pocketknife. We sifted through the ashes pretty carefully, early this morning, and found it right there where the fire started. There's no doubt it's his," he went on, raising his hand as Hilda began to speak. "One of his friends in the fire department recognized it. It's a new one, not very pretty now, going through the fire as it has, but when it's cleaned up it'll be as good as the day his wife gave it to him for a birthday present, last June. It's silver-plated, and it has his initials on it."

He looked anxiously at Hilda. She had gone as white as paper. "Are you all right, ma'am?"

"Yes. I—no. I—I have a headache. Eileen, I would like some coffee. Will you have some, Sergeant?"

"I'm sorry, ma'am. I have to serve this warrant. O'Neill works at Black's still?"

Hilda nodded dumbly.

Lefkowicz looked at her again. "I truly *am* sorry, Mrs. Cavanaugh."

She murmured something, closed the door, and then carefully climbed the stairs without a backward look. The only thing that mattered just now was to get out of the cursed stays so she could breathe.

By the time Eileen came in with a steaming pot of coffee, Hilda had removed her outer garments and was struggling with her corset. "Let me do that for you," said the little maid. "Inventions of the divil, stays are. Beggin' your pardon, ma'am."

Freed of her constraint, Hilda took a deep breath, and then another. "I agree with you, Eileen. I do not know why I wear them." She wrapped herself in a warm robe and sat in front of the fire. "Oh, the coffee is good. And it will help me think. I must think, Eileen."

"Yes, ma'am. It's a poser, isn't it? How do you think Mr. Sean's knife got there in the ashes?"

Hilda was touched by Eileen's loyalty. "Then you do not think he dropped it there?"

"He couldn't have. He was never there. He said so." Eileen's faith was unshakeable.

Hilda drank coffee and racked her brain. "Could he have lent it to someone? A fireman, perhaps, who might have dropped it fighting the fire? He has friends in the fire department. The sergeant said so today, and I think I already knew of it."

"Not that knife, he wouldn't've let nobody borrow. It was his favorite thing. It's a good one, and besides, Norah gave it to him, and you know he thinks the sun rises and sets on Norah."

"How do you know that, about the knife and how much he liked it?"

Eileen shrugged. "Family talk. If an Irishman in this town isn't a relation, then he's a friend of a relation, or a relation of a friend—and we all go to St. Pat's. We all more or less know what's goin' on amongst the Irish. And it was a fine present, silvered and initialed and all. We reckoned Norah must've saved up for a long time, even if it did come from Sears, Roebuck."

"Perhaps he lost it and someone—"

"No, ma'am. Beggin' your pardon, but he would've said. He'd sooner lose his right eye than that knife."

Hilda grimaced. "You had better not say that to anyone else, Eileen. For if he did not lose it or lend it, there seems to be only one way it could have been dropped in the barn. I would like to talk to him, learn if he went to the farm after the fire and lost it then, but I will not be able to talk to him if he is in jail. And this time I do not think it will be so easy to get him out."

"You must, ma'am! You must get him out! He never killed nobody, and his poor lady, and the baby—what will they do? You must help him, ma'am!" Eileen was near tears.

"I will do my best, Eileen." Hilda tried to put confidence into her voice, but Eileen's expression told her she had not succeeded. "Do not tell Norah what has happened. There is no need for her to know just yet. Let her rest and build up her strength while she can."

Drearily Hilda dressed again, this time in an old skirt and waist that did not require stays. Let the doorman at the Oliver Hotel think what he wanted.

She encountered Mr. O'Rourke in the drive, where he was polishing one of the brass carriage lamps. "Was you goin' out, madam?" he asked. "On account of, the horses are needin' some exercise."

"I am, Mr. O'Rourke, but I was going to ride the streetcar. I do not know if the streets are clear enough for a carriage. "

"Downtown, they are. Mr. Patrick, he walked to the store, but Mr. Malloy went in his coach, and when his coachman come back this way he stopped to chat. English, he is, but he's not got his nose so high in the air as some of them English. He said the streets are fine as far as the river, maybe not so good on the other side." Mr. O'Rourke, looking jaunty in his new coat and hat, seemed inclined to friendliness this morning.

"I go to Fire Station Five. It is near the river, on Sample Street."

The coachman cocked his head. "Might be all right, might not. I reckon they'd clear the streets for the fire wagons. I'm willin' to try if you are."

"Thank you, Mr. O'Rourke." Hilda nodded gravely.

"You'll want to wait inside while I get the horses hitched up, ma'am. Perishin' cold it is, never mind all the sunshine. And if ye can't bring yerself to call me O'Rourke," he added as he turned away, "me given name's Kevin."

There was not a great deal of traffic on the streets, and what

there was moved in an eerie quiet. Snow had been shoveled off
the streets, but enough was left to soften the footfalls of the horses
and the rattle of steel tires against pavement. Mr. O'Rourke—
Kevin, Hilda reminded herself—kept the horses to a moderate
pace, but the wind still whistled past, and made Hilda very glad
for the plush carriage robe tucked around her. Indeed, if she was
going to travel often in winter, perhaps a carriage heater would
be a good idea.

Hilda was thinking about creature comforts, deliberately
thinking about them and about the beauty of the snow-covered
city, to avoid thinking about other things. About Sean under
arrest for murder. About Norah, who would soon be cast once
more into despair, and her helpless week-old infant. What would
happen to them if Sean—face it, Hilda—if Sean were hanged for
murder?

"Here we are, ma'am, safe and sound. Was you wantin' me
to wait, or come back?"

Hilda roused herself from her despondent thoughts and
freed herself from the carriage robe. "Wait, I think, please, Mr.—
Kevin. I do not know how long I might be."

"Yes, ma'am. I'll be walkin' the horses up and down a bit, to
keep 'em warm, but I'll keep watch." He handed her down, and
she knocked on the door of the firehouse. Patrick, in his years as
a fireman, had taught her that a woman did not simply walk in
to the place where the men lived during their shift. A married
woman could visit more readily—and with less scandal—than
an unmarried girl, but there were still courtesies to be observed.

The fireman who answered the door knew Hilda by sight,
though she did not know him. The city's firefighters, who
worked together on big blazes no matter which station they belonged to, were a close-knit group. Facing death together will do
that to people, and every fire was a possible death trap. So they
all knew that Patrick Cavanaugh had finally won the beautiful
Swedish bride he had courted for so long. They knew, too, that
marriage had not dampened her enthusiasm for poking her nose
into crime.

"Mrs. Cavanaugh! We've been expecting you. Come in, and

forgive the untidiness. We had a fire early this morning, and we're still sorting ourselves out."

Hilda frowned. "You have expected me? But I did not tell anyone I was coming here."

"We knew you would, though. We knew you'd find out it was one of our men found that billfold, and you'd want to know all about it. Sit down, ma'am—that there's the best chair—and I'll just go and get Joe Brady. He's the one as found it."

This was better than she had dared hope. Now if only the man's answers were the right ones!

Joe Brady, when he came into the room, looked tired. He was shrugging into a coat, but he was unshaven and wore no collar. "I'm sorry, ma'am. I'm not fit to be seen by a lady, but I haven't had time to clean myself up properly."

"Was it a bad fire, Mr. Brady?" Hilda's voice was sympathetic. Fighting a fire in last night's bitter cold wouldn't have been any fun.

"Not what you'd call bad. Some fool a couple of houses down from here put ashes outside before they were dead, and the wind fanned them up and caught the shed on fire. Not much to it, but the cold was somethin' cruel, and the wind, and we had to make sure the other houses didn't catch, or the school." Franklin School was just across the street from the fire station, and even at night, with no one in the building, the firemen would, Hilda knew, have done all they could to preserve it. Schools were important.

Joe Brady yawned hugely, covering his mouth with his hand and making Hilda want to yawn, too. "Sorry, ma'am. You'll be wanting to know about the billfold."

She pulled herself together and nodded. "Yes, please. Especially I want to know where you found it."

"It was in the drive, well away from the barn. We'd pulled in with the wagons, the pumper and the hose wagon, and I was unhitching the horses and leading them away so they weren't so close to the blaze. They're trained about fire, you know, but they get nervous all the same, and we can't have them running away or pulling the wagons around. So I had got one of 'em out of the traces and away safe, and I was tyin' him to the fence when I dropped one of the reins. And when I stooped down to pick it up I saw somethin' lyin' on the ground. I just shoved it in my pocket, havin' other things to think about at the time, but later, when the horses were okay, I thought about it and took a look. It didn't look like it was worth much, kind of worn, and no money in it, but I thought somebody might miss it, and maybe I'd better put it back where I found it. So I did."

"And were the other men still there? The ones from the next farm, who had come to try to help?"

"They were just beginnin' to head back across the field. They'd stuck around for a while, thinkin' to help us out, but if a man's not a firefighter, he gets in the way more than he helps. Not that they weren't goodhearted and all, but they were more trouble than they were worth, and I guess the station chief finally told 'em so."

"Did you see Mr. O'Neill pick up the billfold?"

"No, ma'am. I went back to the fire, and we were pretty busy for a while there. A barn fire's always bad, with so much straw around, and we had all we could do to keep it from spreadin' to the house. Lucky there was no animals inside, but we all feel real bad about the hired man. If we'd knowed he was there, we could've got him out easy. He was up in the loft, well away from the worst of it. But we didn't, and that's all there is to it."

That was, Hilda could see, very far from all there was to it. Joe Brady would probably carry that grief and guilt with him to the end of his days. Every fireman hates it when even an animal dies in a fire, and when a person is lost a little of the fireman dies, too. They hide it, of course, don't talk about it, pretend the canker isn't there, but it eats at them. The more sensitive ones can't take it. They get out of the brigade.

Patrick had nightmares now and then. He didn't like to talk about them the next day, but one day Hilda was going to make him talk, talk it out of his system, maybe. Then she would remind him about the baby whose life he'd saved in a boarding-house fire, about the horses he'd led from a burning stable, about the fellow fireman who owed his life to Patrick's quick actions when a fire wagon overturned.

Hilda knew better than to ask Joe Brady to talk about the dead hired hand. Instead she asked her last question. "Mr. Brady, I have heard there were some initials on the billfold. Can you tell me anything about that?"

But there her luck ran out. "No, ma'am. I only saw it for a minute or two. The light was bad and I was in the middle of fightin' a pretty awful fire. I thought maybe I saw what might have been initials, but they was worn off. And then Sean found it, and when he came back, later, to ask if one of us had dropped it, the fire was almost out, and there wasn't no light at all. I couldn't tell you what those initials were to save me."

"Oh. Well, that is too bad, but I can maybe find out somehow."

"The police'll have it now, I reckon. Maybe they'll tell you. You're friends with that Lefkowicz, aren't you?"

Hilda stood. Her face suddenly felt stiff. She said nothing for a moment, and then decided. There was no reason not to tell him. Everyone would know soon enough. "I am not certain that Sergeant Lefkowicz would help me. He came to my house this morning to arrest Sean O'Neill for murder."

Mr. Brady had of course stood when Hilda did, and now his mouth dropped open. "But that's impossible! O'Neill couldn't have set that fire! We told the police that. It got started while he and the others were still workin' on the new barn next door. And he didn't steal anything from that billfold, neither. There was nothin' in it to begin with. What do the fools think they're doin?"

"They found something that belonged to Sean—his pocketknife—in the remains of the barn. They think he dropped it when he started the fire."

Mr. Brady frowned. "When did they find that? I didn't hear about them findin' anything, and believe me, as soon as that fellow Robert Jenkins started kickin' up a fuss about the fire not being an accident, they looked, the police and the fire department, too."

Hilda tried to think. "I believe Sergeant Lefkowicz said it was this morning that they found it."

"Why?"

"Excuse me?"

"Why did they—look, ma'am, do you mind if we sit down? My mind's whirlin' and I'd feel a lot better off my feet."

Hilda sat, and Mr. Brady folded into the chair opposite her rather like a limp doll. "Look, here. This don't make no sense. It snowed hard day before yesterday, right?"

She nodded, still puzzled.

"And yesterday couldn't nobody get out, hardly. We was all worried for fear there'd be a bad fire we couldn't get to, 'cause the roads were all full of snow. Took us, the brigade, I mean, and the city men, too, all day to clean things up enough so we'd be able to get where we needed to go. And you can bet the roads farther away from the middle of town are still just snow banks, not to mention the country."

Hilda was beginning to get a glimmer of Mr. Brady's thinking.

"So will you tell me why in tarnation the police would take it into their heads to go out to Miller's farm this mornin', all of a sudden, and poke through the ashes?"

Only 11 Trading Days Before Christmas…
You can buy at 25¢ each: Dolls, Friction
Boats, Magic Lanterns, Steam Engine
Attachments, Chimes…

—Geo. Wyman & Co. ad
South Bend *Tribune*
December 8, 1904

23

HILDA THOUGHT ABOUT that all the way to the Oliver Hotel. It was an excellent question, and she was furious with herself for not thinking of it. Of course it was absurd that the police fought their way out to the farm on a day when ordinary travel was nearly impossible. Why not wait until the roads were clear, next week sometime? Why, for that matter, go out there at all? Joe Brady had said it. The barn had been thoroughly searched when Robert Jenkins had brought the accusation of murder. Why hadn't anyone found the pocketknife then?

Because it wasn't there, said a voice somewhere deep in Hilda's head.

She didn't like the thoughts that were crowding in on her. Like most other people in South Bend, she had thought the police more or less competent, and more or less honest. Oh, they could be somewhat lazy, eager to accept the obvious solution, and certainly prejudiced against immigrants—which in turn prejudiced Hilda against them, or most of them. There were exceptions like Sergeant Lefkowicz, hard working, intelligent men whose quest was the truth, not the easy answer.

Or so she had believed. Now she wasn't sure what to believe. She had accepted, with dismay, the sergeant's tale of the discovery of Sean's knife. Now it seemed ridiculous. Where was the proof that anyone had been out to the farm at all? How very much easier to go to Sean's house while he was elsewhere, take a conveniently small object that was obviously his, and make up a story about finding it at the scene of the fire? Drop it in a hearth fire for a little while to give the thing a convincing look, and there was evidence against the only suspect you had. End of case, everybody can relax into their preparations for Christmas.

Would Sergeant Lefkowicz do something like that? Hilda hated to think so. She tried to remember. Had he actually said *he* had found the pocketknife? Or only that it had been found? The news had upset her so much she hadn't concentrated on details. Maybe it was that Sergeant Applegate who had found it. Or pretended to find it? Well, that was something for Patrick to pursue. She could not go to the police station and ask questions, not with any hope of getting answers, and now she hesitated to go to Sergeant Lefkowicz privately.

Andy was on duty in front of the Oliver Hotel. He popped out the door when the carriage pulled up. Given the day's numbing cold, he had been allowed to wait inside for guests, but his face was still bright red. So were his hands, when he took them out of his pockets and blew on them.

"Miss Hilda! Didn't think I'd see you today. Nothin' to report to you, anyway. Snow was so bad on Tuesday that I had to spend the night at the hotel, and most of the boys didn't make it in yesterday. Reckon they was helpin' at home, diggin' out and that. Biggest snow I ever seen!"

"Biggest you ever *saw*, Andy. And the other boys *were* helping at home."

"Yes, ma'am. Anyway it was some storm, huh!"

Hilda was pleased that Andy was still child enough, despite his often hard life, to find pure enjoyment in a blizzard. "It was, indeed. And it is still very beautiful today. But terribly cold. May we go inside for a minute?"

"I have to stay by the door, Miss Hilda. The doorman's down sick, so I'm takin' over for the day. We could talk there, though. It's warmer, unless a lot of people go in and out. And today there's hardly nobody—hardly anybody in the hotel. Most people left this mornin' and nobody new's come yet."

"Good. We will go in. I need to talk to you about the Christmas party."

He grinned. "Reckon you're goin' to have to rent the biggest hall in town for it, Miss Hilda. I've been tellin' everybody, and they're all comin' and bringin' other boys. I started to make a list of names, but it got to be too long, so I gave up and just counted." He reached into his pocket and awkwardly with his stiff hands pulled out a grubby piece of paper. "Let's see. That's ten...and those there, squished up in the corner, that's another seventeen... so twenty-seven..." He muttered to himself for a moment, turning the paper over and frowning at it. "I can't make it come out the same twice, miss, but it's sixty-three or sixty-five. And me and my little brother."

Hilda was staggered. Sixty-seven boys, and that was only the ones Andy had invited. She had been thinking of perhaps a hundred in total. She took a deep breath. "Good, Andy, that is very good. Now, first I want to pay you a little more money. Your information has helped me, and you have also worked hard to invite boys to the party." Gravely she handed him a quarter. "Also, I need to consult you about presents. I am not in charge of that part, but I think maybe the women who are might not know what boys would want, so I will help them." She took a small writing tablet and a pencil out of her handbag. "My brother is making wooden toys, wagons and carved horses and the like, and my mother and sisters are knitting. I think you would like a pair of warm mittens, yes? And perhaps a baseball."

"I don't need nothin'—anything—Miss Hilda. My brother would like a baseball, though. And lots of the little boys I talked to want balls to play with, any kind. Oh, and whistles. The bigger ones are kind of hoping for skates, if they don't cost too much. And some of them would like sleds, but I told them I don't think—"

"We will see if we can find some sleds," said Hilda. "I cannot promise, but I have had an idea. And perhaps small wagons. Banks for saving money?"

"Yes! Not that we've got a lot to save, but I've been puttin' what you pay me in an old sock. A bank would be better."

By the time Andy had to deal with a hotel guest, Hilda had

added tops and checkers and marbles and magnets to her list, along with, of course, candy canes and oranges. She also made a note of several more errands she had to run. First to the churches she had asked to spread the word about the party, and then to Mrs. Elbel's. To that lady she would give the long list of toys, and a suggestion. It had occurred to her that the South Bend Toy Company might well be persuaded to donate some of their famous miniature Studebaker wagons. And didn't she remember that one of the bicycle factories in town also made sleds? It was no good her approaching them, but Mrs. Elbel would know which of the wealthy ladies might be best at soliciting contributions. Oh, and surely the Philadelphia would sell them candy at a discounted price, or even give it to them. And naturally they could get anything they needed from Malloy's Dry Goods at wholesale prices or better! Even if Mrs. Elbel had already thought of all these things, it made Hilda proud that she, too, had thought of them. She was maybe learning to think like a privileged lady.

She was busy all day, stopping only for a sandwich and a cup of tea at Osborn's, a café on Michigan Street. Instead of going home, she sent O'Rourke home to get his own dinner, take a message to his wife that she would be away all day, and come back for her when he had finished.

It was cowardly of her, and she knew it, but she simply could not face Norah. Not yet. Not until she had made some progress towards clearing Sean's name.

In midafternoon, having visited all the churches and added nearly two hundred more party-goers to her list, she asked the coachman to take her to Uncle Dan's store. She tried never to bother Patrick at work, but the situation was critical. She had to talk to him about Sean. "Do not wait for me, Mr.—Kevin. I do not know how long I will be. I will walk home, maybe."

"Mighty cold for that, ma'am. You could phone," he added somewhat grudgingly.

Hilda smiled to herself. If O'Rourke was beginning to accept the telephone, it was progress, indeed.

Trade was no brisker at Malloy's than at the Oliver Hotel.

Clerks stood around tidying the merchandise, quite unnecessarily as far as Hilda could see, or gossiping in small groups. Hilda approached one bored woman who straightened up and tried to look busy when she saw Hilda.

"Good afternoon, Mrs. Cavanaugh. And how can I help you today? We have some lovely new silk mufflers in—just the thing for a Christmas present for Mr. Cavanaugh."

"Thank you, Miss—Miss Forbes." She was learning the clerks' names, but slowly. "I would like to look at them, but not right now. I want to talk to Mr. Cavanaugh for a little. Is he in his office?"

"I expect he is. Mr. Malloy is upstairs, I know."

"I will go up, then. Thank you, Miss Forbes, and I will look at the mufflers before I leave."

The sales clerks received a small commission for every item they sold, Hilda knew. It wouldn't be much, since Hilda was entitled to a big discount on her purchases, but it would help a bit. Christmas was coming as surely for Miss Forbes as for everyone else, and she probably needed all the extra cash she could get in these hard times.

Malloy's Dry Goods Store was modern in every way. It was lit by electricity and there was an elevator to the upper floors, run by a boy whom Hilda knew slightly. "Hello, ma'am," he said brightly when she entered the cage. "Where to?"

"The third floor, please, Mike. Oh, and Mike, has anyone told you about the Christmas party a week from Saturday?"

"Yes, ma'am! I'm comin', and so are my three brothers. It's the first party we've ever been to. What's it gonna be like, ma'am?"

Absolute chaos, Hilda's mind replied. Aloud, she said, "There will be a Christmas tree, and decorations, and plenty of food, and games and gifts. It will be fun, Mike. I am happy you are coming."

"Me, too! Here we are, ma'am."

Patrick was sitting at his desk, frowning at a big ledger. He looked up as Hilda came in, and a smile replaced the frown. "Darlin' girl! It's a pleasure to see you, and no mistake. Sit down."

She looked around. The two other chairs in the small office were covered with wallpaper sample books, fabric swatches, wholesalers' catalogues, and odd sheets of paper. "Where?"

"Oh. Just throw that on the floor. None of it's important."

She did as he suggested, not even remembering to scold him for his untidiness. Patrick saw that something was up. "What is it, darlin'?"

"They have arrested Sean for murder." Her voice quivered a little in spite of herself, and Patrick was at her side in an instant.

"Tell me," he said, his arm around her shoulders.

So Hilda told him, told him everything in an increasingly unsteady voice, what Lefkowicz had told her about the pocket-knife, what Joe Brady had said. "So you see," she finished, "I do not even like to go to Sergeant Lefkowicz now, for I am not sure I can trust him. And I do not like that, Patrick! I do not like losing a friend. And oh, more than one, my best friend even, maybe, for if I cannot clear Sean's name, Norah will—she will not be my friend anymore and even she might die!"

That unleashed real tears, and for a few minutes Patrick knelt at her side and held her and let her cry in his arms. When her sobs had subsided to sniffles he fished a handkerchief out of his pocket, dabbed her cheeks, and then handed it to her.

She sat back, blew her nose, and sniffed. "I did not mean to weep," she murmured.

"I'd hope not," said Patrick, raising one eyebrow. "Got me best suit coat all wet. It'll shrink, like as not."

"Patrick! It will not. It is not that wet, and anyway, the goods came from here. It is fine wool."

He grinned. "Feelin' a little better, are you?"

She was able to muster up a small smile. "Always you distract me, and never do I catch up."

"Catch on," said Patrick. "We'll have you speakin' English yet."

"I do speak English! I—oh. You are doing it again."

"Right you are. Now, you ready to talk about it, sensible-like?"

"I will be sensible." Hilda blew her nose once more and put the handkerchief in her pocket. "Patrick, what are we to do? And do not tell me we can do nothing and must leave all to the police, because I will not listen."

"No, you're right. Somethin' has to be done, and it's somethin' neither of us can do. No, darlin', let me finish. If we're talkin' about the police maybe plantin' evidence, that's a serious thing, serious enough to take to the mayor. I think it's time we had a talk with Uncle Dan."

He led her to the next office and tapped on the open door. "Uncle Dan, if you're not too busy, we've got ourselves a big problem, and we'd like to talk to you about it."

24

Power tends to corrupt...

—Lord Acton, letter to
   Bishop Creighton, 1887

S o you see," Patrick concluded, "it's lookin' more and more like there's some funny business goin' on, and Hilda and me, we don't see as we can do much to get to the bottom of that. But what with you bein' on the County Council, and a friend to Mayor Fogarty, and all, we reckoned you might take a look-see."

Daniel Malloy's face had been growing redder and redder as Patrick told his story. Now he slammed his fist down on the desk. Hilda jumped.

"By God!" he shouted. "You'll be forgivin' me for my language, Hilda, darlin'. But I'll get to the bottom of this if it's the last thing I do! The *Tribune*'s been hintin' for years at dirty doin's in the police force, only on account of the chief's an Irishman. If they get hold of this business, they'll go to town with it, whether it's true or it isn't. Myself, I've been thinkin' the police were a lazy bunch o' slackers, but no worse. I never really believed what was bein' said about Applegate, but maybe it's true! I know for meself that Ed Fogarty's none too pleased with the job they're doin', either. I'm goin' over there this minute to talk to him, and you're comin' with me, Patrick. And Hilda, I'd be obliged if you'd come, too. His Honor has a lot o' respect for the brains you carry around in that pretty head o' yours, and so've I."

Hilda opened her mouth to protest that she was not suitably dressed for calling on the mayor, and then shut it again. Mayor Fogarty had met her often enough in the days when she wore a maid's uniform. He was not a man to judge a person by her clothes.

Dan Malloy was one of the men who was always welcome

in the mayor's office. The Honorable Edward Fogarty greeted them all with smiles and handshakes and a courtly bow to Hilda. "My belated congratulations on your marriage, Mr. and Mrs. Cavanaugh. You're a fortunate man, Patrick, my lad. A wife as bright as she is beautiful is a rare jewel. Sit down, sit down, my dear." He solicitously held a chair for Hilda, who pondered the change in status that her marriage had brought about. She wasn't sure, actually, that she liked it. She was the same person who, a few months ago, would have curtseyed to the mayor; now he was bowing to her. Why should marriage create such a change? Marriage, moreover, to a man who had been a fireman for years before becoming, overnight, a partner to his uncle and thus a wealthy businessman. She shook her head.

"Is something the matter, Mrs. Cavanaugh?"

"No, sir. Nothing." Her feelings were too complicated to explain. She wasn't sure she understood them herself.

The mayor waved the two men to chairs and then said, "Now. What can I do for you today?"

At a nod from Patrick, Dan explained the situation. "And what we'd like to know is, where did the police get that pocket-knife? Sounds to us like there's funny business goin' on."

The mayor looked grave. "Mrs. Cavanaugh, what exactly did the fireman say to you about the knife?"

Hilda repeated the conversation as nearly as she could re-member, and added, "It did not seem likely to him that the police and fire inspectors would have overlooked the knife the first time they examined the remains of the fire. And it does not seem likely to me, either. And, Mr. Mayor, I am certain that Sean—that Mr. O'Neill found that billfold the way he said he did, and that there was no money in it. So why would he have set the fire? Even if he could have done so, working all the time a quarter mile away?" Her voice had become vehement. She cleared her throat. "I am sorry, sir. I did not mean to become angry. But it does seem that the police had no reason to hold Sean, and no other suspect, so it is very—very *convenient* that they found this knife when they did." She hoped it was the right word.

"Hmm." The mayor frowned, picked up a pencil, and began drawing little circles on his desk blotter. "Yes. Hmm."

Dan Malloy was getting red in the face again. "Now look here, Ed," he began.

Hilda's eyes grew wide. She, too, was irritated, but calling the mayor by his first name!

"Don't blow a gasket, Dan. That temper's not good for your health. Molly'd have my head if I let you get so mad in my office you dropped dead of a heart attack. I'm thinkin', that's all." Mayor Fogarty drew a few more circles, puffed out his cheeks, pursed his lips.

Then he stood up, when Hilda was ready to scream with impatience. "All right. It wants explaining. I'd better go talk to the chief. Any of you want to come along?"

Hilda shook her head. The police chief didn't like her, nor she him. They had crossed swords more than once, particularly a while back when Uncle Dan had disappeared, under false suspicion of murder. It was better to let the mayor handle this confrontation.

Patrick looked at his uncle. Dan heaved a sigh. "Ah, I'd just lose me temper. Better you do it, Ed. Mind you rake the fellow over the coals, though!"

"I'll get the truth out of him," said the mayor grimly, "but I'll do it my own way. You'll be at the store?"

"All afternoon. What with business as slow as it is, I'll be twiddlin' me thumbs waitin' for you to show up with news."

Hilda went back to the store with them. There was, after all, shopping to do. Her heart wasn't in it, but she bought the muffler for Patrick and some cologne for Aunt Molly. Her own family didn't want expensive presents, though Hilda longed to give them some pretty things. She compromised on warm, attractive shawls for Mama and the older girls and lace-trimmed handkerchiefs for the younger ones. Erik was easy; he'd wanted really good ice skates for a long time. Sven, as usual, was almost impossible. Mama knitted him all the mufflers and mittens and caps he needed, and he had no time for such things as skating. His only pipe was a cherished companion of many years; he wouldn't care for another one. She browsed various departments, seeing nothing suitable, and at last gave up. There was still time before Christmas, and her mind was with the mayor and the chief of police.

Well, there *was* another problem she could deal with. She went upstairs to Uncle Dan's office, where she found him staring into space. "No word," he said when she came in.

"No. I knew you would tell me if he called you on the telephone, and I would have seen him if he came in the door. I have been watching. No, I came to ask you about gifts for the Boys' Club Christmas party. There are so many boys, about three hundred I think, and I do not know how we can raise enough money in such a short time to buy the food and give them presents, too."

Dan chuckled, a sound with little humor in it. "Welcome to the world of ladies doing good! If I had a nickel for every do-gooder who's done me out of me money or me merchandise, now, I'd be a wealthy man."

Hilda studied his face for a moment and then ventured, "Uncle Dan, you *are* a wealthy man."

"Ah, called me bluff, have you?" His laughter this time was genuine. "All right, all right, they've not beggared me yet. You tell me what you want of me, and I'll see what I can do."

"I have a list," said Hilda. "I do not expect you to give us the things, but maybe you could sell them to us at a good price? And I thought perhaps you could ask for some sleds from someone. Is there not a company in town that makes them? And—do you know any of the owners of South Bend Toy? Because it would be wonderful if they would give us a wagon, maybe two. I know they are expensive, but—"

Dan Malloy's secretary tapped on the door and opened it. "The mayor is here to see you, sir."

"Thank you, Sadie. Come in, Ed, and have a seat. No, stay, Hilda. This is more your problem than mine. And Sadie, ask Mr. Patrick to join us."

The mayor tipped his hat to Hilda, waited until Patrick had come in and they had seated themselves, and then sat down and took out a cigar. "You don't mind if I smoke, do you, Mrs. Cavanaugh?"

Hilda, who hated the smell of cigar smoke, knew when to insist on her way and when to give in. She smiled and shook her head, but Dan spoke up. "But I mind, Ed. So does Sadie. She says the smell never gets out of the office and even drifts down to the sales floors. The ladies don't want to buy dress goods and linens that stink like a men's club. So what do you have to tell us?"

The mayor grimaced, but put the cigar back in his breast pocket. "Don't be tellin' my wife that. I've convinced her it's the best smell in the world. Well, I've been to see the chief, and unless he and Applegate and two of his officers are lyin' themselves blue in the face, they did find that knife in the ashes of the barn this mornin'."

"But why?" Hilda burst out. "It makes no sense! Why would they decide to drive out there on a morning when the roads are deep with snow and it is bitter cold, to look again at what they have already looked at carefully?"

"That's just what I asked him," said the mayor with satisfaction. "Told him it looked fishy to me. And do you know what he told me?"

Since they obviously did not know, all three of them just looked at him.

"He told me he got a tip."

Hilda frowned.

"A piece of information. A suggestion," Patrick translated. "What kind of tip, sir?"

"A letter. Unsigned, of course. They always are. Said the police had better look through those ashes again, because they—whoever wrote the letter—knew Sean O'Neill set the fire and knew he was missing something he always carried. They figured he'd lost it when he set that barn on fire. So the chief took some of his boys out first thing this morning, and sure enough. There was that knife."

"Where was the letter mailed? And when?" asked Hilda, trying to comprehend this unbelievable thing.

"Wasn't mailed. Stuck through the letter drop at the police station yesterday afternoon late, but they couldn't do anything about it till today."

"And when was the last time anybody looked in that same spot before?" asked Dan, his jaw thrust forward pugnaciously.

"Asked 'em that, too. That was when the chief got a little cagey. See, he had to either admit they didn't do such a good job lookin' before, or admit it looked funny findin' the knife now. So he said they'd looked, real carefully, a couple of weeks ago when Jenkins's brother first cried murder. But, he said, there was all that strong wind on Tuesday with the blizzard and all, and probably things shifted some and this was buried before so they couldn't find it."

They were all silent, thinking. Finally Dan said, "And you believed him?"

"I believe he did what he said, and found what he said. I don't believe, any more than you do, that this-here knife was there before. I believe somebody planted it and then wrote that note. And it must be awful important to them, because the only time they could have done it was yesterday or the day before, and the chief said it was as much as the police could do to get out there and back this mornin', with a sleigh and four good strong horses. And that's with most of the roads in town cleared."

"Did they see any sign of anyone going before them? Hoof prints, the marks of sleigh runners?" asked Dan.

"Not a thing. The chief pretended he believed that meant the knife had been there all along, but he really believes the same as I do, that some durn fool went out there in that blizzard and the snow covered up all their tracks. And that means somebody risked their life, not to mention the lives of their horses, to do it."

"Someone had to steal Sean's knife," said Hilda, thinking hard. "And it must have been during the blizzard, because he went home early that day and changed his clothes, and then went out in the storm to look for a job. After that he came to our house to see Norah and the baby, and then the storm got so bad he didn't leave again until they arrested him this morning."

"According to the chief, O'Neill's story is that he went home to clean up a bit after workin'. He says he was in a hurry because he wanted to get to as many places as he could before they closed, and maybe he forgot to put the knife back in his pocket. And then he forgot about it, what with the storm gettin' so bad and all. He acted real broke up about losin' it, claims he's had it since the fire and other people have seen him with it. He wanted the police to give it back to him, claimed again he was never near the barn till after the fire started. Made sense to me."

"So you told the police to let him go?" said Hilda eagerly.

"No." The mayor settled back into his chair and took his cigar out of his pocket.

"*No?* But you said—"

"I think he's an innocent man, and he's been set up for this." All trace of the mayor's folksy Irish accent was gone. "I also think the safest place for him right now is the city jail. As long as— whoever it is—thinks Sean's under suspicion, they won't try to get him. We let him out, the murderer feels threatened again, and who knows what they might do? As long as Sean O'Neill is alive, he can tell his story, and might think of something that would lead the police to the truth. And that's why he's going to stay right where he is until the chief gets those boys of his off their—er—chairs and out working to find out what really happened."

"And what," said Hilda, her Swedish lilt coming to the fore, "am I to tell Norah when she asks me what I do to free her husband?"

"I'm sorry, Mrs. Cavanaugh, but you can't tell her anything. No one must know that the police believe Sean to be innocent."

25

Women, who are, beyond all doubt,
the mothers of all mischief...

—R. D. Blackmore
Lorna Doone, 1869

PATRICK WENT HOME with Hilda. "She needs you more than I do this minute, me boy," said Uncle Dan. "It'll not be such a pleasant time she'll be havin' at home, I reckon."

If Hilda had known just how unpleasant it was to be, she might have elected to stay with the Malloys for a while. But she was mildly optimistic. "Norah is still not well enough to get really angry," she said to Patrick as O'Rourke drove them through the frosty twilight. "I will tell her part of the truth, that I do not think it will be long before Sean is free. She will not be happy, but she will think of the baby and she will be reasonable."

That was reckoning without Norah's mother.

Mrs. Murphy was standing in the hall when Hilda and Patrick approached the front porch. They could hear her through the stout oak door.

"...come to take my daughter and her babe, and no chit of a girl like you is goin' to stop me!"

Hilda hesitated, her hand on Patrick's arm, but he covered her hand with his own and led her up the steps and into the house.

In the entryway, with only the inner door between, the voices were much louder. "But ma'am," pleaded little Eileen, "the nurse and the doctor both, they say she isn't to be moved, 'specially not in this cold. And Mrs. Cavanaugh—"

Hilda opened the door and stepped into the hall. "Mrs. Cavanaugh is here," she said. "Thank you, Eileen. Please go and telephone the doctor. Mr. Cavanaugh and I will speak to Mrs. Murphy."

"And there's no need for that," said that good lady, hands on hips, her hat askew, her shawl dragging on the floor, her face red in the warm hall. "I've done all the talkin' I'm goin' to. I'm takin' me daughter and me granddaughter home with me, and that's flat!"

"Indeed you are not going to do any such thing." A new combatant entered the fray, Nurse Pickerell marching down the stairs, disapproval written in every line of her face. "And you will please stop shouting. Mrs. O'Neill is asleep, as is the baby, and I cannot have you disturbing them."

"I'll not be ordered about by you or anybody else," roared Mrs. Murphy. "Is this a free country, or isn't it?"

A lusty wail issued from somewhere upstairs. The nurse glanced up, a ferocious frown on her face, but stood her ground. "Now see what you've done! You've gone and wakened the baby. If you insist on screaming, will you *please* go into the kitchen to do it!"

"Oh, so you think the likes of me belong in the kitchen, do you! Well, let me just tell you a thing or two, you jumped-up hussy, think you're so fine in that apron and that silly hat, when everybody knows a nurse is the one what carries the slops and—"

"Now, now," Patrick interrupted hastily, "we're all of us a bit upset. What we need is a nice cup o' tea. And it's lovely and warm in the kitchen. Come along, now, do." He attempted to take Mrs. Murphy's arm, but this time she was too angry to be beguiled.

"And you needn't think you'll get around me with your blarney, Patrick Cavanaugh. Fine kind of an Irishman you call yourself, marryin' a Protestant and lettin' her lead you around by the nose while she lets my son-in-law rot in jail, too much of a fine lady to lift a finger to prove he's innocent as a newborn babe, while my poor daughter's grievin' her life away—"

"I do *not* lead Patrick by the nose!" said Hilda, stung at last into angry speech. "He is as stubborn as I. And I let no one rot. I do everything I can—"

"And a fine lot of good it does, oh, I can see that, when you let 'em drag him out of your very house without liftin' a finger…"

There was more. There was much more. The sound level

rose and rose as Patrick and the nurse tried to move Mrs. Murphy to the kitchen, while she tried to reach the stairs, screaming insults at Hilda, who tried to defend herself, baby Fiona howling all the time with greater and greater urgency. Eileen and the O'Rourkes, coming in from the kitchen, stood on the periphery, Eileen afraid to enter the battle, the O'Rourkes unsure of where their loyalty lay. At last Mrs. Murphy, clinging to the newel post, kicked out at Hilda. She didn't connect, but Hilda, losing her temper completely, might have been driven to physical retaliation if two things hadn't happened, more or less at the same time.

Norah appeared at the head of the stairs. Her red hair hung in limp strings down to her waist. Her nightgown was wrinkled, her feet bare, her face pale. Mrs. Murphy caught a glimpse of her, took a shocked breath, and stopped screaming imprecations. In the sudden near-silence, broken only by the baby's cries, the entryway door opened.

"And what in the name of God is going on here?" said the doctor in the voice of doom. "Miss Pickerell, get your patient back to bed at once, and then see to that baby! And the rest of you, I want an explanation of this disgraceful scene as soon as I've finished examining Mrs. O'Neill."

"But, Doctor," said at least three voices at once.

"Quiet!" he bellowed.

"Tea," said Patrick, putting one arm around the sobbing Mrs. Murphy's shoulders and the other around his wife's waist. "With maybe somethin' a little stronger in it."

He must have put quite a little bit of the stronger stuff into Mrs. Murphy's tea, because by the time the doctor came downstairs and put his head in the kitchen door she was no longer crying. Indeed, she was singing, along with Patrick, a quavery rendition of "I Dreamt I Dwelt in Marble Halls." Hilda, with a headache growing more and more insistent, had asked for coffee. Mrs. O'Rourke made it, but she was not pleased. She hated having the family in her domain, especially so close to suppertime.

"We could go to the parlor," said Hilda to the doctor, looking a little doubtfully at Mrs. Murphy.

Patrick shook his head. "Better to let sleepin' dogs lie," he said under his breath. "She's happy at the moment."

"And *she's* welcome to stay," said Mrs. O'Rourke. "The poor woman's had a hard day, and another drop of whiskey won't do her no harm. But I'd be obliged if the rest of you would let me get on with me work, or the saints alone know when you'll get your supper."

Hilda had noticed that all the Irish men and women in her life—and the good Lord knew there were enough of them!—became much more Irish when they were in an emotional state. But then she, herself, reverted to her Swedish lilt and accent when upset, and occasionally even to a little Swedish profanity. To each his own, she thought with a shrug, and watched Patrick remove his arm from Mrs. Murphy's grasp—carefully, lest she fall from her chair. Mrs. Murphy hiccupped and went on with another verse of her song.

"Well, I've got them settled," said Doctor Clark, accepting a glass of whiskey from Patrick. "Took some doing. Norah wanted to go on about her husband, and the baby'd cried herself into near hysterics. I gave 'em both some laudanum. Don't like to give drugs to a baby that young, but she was heading for a fit. Who I'd like to dose is that mother of Norah's."

"I've done that for you," said Patrick with a grin. "She's feelin' no pain. What she'll feel in the mornin' is another question. Hilda, a little brandy?"

She shook her head, and instantly regretted it. Her temples were throbbing. "Patrick, you should not have made her drunk."

"Ah, you can scold me better than that, darlin'. Your heart's not in it. You know you'd rather have her drunk and quiet than sober and raisin' Hail Columbia." He poured himself some whiskey and sat down next to Hilda on the settee. Hilda rested her aching head on his shoulder. It was not proper, with someone else present, but she was too tired to care.

"So what's it all about, then?" asked the doctor. "I've been out on rounds all day and didn't know anything about anything until I got a frantic phone call from that little maid of yours. And Norah wasn't making a lot of sense."

Hilda opened her mouth, but Patrick got in first. "Let me, darlin'. You're fair worn out, what with runnin' errands all day and worryin' on top of it. The short of it is, Doctor, that Sean O'Neill's been arrested for murderin' that man that died in the barn fire."

The doctor was tired, too. He sipped from his glass before saying, "And why is that? I thought they'd pretty nearly decided he couldn't have done it."

Patrick and Hilda looked at each other. "Um…" said Hilda. "Well…" said Patrick.

Doctor Clark shook his head impatiently. "Out with it, then. It's Norah's health I'm worried about, you know that. Don't give a hoot what Sean's done, unless worry over it kills his wife."

Hilda made up her mind. If a doctor could not be trusted to keep secrets, the world was a sorry place. "The police do not really suspect Sean, not now." She spoke very quietly. "There was some evidence against him, but they have decided it was seeded—"

"Planted," put in Patrick.

"—planted, and they believe what Sean says. But they think he is not safe, because the person who would do such a thing as plant evidence against him might even want to kill him. So they keep him in the jail, to keep him from danger. And we are not to tell anyone."

"I'm safe enough, you know that." The doctor yawned.

"Yes, I know, and that is why I told you. But, Doctor, Norah is not safe. She would tell her mother, and Mrs. Murphy would tell her friends, and the whole town would know soon. And that could be very bad for Sean." She massaged her temples.

"And if Norah doesn't know, it could be very bad for Norah. Now look here, Mrs. Cavanaugh. I can see you're not feeling very well. Headache?"

Hilda nodded. Carefully.

"I'll give you something for it before I go, and I'm sorry to keep you from your supper and your bed, but you need to understand. What's wrong with Norah is anemia, and it's a funny disease. We don't know a lot about it, but we do know that a person who has it *must* eat the right kind of food. Often that'll be enough to cure it. Norah's doing well, better than I expected."

"We make her take the tonic," said Hilda. "The nurse and Mrs. O'Rourke and I, we all make sure she takes it, and eats what she should, too."

"In her case, that seems to be working, that and being kept calm and quiet, and getting lots of sleep. But she's not well yet, not by a long shot. This worry could keep her from eating and sleeping, and that's bad. And worry by itself is an awful strain on a person, even one who isn't sick. Norah's just had a baby, and she lost a lot of blood in the process. Now she's got this to worry about again. It's doing her no good, I tell you frankly."

Hilda stood up and began to pace the floor. "I do not know what is best to do. I promised the mayor I would not tell anyone about Sean. Now I have told you, and you tell me I should tell Norah. But telling her is telling the world."

"Well, you've until tomorrow to decide. Norah's dead to the world for the next ten hours or so. I know what I'd do—tell her and let the devil take the hindmost. As long as the man's in jail, what harm can come to him from outside? But I'll leave it up to you. You told me in confidence, and I won't spill the beans myself. Now." He stood, put down his glass, and reached into his bag. "You're to take one of these powders now and one just before bed. Have a light supper and some strong coffee, and put an ice bag on your head when you go to bed. I'm off to check on another soul who's about to come into the world. If you want, I'll take Mrs. Murphy home and give her something that'll make *her* head better in the morning."

Patrick and Hilda gratefully agreed. Mrs. Murphy on the rampage was bad enough. Mrs. Murphy with a hangover—they shuddered to think. They eased her out the door, still singing and clinging to the doctor's arm, and retired to lick their wounds.

Portlands and Speeding Cutters
One and Two-horse
"Sensible" Bob Sleds...
At Studebaker's

—Advertisement
   South Bend *Tribune*
   December 1904

26

"SHALL I STAY HOME this mornin' and help you fend off any wild Irish matrons that might come callin'?" Patrick folded his newspaper and finished his coffee.

"No, Patrick. I have told Eileen to keep the doors locked and not let Mrs. Murphy in. It seems cruel, but it is better for Norah. And I will be out. I have been thinking."

"So that's why you were so restless last night. Was your head bad? I thought you'd sleep like the dead after the day you'd had and those headache powders, but you were up and down like a jack-in-the-box."

"Ooh, that is another toy for the list." She made a note on a pad she kept by her plate. "No, the medicine helped, or maybe the ice. My headache went away, but the coffee, maybe, kept me awake. And then I had to think out what to do, and there are many things. One thing there is that I want you to do."

"I'm at your feet, darlin'."

"I want you to go to the police station and look at the billfold, the one that started all the trouble. There may be initials on it. If there are, they are hard to read, but I want you to try. I think it is important to know whose billfold that was."

"It could have been lyin' there for a long time, you know. I expect that's why the police haven't followed up on it."

"Yes, but I want to know about the initials. I think they might be important. Also, I want to go to see Mr. Miller."

Patrick frowned. "I'm not sure that's such a good idea. We don't know a lot about the man. For all we know, he set that fire himself."

"Patrick! Do not be foolish! He could not have set it himself; he was not there. But I want to know where he was, and the only way to find out is to ask him."

"Can't you leave that to the police?"

"I do not trust the police. Oh, I believe the mayor when he says they did not seed—plant—that knife. But they were not smart about it, either. I think some of them are stupid and lazy, and Sergeant Applegate, he might be worse than that. Now that the mayor has scolded them, they will maybe do better, but they are not in a hurry about it. For Norah, I must be in a hurry."

Patrick gave up. Much as he would like to protect his wife, she would have none of it. "Then make sure O'Rourke is close by the whole time. I'm buyin' you that beautiful indigo wool today and droppin' it by your dressmaker's, and I want to make sure I've got a wife to put in it when it's done."

"That is kind of you, Patrick. And I will be careful. But you know I must do these things, or I will be as—as blue as that wool."

"I ought to know that by now. Determination is your middle name, darlin' girl."

He kissed her quite thoroughly and hurried off to work. Hilda was glad to see him go, for it allowed her to put into operation the other part of her plan. She went to the telephone and called the home of her old employers.

"Tippecanoe Place." Mr. Williams's voice on the other end of the line was cold. It was not the proper time of day for phone calls.

"This is Mrs. Cavanaugh, Williams." She got that out without giggling, much to her satisfaction. "I am sorry to call so early, but I need to speak to Mrs. Clem, if she is able to come to the telephone."

"Mrs. Clem is not feeling well, Hil—madam. She cannot come to the telephone."

"Oh, then she will not be wanting the carriage today. Will Colonel George need it, do you know, or Mrs. George?"

"Colonel George and Mrs. George are away, madam."

"Oh, good. Then would you please ask Mrs. Clem if she would mind if I borrowed John Bolton and the sleigh for the day, or the morning anyway?"

"Er—is your coachman ill, madam?"

"No, Williams. O'Rourke is well. Will you ask her, please?"

"Yes, madam."

The chill in his voice could almost be felt. Once it would have frozen Hilda to the bone. Today, she was delighted to realize, she didn't care. She only wanted him to hurry with a reply.

"Hilda, my dear, why do you need my coachman? You're quite welcome to him, of course, but is something wrong?"

Hilda was so delighted to hear Mrs. Clem's voice she almost fell back into her servant mode. "Oh, mad—er—Mrs. Clem, I am so glad to talk to you. Williams said you were ill."

"Silly man. Not ill, just tired. I have no plans for today, though, so if you want Bolton, I'll send him over."

"Thank you. You see, I want to leave Mr.—that is, to leave O'Rourke here today." Briefly Hilda told the old lady the story of Mrs. Murphy's invasion. "And I do not think Eileen will be able to keep her out if she decides to come back, so I want a strong man here. But I have things I must do, in the country. I could hire a sleigh, but I need a coachman."

The chuckle came clearly over the line. "I won't ask what things, my dear. Good luck to you. And when you've finished for the day, why don't you stop in here? We do need to talk a bit about the party, as it's a week from tomorrow."

"I have not forgotten. I have been planning. Thank you for letting me use your sleigh, and John Bolton, and I will call in late this afternoon."

Patrick would not like her using John. There had been times in the past when John's flirtation with Hilda had been on the heavy side. But Hilda knew he had meant little by it, and had put him in his place when necessary. And John was strong, and essentially loyal to her. He would do nicely as an escort for today.

She had barely had time to inform the O'Rourkes about her plans when John was at the door, with a dashing cutter pulled by

Star and Bright, Hilda's favorites among the Studebaker horses. She slipped some sugar lumps into her pocket and went out into another day of brilliant winter sunshine.

She had not seen John since her wedding. He took off his hat and swept a bow, a pronounced twinkle in his eye. "Good morning, madam. You're looking very fine today, if you don't mind me saying so."

"Good morning, John. You are looking well yourself. It is good to see you again. And my name is Hilda."

He grinned. "So long as nobody's around."

"Yes. We are friends. I do not see why we should be formal when we are private. With others, I suppose we are Mrs. Cavanaugh and Bolton. Yes?"

"Agreed. You really are looking beautiful, Hilda. Regular Gibson Girl. So where do I have the privilege of driving you today?"

"We go first to Firehouse Five, then out to the country. South of town; I do not know exactly where. That is what I must find out at the firehouse."

❧

Given explicit directions from an admiring fire crew, Hilda climbed back up into the sleigh. John wrapped her well in Mrs. Clem's fur carriage robes, and they were off, harness bells jingling.

It was truly a beautiful day. Since the snow, the weather had been so cold that very little had turned to dirty brown slush. The small factory workers' houses they were driving past looked brighter, cleaner than usual, snow turning stunted bushes into sparkling white mounds, snow covering dirt front yards, snow hiding roofs that needed repair. On a few of the houses were hung small wreaths of holly or pine, bright with red ribbons. The people they passed waved cheerily, and Hilda returned the waves. Snow and sunshine—a merry combination.

Soon, though, the snow would melt. The poverty and ugliness it hid would be seen again. The sky would darken, and so would the spirits of the poor. She must, Hilda thought, she *must* see to it that the boys' party was a great success. And if she could bring Sean home soon, she would ensure that one poor family, at any rate, had a happy Christmas.

She leaned forward. "Can we go no faster, John?"

"Not unless you want your ears froze off," he called back. "It's cold out, in case you hadn't noticed."

Hilda sat back and shook her head. John would never change.

In fact it took only half an hour to get to the Miller farm. Once they were near, it was easy to spot. The blackened ruins of the barn loomed over the property like an ugly sentinel. Even after more than a month of rain and snow, the smell of smoke still hung heavy in the air.

"You sure this is the place?"

"John! This is the farm where the hired man was killed. Of course it is where I want to visit."

"Ah. Snooping again, I see."

"I try," said Hilda with dignity, "to find out who set the fire. I know it could not have been Sean O'Neill, but Norah is very afraid. And with her new baby, she should not be worrying."

"That's true enough," said John seriously. "It's a bad business, that. Sean's all right, if he is an Irishman, and I'll swear on forty stacks of Bibles he never killed anybody. Right you are. I'll deliver you to the door, and I'll be right here, in case of any funny business."

"Thank you, John. That is why I wanted you to come. I can trust you."

He helped her down, and she made her way to the side door, knowing better than to go to the seldom-used front door of a farmhouse.

Her knock set off a cacophony of barking. "Hold your horses, I'm coming!" A female voice responded to her knock, and a moment later, the door was flung open. Two large dogs stood panting next to a rosy-cheeked woman in a print dress and an apron, with flour on her hands and a smudge of it on her nose.

They looked at each other in equal astonishment. Hilda

recovered first. "I am sorry. I did not know Mr. Miller had a housekeeper. That is—I am at the right house, am I not? This is Mr. Miller's farm?"

"It is, though I'm sure I don't know who you might be. As for me, I'm not the housekeeper. Or, I suppose in a way I am. I'm Mrs. Miller. Here, now, don't stand there in the cold letting your mouth gape open like a fish. Come on in, come on in."

It was warm in the kitchen, and fragrant with the smell of apple pie. "Thank you," said Hilda, grasping at her manners. "My name is Hilda Joh—Hilda Cavanaugh. I was surprised, Mrs. Miller, because I did not know Mr. Miller was married."

"He wasn't, was he, till about a month ago. And I only moved out here last week. So nobody much knows about me yet. We don't have close neighbors and we don't get into town much, what with all the work to be done here. Sit down, child, and take your things off. My, that's a pretty hat! Mind you don't get flour on your skirt. I'm afraid the kitchen's not very tidy, but I've been baking. Wanted to get my pies done well before Christmas. I've finished with the apple now, and before I start on the mince I was just about to sit down and have a piece myself. Want one?"

The kitchen was a model of cleanliness, except for the table, where a dusting of flour covered the oilcloth and a rolling pin sat amidst a few scraps of dough. Hilda assessed the situation and made a decision. "I would like a piece of pie. It is very kind of you. But may I ask my—my friend to come in? He drove me here, and he will get very cold waiting."

"He's welcome as the day!" Mrs. Miller went to the door. "Yoo-hoo! Come on inside and warm yourself!"

When John had come in and surrendered his coat and hat, he exchanged glances with Hilda, who shrugged slightly. Mrs. Miller didn't notice. "Those are beautiful horses you've got. I'm sorry I can't ask you to put them in the barn, but our barn burned a while back and the insurance company hasn't paid us yet, so we haven't rebuilt."

"They'll be all right for a little, what with the sunshine, thank you kindly, ma'am."

"So you'd be Mr. Cavanaugh, then?"

"No," said John and Hilda at the same moment. Hilda went on. "I must tell you, Mrs. Miller. Mr. Cavanaugh and I do not own a sleigh, so I borrowed this one from a friend. Bolton is my friend's coachman."

"Oh." Mrs. Miller was clearly puzzled. "But what I don't quite understand is what you wanted to traipse out here for in the first place, with the snow and all. Is Mr. Miller a friend of yours? Oh, would you like some coffee with your pie?"

"No, thank you," said Hilda, knowing how most American coffee tasted. She took a deep breath. "No, I have never met Mr. Miller. I hope you do not mind, but I came to ask him some questions about the barn fire. You see, the man who has been accused of setting it is a good friend of mine, and I am sure he did not do it. I thought maybe if I asked Mr. Miller a few questions about it, I might learn something to help my friend."

"Well, you'd be welcome, I'm sure. He wants to get to the bottom of it, too, so the insurance people will be satisfied and give us our money. But he's not here right now. Went to town this morning to try to find a new man to hire. He and I've been able to keep up with the work so far, it being winter and all, but come the spring planting, he'll have to have help."

It was a blow. She had counted heavily on talking to Miller. But perhaps this unexpected wife could help. "Does he have any idea who might have started the fire?"

"Dearie, if he knew, he'd horsewhip him! He's lost a lot that'll never be repaid, even when the insurance settles up, not to mention that Jim Jenkins was a good worker, if a mite too fond of the bottle, and didn't deserve to die that way. The only thing my Walter can think is maybe some tramp went in there and turned over the lantern by accident, and then got scared and ran when the straw caught."

Hilda frowned. "Do you get tramps out here very often?"

"Well, I wouldn't know, would I, bein' as I've only lived out here a week or so. Walter says no, hardly ever, except in summer when they maybe want a handout. But there's not much to give anybody in November, except apples. And it's a long way to walk from the nearest train tracks for an apple. Only he couldn't think of anything else. Another piece of pie?"

"No, thank you. It was very good, but I cannot eat any more. Is there anyone who—who does not like Mr. Miller? Who would have a reason to want to hurt him?"

"Don't know as there is. He's a shy kind of a man, y'see. Keeps pretty much to himself out here, away from town, except for buying supplies and that. We met one day in Harper's feed store. I worked there then, and he could hardly get himself to say two words to me. He kept coming in, though, and we'd talk a little, and after about a year I got brave and asked him if he'd like to go to the ice cream social at the Methodist church with me. I knew he'd never have the nerve to ask me himself. Well, so we went, and had a real nice time, and after that sometimes he'd take me to a spelling bee or a church social, and once to a barn dance. Took him two more years to work himself up to asking me to marry him! I declare, *I* was gonna ask *him* if he didn't get a move on." She laughed richly.

Hilda had a sudden idea. "And on the day of the fire—that was your wedding day, was it not?"

"It was. And we'd planned a nice little wedding trip, only he had to come right back out here next day, the minute he heard about the fire."

"Mrs. Miller," said Hilda, unable to resist an irrelevant question, "why would Mr. Miller drive to his wedding in a farm wagon, when he owns a buggy? And with his dogs? And why did he not tell the police when they asked him what he was doing on the day of the fire?"

"He doesn't own a buggy anymore, dear. It got burnt up in the fire. And he'd as soon go without his shirt as without these two mutts." She rubbed their heads affectionately. "But he didn't drive us to the church in a wagon. Catch me climbin' up on one o' those contraptions in my wedding dress! He drove the wagon to the livery stable and hired a nice little surrey for us. I was right

sorry when he had to take it back. As for tellin' the police, he said
to me it was nobody's business except ours. He's shy about it, is
what I think, gettin' married at his age. Me, I think it's grand—
and I'm as old as him!"

Great Holiday Furniture Sale…
5 Piece Parlor Suites—a durable gift,
handsomely upholstered in velour or
plush. Best construction. Up from $22.50

—Household Outfitting Co. ad
South Bend *Tribune*
December 1904

27

S O THERE, THOUGHT Hilda as John drove her back to town, went another lovely theory. Mr. Miller had been doing nothing shameful, nothing to provide a reason for blackmail. He had been courting. And on the day of the fire, he had been, finally, getting married.

The voluble Mrs. Miller had explained further. She had planned to move out to the farm as soon as they had come back from their "little wedding trip" to Niles. But the fire had so disrupted life at the farm that they had decided she should stay where she was, in a respectable boarding house in South Bend, until Mr. Miller could put things to rights. He had been distressed by the accusations of arson and murder, and thought Mrs. Miller had better wait a while longer, but she had put her foot down. "I told him he needed somebody to look after him. He wasn't eating right, I could tell that, getting thin as a rail, and I could only imagine what the house looked like. So I moved myself in, bag and baggage, and to tell the truth, the place wasn't too bad. Not much cheerfulness to the house, you know, what with a man living here all by himself all those years, but I soon put up my own curtains and put down my own rugs. I'm plannin' to buy new furniture, too, as soon as that insurance pays up. Wish I could do it now, with the Christmas sales, but when I do, the place is going to look right nice!"

Hilda assured her that it looked nice already, and refusing more pie, set off for home.

"Where to now?" asked John when they were close to home.

"I promised Mrs. Clem that I would stop and talk with her

about the Christmas party for the boys. This is not a good time, though. It is nearly time for her lunch."

"She doesn't eat much when she's home alone, remember? Usually just a little from a tray in her room. She'd welcome the company, Hilda. She misses you. We all do."

"But I was only a maid! Why would Mrs. Clem miss me?"

"She doesn't look at servants the way most people do, Hilda. You ought to know that. We're people to her. She likes you, always did. She thinks you're interesting, and she's happy you've done so well for yourself. As for the rest of us—well, life is pretty dull around the place without you to stir things up. Normal, comfortable, but dull."

Hilda didn't know what to say to that, so she was silent the rest of the way back to Tippecanoe Place.

Mrs. Clem was indeed taking a tray in her room and invited Hilda to join her. Hilda, full of pie, declined anything but a cup of coffee. Mrs. Sullivan, the cook, would, Hilda knew, make it properly. Hilda had taught her herself.

"And are you any closer, my dear, to learning how that poor man died?" asked Mrs. Clem when Hilda was comfortably settled with her coffee.

"No closer. Further away, even. I thought Mr. Miller—the farmer, you know?—that he maybe had a reason to keep the hired man quiet, blackmail, perhaps. It was Norah who gave me the idea. I had learned that Mr. Miller was not where he said he was on the day of the fire, and Norah thought he was maybe carrying on with a married woman. But today I learned what he was really doing."

"And that was?" Mrs. Clem leaned forward eagerly, her face pink with excitement.

"He was attending a wedding. His own wedding. He has a new wife." She told the story.

Mrs. Clem laughed and sat back. "And how old a man is he?

"I do not know, but Mrs. Miller is fifty, at least. I believe her when she says it takes Mr. Miller some time to make up his mind to do a thing."

"Indeed. So that takes care of that."

"Yes, and I am not sure what to do next. If Mr. Miller had been there today, I had planned to ask him about the mortgage on the farm, to see if there was any way he could profit from the fire. But I could not ask his new wife such a thing, and anyway I do not see how he could make money from a fire. Mrs. Miller says he has lost things that cannot be replaced, and that he is very upset about the death of Mr. Jenkins."

Mrs. Clem considered for a moment, and then shook her head. "I don't see any help in that direction, either. Well, for Norah's sake, and the baby's, I hope you can see your way out of the woods soon. Now, what is happening about the Christmas party?"

Hilda reported on the hall Riggs had reserved for the party, and the growing number of attendees. "So we will need many gifts, not just toys but warm clothing. Do you know what Mrs. Ford and Mrs. Cushing have done about the gifts?"

"Not a lot, I expect. They are probably waiting to know how many would be needed, and for what ages."

"I thought so. Do you think we have enough money to buy so many? There is the food, too, and I think it should be more than punch and cookies. These boys do not have enough to eat at home, Mrs. Clem. We should have sandwiches for them, too, and not just tea sandwiches, but real ones, with meat. They do not get very much meat."

Mrs. Clem nodded thoughtfully. "I think if you will give me your list of possible gifts, I will talk to Mrs. Ford and Mrs. Cushing. We can probably find donors for most of them. George gets home on Monday, and he can put a little pressure on South Bend Toy for a wagon or two. They're expensive, you know, five dollars or more."

"I know. We cannot give them away like the rest of the toys. It would not be fair. I thought we could have a drawing, and some lucky boys would get them."

"Better to make them a prize for doing something good. I'll think about that. Reward for accomplishment is better than reliance on luck, especially as a lesson in life. And shall I take over the planning of the food? I had boys of my own, remember. I know what they like to eat."

"Yes, please! If you think it will not make Mrs. Brick angry," she added anxiously.

"Anna Brick is a sensible woman. Oh, and speaking of sensible. I had a phone call this morning from Mrs. Townsend, as sweet and pleasant as you could wish. She wanted to know if I thought a game of musical chairs would amuse the smaller boys. Mrs. Witwer is working on finding a pianist for the afternoon. So the entertainment seems to be coming along."

Hilda nodded. "That is good. There are other details, though—decorations, and the Christmas tree, and other games for the bigger boys. I hope the other ladies are working on those things."

"Perhaps we should have another committee meeting to make final plans. Let's see. Today is Friday. The party is a week from tomorrow. I have other obligations on Monday. Tuesday afternoon, here?"

"That will be good."

"Fine. Then I'll have Williams telephone everybody. And if you can get that list to me today, we'll have most of the toys lined up by the time of the meeting."

It must, thought Hilda as John drove her home, be nice to be the Queen of South Bend and know that everyone would do your bidding.

When Hilda reached home all was serene, on the surface, at least. Patrick had been home for his midday dinner and gone back to the store again. Hilda was glad of that. She wanted time to prepare herself for his displeasure about John Bolton.

She had to face Norah now, though. With leaden feet she climbed the stairway and tapped on Norah's door.

Norah was in bed with her face to the wall. The nurse, in one corner with the baby in her arms, stood and came to the door. "She's not asleep," she said in a low tone. "She won't talk to you. She won't do anything. I've had to force her medicine down, and I thought she'd spit it right back at me. She won't even nurse Fiona, and she must, or her milk will go dry. If you think you can do anything, Mrs. Cavanaugh, I wish you'd try. I'm not one to let a patient get the best of me, but this one…" She shook her head.

Hilda made up her mind, and said, rather loudly, "Yes, I will try, but you must leave the room. I am going to tell her a secret I promised to tell no one. I know you can be trusted, but I do not wish to break my word any more than I have to."

When she went into the room, the lump in the bed hadn't moved, but it seemed to Hilda to have a certain alert attitude. She seated herself by the side of the bed. "Norah, I am going to tell you something I should not. If you say anything to anyone—anyone at all, even your mother—it could harm Sean. Do you understand that?"

There was no response from the lump.

"Very well. I am angry with you, Norah. You are being stubborn and foolish. It is your mother who has put this into your head, I think, or I would be *very* angry. You are safe here, and comfortable, and you and your baby are getting good care. There is no reason for you to refuse to eat, or talk, or do anything like a sensible person. I never thought you were stupid. Always I thought you had a good mind, but now I wonder. Maybe the people who say the Irish are stupid are right, after all."

The lump stirred. There was a sound remarkably like a snort.

"And there is no reason for you not to trust me. We have been friends for many years now. It hurts me, Norah, it hurts me very much that now you think I will not help you and Sean. I do everything I can, and you lie there and sulk. Eileen says you and your mother are ungrateful, and maybe she is right. Or maybe you are just afraid of what I will find out, because you know Sean is guilty after all."

That did it, finally. Norah rolled over and sat up. "Don't you dare say that, you—you—Swede! Me mother's right! I'm gettin' out of here this minute, and takin' the babe with me, and I'm findin' a new name for her as soon as I can think of one!" Then she collapsed onto the pillows in a storm of sobs.

"That is better," said Hilda calmly. "I thought I could make you lose your temper. When you have finished feeling sorry for yourself, I will tell you what I said I would. It is about Sean, and it will make you happier. But you must promise by all your Catholic saints not to tell anyone at all."

"What? What about Sean? Is it something good? Tell me this minute!"

"Not until you promise."

Norah uttered a rich curse and threw a pillow across the room, narrowly missing the water pitcher.

"And do not destroy my property, if you please."

Norah's eyes, Hilda had always thought, were beautiful, dark blue with long, long lashes. Now they were filled with fury. "All right. I promise. Now *tell me!*"

"By the saints."

Norah's breasts heaved as she made the sign of the cross over them. "By all the saints. I swear."

"Good. The police do not think Sean set the fire."

"Then why in the name of all that's holy haven't they let him go?" Norah's voice rose to a scream.

"Because he is safer in jail. I will tell you the story if you will lie back and be calm and take your tonic."

"To the divil with my tonic!"

But Hilda stood with the bottle in her hand and refused to speak a word until Norah allowed a spoonful down her throat. Then she lay back on the pillow Hilda returned to her. "There. Now are you satisfied?"

Hilda sighed. "You are not calm, but I suppose that is asking too much. I will tell you all I know." She sat down beside the bed. "The police think the real murderer has tried to make them believe Sean is guilty. If the murderer knows he has not succeeded, he will maybe try to keep Sean quiet. The best way to do that would be to kill him. So he is being kept in jail for his own safety, while they—and I—try to find the real killer. Now. Does that make you feel better?"

"Is this the truth you're tellin' me?"

"Norah! Have I ever lied to you?"

"Yes. Often."

Hilda made a face. "Well—but only when it was better that

you should not know the truth. This time I tell no lie. The mayor went to the police yesterday and made them understand that the evidence they thought they had against Sean was no good."

"What evidence? Why did they arrest him? Nobody ever tells me anything!"

"We did not want to make you unhappy," said Hilda reluctantly, "but I expect I will have to tell you now. Yesterday morning the police found Sean's pocketknife in the ashes of the barn."

"His knife? The one I gave him? But he's had that with him, all the time. I've seen it every day, ever since his birthday when he got it. He couldn't have left it in that barn. I can tell that to any policeman who bothers to ask me! What do they think they're doin', makin' up a thing like that?" Norah was sitting bolt upright again, and the fire was back in her eyes.

"*They* did not make it up, Norah. Someone stole it, we think during the blizzard on Tuesday, and planted it in the ashes. Then they told the police it was there. So the police really did find it, and for a time the police believed—or pretended to believe—that it meant Sean must have dropped it while setting the fire. But I thought that did not make sense, and Patrick thought the same, so he and I and Uncle Dan went to the mayor about it, and he went to the police chief, and the rest is as I told you."

"Don't know why nobody asked me," said Norah. She lay back, but her tone was sulky. "I could've told them."

"But you are Sean's wife," said Hilda patiently. "You would say anything that would protect him. So would his friends. And we did not want you to know the knife had been used in that way, because you gave it to him and it is precious to both of you."

"It's all right?"

"Dented a little, and black from the ashes. We think the person who stole it maybe dropped it in a fireplace for a bit to make it look right. But it can be made to look like new."

"Oh. Well, then." Norah was silent for a time, absorbing all she had been told. "But when will they let Sean go?"

That was the question Hilda had been dreading. "Probably not until they catch the real murderer. Do you not see, Norah? It will not be safe for him until then."

"And what, may I humbly ask Your Majesty, are they doin' to catch him?"

"I do not know. Patrick is talking to them today, and will tell me when he comes home tonight. Me, I tried to find out something this morning, and I did, but it did not help." She related the story of Mr. Miller and his bride.

Norah laughed a little at that, and then said, "Hilda, I'm sorry I got so mad at you. It was just worry about Sean, and not feelin' so good, and that. And you were tauntin' me, y'know."

"I know. I was not really angry with you. I needed only to make you pay attention to me. But Norah, I am serious about you saying nothing. No one must know that the police no longer suspect Sean. If you tell one person, and she tells someone else—you see?"

"I see," said Norah. "But if I don't tell me mother, she'll stay on the warpath, and I warn ye, she can be—"

"I know," said Hilda again. "But Patrick knows how to handle her. Last night he gave her so much whiskey that I think she will not feel very good today. I am sorry, but it was the only way. She was determined to take you and Fiona away, and that would have been very bad for both of you."

Norah stirred restlessly. "Ye-es. I suppose so. But Hilda, we can't stay here forever, Fiona and me."

"You have not been here forever, only a week. Fiona is a week old today, think of that!"

Perhaps it was the sound of her name. Or perhaps not. At any rate, Fiona, wherever she was with Nurse Pickerell, began to wail. Norah perked up. "Ah, the little beggar! She's hungry. Get her, Hilda, and bring her to me."

When Fiona had settled to comfortable suckling, Hilda stole out of the room.

MANY FINE WINDOWS
Local Merchants Make
an Unusual Showing—
Displays Very Attractive

—South Bend *Tribune*
December 1904

28

HILDA COMPLETED HER list of needed toys and sent it to Mrs. Clem, but her mind was entirely on Sean's problem and what Patrick might have learned. When she heard Patrick's footstep on the porch, she flew to the hall and barely let him get his coat off before accosting him. "Did you have time to go to the police station? Did you find out anything about the billfold?"

"I did better than that," said Patrick with satisfaction. "I brought it home with me." He reached into his breast pocket, got out the billfold, and handed it to Hilda.

"Ooh! I did not think the police would let you have it."

"They've decided it had nothin' to do with the fire, so there was no reason to hold onto it. I stopped by the jail and told Sean I had it and he'd get it back as soon as he's walkin' free again."

Hilda was examining the billfold. "I can see why Sean wanted it. It is dirty and a little worn, but it is very good leather. It will last for a long time yet. And I think the police are wrong to say it is not important. It does not tie Sean to the fire, of course, but it might be a clue to someone else." She took it to the gas fixture on the wall and squinted. "I think there have been initials on it, here, but they are nearly gone."

"I couldn't make anything of them meself. Better wait until the mornin' light."

Hilda sighed. "I suppose so. I wanted to know now."

"I don't see why you're carryin' on about that billfold. It never belonged to the hired man, that's certain. No hired man ever carried a fine thing like that."

"You are right about that. I do not know why the police were so stupid as to think it might have been Mr. Jenkins's. But someone carried it, Patrick. Someone lost it. Oh!" She clapped a hand to her head. "I should have asked Mrs. Miller if her husband had lost a billfold."

"Mrs. Miller? Husband? What're ye talkin' about?"

So she told him about her morning. "And I was so surprised to see her there that I forgot to ask about the billfold. And I could not ask about the mortgage."

Patrick whistled. "Ye did well to remember anything at all. That's a turn-up for the books, Old Man Miller married. Well, in the mornin' when you can look proper, you can maybe see if the initials could be his. I don't know what his Christian name is."

"Mrs. Miller called him Walter."

"It'll probably turn out to be WM on the billfold, then. We'll know tomorrow. Meanwhile, I can tell you a bit about the mortgage. I asked Uncle Dan about it this afternoon."

"Uncle Dan? Why would he know about Mr. Miller's mortgage?"

"Well, he doesn't, not to say know. But he keeps a weather eye on the finances around town, as ye might say. He has to. A merchant can't sell fancy goods when a town's havin' hard times, but folks as are doin' all right don't want plain goods. So he has to trim his sails, like. So I asked him whether he knew where Miller did his bankin'. I thought he might, seein' as Miller's been the subject of a good deal of conversation just lately. And he said he'd heard it was Farmer's Bank."

"But did you not say, last week—"

"That Farmer's isn't doin' too good? That I did. It was the word around town. So I asked Uncle Dan about that, and he said it was true. They're callin' in loans left and right. Turns out that's why Black's Bicycle Works is closin'. And if Miller has a mortgage with them…"

Hilda was thinking hard. "But Mrs. Miller did not seem worried, today. She talked about rebuilding the barn soon—yes, and buying new furniture."

Patrick shrugged. "Don't know. But it's another road that seems to go nowhere. By the by, how was the going out in the country? I'd've thought the snow would still be too deep for a carriage."

"I borrowed Mrs. Clem's sleigh," said Hilda. "Colonel George and Mrs. George are out of town, and Mrs. Clem was not going out today, so she was happy to lend it to me."

"We're going to have to get one of our own. Business was much better at the store today. People makin' up for lost time, I guess, and realizin' Christmas is in just two weeks. And our window displays are new, and they're fine, Hilda. You ought to see! So maybe there'll be enough extra money that I can buy you a nice sleigh as a Christmas present. What kind would you like?"

"A Studebaker, of course! Oh—you are teasing me again!"

He gave her a hug and a peck on the cheek. "I am that. I wouldn't get you anything but the best, darlin' girl. Now, is that beef stew I smell?"

Eileen announced supper just then, greatly to Hilda's relief. She hadn't had to confess about borrowing John Bolton along with the sleigh!

∾

Saturday morning dawned clear and cold once more. Hilda was able to examine the billfold by the hard light of sunshine on snow, and decided that the initials could not possibly be WM. The first might have been M, or possibly H. The second was, she thought, T. But it could have been F or even R. Assuming she was reading them right-side up. She gave it up for the time being and concentrated on other aspects of the problem.

Did the difficulties at Farmer's Bank have anything to do with the fire? Hilda knew little about high finance, though she was learning. She could not imagine how it would be to anyone's benefit to burn down Mr. Miller's barn. He might have lost valuable stock. It was only by luck that the horses were away, and only because of the hired man's drunken idleness that the cows were still out to pasture when the fire started.

So. *Think, Hilda.* Mr. Miller could not have burned down

the barn himself, but suppose he hired someone to do it, maybe. Why? He would get the insurance money, but he would have to use it to rebuild the barn. And the insurance would not pay for everything. And the fire cost him a hired man and a great deal of inconvenience. No, she could see no reason why he would burn it himself.

Could Jenkins have had a grudge against his employer? Even if so, what good would it do him to burn down the barn? It was doing Miller a bad deed, but it wasn't doing Jenkins any good. And in any case, Jenkins died in the fire. And he could not have set it himself and then fallen asleep in the far corner of the hayloft.

Someone who hated Miller. True, there was no such person, according to Mrs. Miller, but she might be wrong. Someone from Mr. Miller's past? But again, what point was there? No permanent harm was done to Miller or his farm.

Really, the only one who truly suffered was poor Jenkins. Could someone have hated him? He was an unreliable type, but apparently a hard enough worker. He might have made some enemies among the men at a tavern. But even if someone had wanted to kill him, why choose such an uncertain way? Jenkins might have wakened out of his drunken stupor and escaped. He might even have put out the fire, if he had seen it early enough. There were so many easier ways to kill a drunken man, easier and surer. Push him into a creek, or in front of a train. Hit him on the head. Put a bullet into his back.

Hilda shuddered. Thinking about murder methods was not pleasant, nor was it productive. The fact was, she could think of no possible reason for anyone to set that fire.

Maybe everyone was wrong. Maybe it was an accident after all.

Then why was someone planting false evidence against Sean O'Neill, if not to cover their own tracks?

Her head was beginning to ache, and she was making no progress at all towards a solution. She would stop for a little, and go up and see how Norah was doing.

Norah was much better. Her face was pink, she had (according to the nurse) eaten all her breakfast and asked for more, and she was nursing Fiona and crooning to her when Hilda came in.

"There's a little love of a colleen, then. Isn't she, Hilda?"

"She is beautiful," said Hilda honestly. The baby had filled out wonderfully in a week's time, and she had her mother's eyelashes.

"That nurse won't let me give her all she wants. She says it's too hard on me. But I've plenty of milk now, and she cries when I take her away from the breast."

Never having been a mother, Hilda had no useful advice to offer. "Have you talked to the doctor?"

"Haven't seen him since Thursday, have I? And then I was—not meself."

"No," said Hilda. "You were hysterical."

"Well, you can call a spade a spade, can't you?"

"If not," said Hilda in as near to John Bolton's accent as she could manage, "a bloody shovel."

"Hilda!"

"I think," said Hilda, settling herself beside the bed, "that is the first time I have ever sworn. In English," she added.

"You're gettin' above yourself, me girl."

The nurse bustled in to take the baby, who promptly began to howl. "There now, lovey," said Nurse Pickerell, "I have a nice warm bottle for you."

"She doesn't want a bottle," said Norah. "She wants her mother."

"And we can't allow that just yet, can we? We'll wait until Doctor tells us we can do that."

"I think," said Hilda before Norah could speak, "that you should call the doctor and ask him if Norah can nurse all she wants. It is plain that she is getting well, and mother's milk must be better for Fiona than cow's milk."

"Well, really! Anyone would think the two of you knew something about nursing!"

"I know something," said Norah in a dangerous tone, "about being a mother. And you don't."

"Go and call, Nurse," said Hilda quickly. "I will look after Fiona for a little."

Miss Pickerell stalked out, and the minute she had gone Hilda handed the redfaced baby back to Norah. "Now," she said, when the baby was contentedly back at the breast, "I want to talk to you, Norah. If you are feeling strong," she added.

"I'm feelin' fine," said Norah. "Nothin's gone wrong, has it?"

"No. Except I cannot make sense of anything. Norah, I think my mind has turned to—to something soft and woolly. I can find no answers."

"Well, what's your questions?"

"I cannot understand why anyone would want to burn down Mr. Miller's barn."

Norah thought about that while the baby suckled greedily. "Maybe nobody did."

"No, it was not an accident. That is certain. Someone set that fire on purpose."

"That isn't what I meant." She shifted the baby's position a bit. "I mean, suppose whoever it was meant to start just a little fire, or something. Suppose things didn't work out the way they intended. Then it would make sense that nothin' made sense. If you see what I'm sayin'."

Hilda did, after a little thought. "You mean—we are seeing what happened, not what someone meant to happen."

"Yes. So of course you can't figger out a reason. There isn't a reason for what really happened."

Hilda held her head in her hands. "Stop! You make it worse! If I cannot make sense of what happened, how can I make sense of what was supposed to happen? When I do not even know what that is?"

Norah shrugged, disturbing Fiona, who made a little grunt of protest. "There, darlin', I didn't mean to move you. You're a fine hungry girl, you are. No, but Hilda, it gives you a different place to start. Instead of tryin' to work from the fire, work from what somebody might have wanted from Mr. Miller and thought they could get by—by doin' somethin' besides what they did."

The nurse came back in, starch and righteousness much in evidence, and Hilda was glad of it. Her head was hurting worse than ever. She didn't stay to listen to the nurse's arguments and instructions. Let the two of them work it out. She had other worries.

Norah had given her a new line of thought, but she didn't know how to follow it. How could one assess a situation, not as it was, but as it was meant to be? No, taking the inquiry from that end was hopeless. She had thought that, if she could work out why the fire was set, she would know who set it. Now she realized that motive was very elusive.

But what other approach was even possible? There was no way to find out who, on the basis of opportunity, could have done the deed. Over forty thousand people lived in South Bend, many more if one counted the inhabitants of the neighboring farms. Any one of them might, presumably, have done it.

Well, but unless it was set by a tramp, it must have been done by someone who knew Mr. Miller. And that, according to the new Mrs. Miller, was not a large group. He was shy. He stayed most of the time alone on his farm, working with his hired man, James Jenkins. He knew, at least slightly, the people he did business with. Those would be the merchants who sold him supplies and equipment, his banker, the men to whom he sold his corn and wheat and apples and milk and whatever else he raised.

Hilda made a list and then looked at it dispiritedly. She could find out who all these people were. She could go and ask them where they all were on that day in November, the day of the fire. And the honest ones probably would not remember, and the guilty one—and perhaps some of the others—would lie. There are many reasons for hiding what one was doing at a particular time, and most of them are not criminal.

It was no use. The police had probably already asked all those questions of all those people, and the police had uncovered nothing at all. Until she got a better idea, she would think about something else.

The party. That growing party. She could go to see Sven

and ask about the toys he was making. Not until this afternoon, though. He worked on Saturday mornings, and Mama and the others worked all day on Saturday at their respective jobs. Even Erik would be working, in the stable at the central fire station. She could go and see him. He would know what progress had been made on the toys, and what Mama and the girls were making.

Ah! She had it! She would go and talk to Aunt Molly. She needed to tell Riggs how large the party was growing, anyway, and Aunt Molly had a way of seeing things clearly that always helped Hilda's state of mind.

She telephoned first. Riggs assured her that Madam was, indeed, at home and would welcome her visit.

She rang for Eileen. "I am going out, Eileen. Only to see Aunt Molly, and I will walk. It is not far, and the day is beautiful."

"Cold, though, ma'am. Be sure and wrap up good. Will you be home for dinner?"

"I do not know. What is Mrs. O'Rourke planning?"

"Baked ham and sweet potatoes and lima beans and custard."

"Ask her, please, to keep something warm for me unless I telephone to say I am eating elsewhere. Thank you, Eileen."

There was, she thought as she walked carefully down the icy porch steps, something to be said for having servants.

At the Malloy house, Riggs greeted her with a smile, the first she had ever seen on his face. "Good morning, madam. But where is your carriage?"

"I walked. The snow is beautiful in the sunshine."

"That it is. Have you news for me, madam?"

"Yes, Riggs. I hope it is not bad news. At the last count, there were at least three hundred boys coming to the party. Will that be an impossible crowd?"

"I have spoken to the Odd Fellows about their largest meeting hall, madam. It will hold over five hundred if necessary. Perhaps we should plan for that many?"

Hilda sighed. "You are probably right. I did not think this would be such a popular event."

"The poorer boys of South Bend have had very little attention for many years, madam. It's high time someone thought of doing something for them. I intend to be there, myself."

"Oh!" Hilda had just had a brilliant idea. "Could you, maybe, dress up like Santa Claus and give out the presents?"

Clearly pleased at the idea, Riggs coughed. "Would it not be better for Mr. Malloy to take that role? Or Mr. Cavanaugh, perhaps?"

"No, Riggs," said Hilda firmly. "You have a rosy face, and when you smile, you look very yolly. Jolly. You do not have a beard, like most pictures of Santa Claus, but we can give you a false one. You will be very good, I think."

He bowed. "Thank you madam. It will be an honor. And may I say, you look a bit like a jolly elf this morning, yourself, with your cheeks rosy from the cold. Very becoming, madam, if you don't mind my saying so."

Hilda could have kissed him. How could she ever have been afraid of this charming man? "Thank you, Riggs. That is very nice of you."

He bowed again, his face once more set in his butler expression. "Mrs. Malloy is in the parlor, madam."

Hilda turned away, but before she did she was sure she saw a tear on the butler's face. So that was why he stayed frozen most of the time. When he let himself thaw, his emotions got the better of him.

If, she mused as Riggs showed her to the parlor, she now knew that butlers were as human as anyone else, she had learned an important lesson.

*The crusade to keep women from earning
their living as stenographers does not
appeal to us with much force, even
though it has its origin in the great
state of Ohio.* [Washington *Post*]

——South Bend *Tribune*
December 1904

"COME IN, CHILD," said Aunt Molly, who was seated by the fire. "I won't get up. My bones ache this morning. They don't care for this run of cold weather. Would you like some coffee or tea, or anything?"

"Yes, thank you, some coffee would be very nice."

"Thanks to you. I could never abide the stuff before you taught Cook how to make it. I'll have some, too, Riggs. Thank you."

"Do you know, Aunt Molly, he is *nice,*" said Hilda when Riggs had left the room. "I never thought I would say that about a butler. I have asked him to be Santa Claus at the party."

Molly clapped her lace-mitted hands together. "What a good idea! I wish I'd thought of it. He's never really stopped grieving for his son, you know. It will do him a world of good to mix with a lot of boys."

"I did not know about his son until Patrick told me. I think I have not bothered to learn very much about some people. I do not even know anything about Williams, not really, and I worked for him for six years."

"You'll learn, my dear. Very few people can open their eyes to the world around them, but you are one of those few. Your new freedom will help. You're feeling more comfortable now, aren't you?"

Hilda hadn't realized it herself until that moment. "Yes, I am. I have learned—I am learning—to see that I am the same person I always was, and that other people are the same, too. They are not—they do not just—oh, I cannot say what I mean!"

"They're not just actors, perhaps you're trying to say. Not just puppets playing roles in a play, but real people with real problems and emotions. All of them, no matter what their job or their position in society."

"Yes!" said Hilda with the relief of having her ideas expressed clearly. "And I am a real person, too, not just 'a servant' or 'a Swede' or even 'a wealthy wife.' It makes it easier to know what to do. And harder, sometimes."

"Yes, sometimes harder, because society doesn't like us to step outside our roles and come to life. You, my dear, are not a person to put up with that kind of restraint."

"No. And I am not a person to be—to be just a wife. I do not mean that I do not love Patrick. You know I do, and I am happy and proud to be his wife. But that is not all I am. I do not like it that women are so often thought of as just somebody's wife. Mrs. Brick, I was thinking at the meeting last week, is the wife of a politician. Mrs. Elbel is the wife of a musician, Mrs. Darby the wife of a businessman. Oh, and that Mrs. Townsend, the one I do not like. I forgot to ask Mrs. Clem about her. Is she just somebody's wife, too?"

"Her husband is a banker, and I really know very little about either of them. They're from Terre Haute, I think. The others, though, are all quite interesting women."

"That is what I mean. I should not think of them the way I do! They are not just wives. They are people."

"That is beginning to be true, Hilda. It wasn't always. I do think it may not be too many years before women are allowed to vote, and good for them, I say. I was always a rebel—like you. All my life I've said and done what I pleased, and shocked everyone. Now that I'm an old lady, everyone says I'm wonderful. So you see what you have to look forward to."

Hilda made a face. "There is much of life before that. And you are not old, Aunt Molly!"

"Oh, yes, I am. But I seldom think about it, except when my bones tell me. Now, what have you come to see me about? Or was it Riggs you came to call on?"

Hilda giggled. "I think maybe it was. How shocked he would be—"

Molly put up her hand as Riggs came into the room with a silver coffee tray and two delicate bone china cups, along with some thin, crisp cookies.

Hilda smiled at him, the light of mischief in her eyes. She waited until he had set the tray down—for fear of accidents—and then said, "I was saying, Riggs, how shocked you would be if I said I came here to call on you, really."

"Ah, but ladies say many things, do they not, madam? Will that be all, then?"

And he was gone, the lacquered façade perfectly in place.

"He'll not let you in easily, child," said Molly, sipping her coffee. "He used to be much less stiff, before the *Maine*. He was very proud of his son's career, used to read us bits out of his letters. So I knew the boy—now, what was his name? Jonathan, that's it—I knew Jonathan was on a ship near Cuba. When the news came about the *Maine* and a telegram came for Riggs, I called him in and said I hoped it wasn't bad news. I'll never forget it. He said, 'Thank you, madam. I fear the news is very bad. Will there be anything else, madam?' And of course I let him go, because I could see he was controlling himself by sheer force. Ever since, he's been the way you know him. He has never once mentioned Jonathan's name."

"He wept today," said Hilda softly, "when I asked him to be Santa Claus. One tear."

"That's good. You're good for him, I think. But take it slowly. He's worked hard at building up that shell, and it's very thick now. If it cracked suddenly, I don't know what would happen."

Hilda nodded soberly.

"But you did not, after all, come just to talk to Riggs. Or about him. How can I help you? Is it Norah again?"

"No, Norah is getting well very nicely, if only her mother will stop creating scenes. No, it is the fire, and Mr. Miller, and all. I have learned much, but everything seems to make less sense than before. Aunt Molly, we must find out what really happened!"

Molly frowned. "I would have thought Norah would be in a real state, with Sean under arrest."

"Oh, dear. Now I will have to tell you, too!" And quickly she related the story of manufactured evidence and the mayor's intervention.

"Ah! I see. And of course that word must not get out."

"But I think I should not have told Norah. For now others will wonder why she is not upset, and they may guess, or make Norah tell them. It will not be very long, I fear, before everyone knows, and then the police will have to let him go. We do not have very much time, Aunt Molly, to learn the truth."

"Do you know what the police are doing?"

"No. If I can think of nothing to do, no one to ask, how can they?"

Molly laughed. "You *do* have a high opinion of your own brains, don't you? Not that I don't think you're justified. You solved Daniel's problem for him, when the police couldn't, or wouldn't."

"I know I am smart," said Hilda calmly. "And the police are sometimes very stupid. But this time I am as stupid as they. I cannot make a pattern out of the things that have happened. Norah said something this morning that made me think, but it complicated things even more. She said perhaps the fire did not work out as it was intended to, that someone might have meant to start only a small fire, and something went wrong. So we cannot make sense of things as they are, because they are not what the bad person intended."

"That was very astute of Norah," said Molly with a little sigh. "But not, as you say, very helpful. It solves the question of why everything is such a muddle, but unless you can work out what *was* intended, you're no further ahead."

"That is why I wanted to talk to you. Aunt Molly, why would anyone start a small fire in a barn?"

"No one with any sense would!" said Molly fiercely. "A wooden barn full of hay and straw—why, it would flare up in a minute, even without kerosene, which I understand was used."

"A lantern, yes. It turned over and spilled the kerosene. But could that have maybe been an accident?" She had just thought of the possibility. "Suppose someone went to the barn looking for something. And it was dark in there and the person lit a lantern. And then the person dropped the lantern, and the kerosene spilled and caught fire and started the straw burning. And the person was frightened and ran away, and the whole barn burned."

"Hmm. Why would anyone have been there at the time?"

"I do not know. Maybe—maybe it was one of the hired man's friends, coming to check on him. He would have been there, asleep, by the middle of the afternoon."

"No friend would go off and let him burn up."

"Oh. No, I suppose not. Well, it was a robber, maybe. Someone who knew Mr. Miller was away."

"Hilda, my dear, you're not using that excellent brain of yours. A robber would go to the house where there might be money or valuables. Not to the barn, where the only real valuables would be the horses, which were away at the time, and the buggy, which one cannot steal without horses."

"You are right. Aunt Molly, what are we to do? We cannot let Sean stay in jail, and if he gets out he could be in danger, and Norah needs him, and—"

"Yes, my dear girl. Yes, the problem must be solved. But we're not going to solve it by getting our minds so twisted we can hardly think at all. Besides, you have a headache. I can always tell. You need fresh air and exercise, not more study and deliberation. Go spend the rest of the day in the sunshine. Go skating with that handsome big brother of yours; the ponds are all frozen hard. Think about the Christmas party, or future plans for the Boys' Club, or anything but the fire. You'll see. An idea will come."

Unwillingly, Hilda took her leave.

Once outside, she remembered that she had wanted to talk to both of her brothers. Erik, at the central firehouse, was closer, and the sun had warmed the air a bit. She walked briskly and arrived with cheeks rosier than ever.

Erik was currying one of the horses, his favorite, Donner.

"It means thunder, in German," he had explained importantly to Hilda. "Mr. Gruner, he named him. And it's almost the same name as one of Santa's reindeer in that poem. Isn't that funny?"

He was delighted to see Hilda. "Are you all ready for the party? What kind of presents are you getting? Sven's making lots of toys; you should see. And Mama's knitted hundreds of caps and mittens, I bet. What are we having to eat? Will there be candy? What are you getting for me? Sven's making me something, but I don't know what. And he's making something for you, too, and I know what it is, but I can't tell. And I found out something for you, about the fire maybe."

"*Oj då!*" said Hilda. "What do you want to talk about first?"

"My news," said Erik importantly. "I heard it yesterday from one of my friends at school. He has a friend who knows a boy who delivers groceries to some people named Townsend. He's a banker, I guess. Mr. Townsend, I mean. Anyway the boy who works there, Freddy his name is, he likes horses and so he's friends with Mr. Townsend's coachman."

"Yes, Erik," said Hilda with scarcely controlled impatience. "And what did you learn?"

"But it's important, that it's the coachman who told him, because it means it must be true, see."

"No," said Hilda, "I do not see. You have not told me."

"You won't give me a chance! So I was talking to this boy who knows the boy who—"

"Yes, we have had all that. Erik if you do not tell me, I will leave. It is cold standing here."

"You can sit," said Erik with a cheeky grin. He tugged over a bale of hay.

"Erik…" she said dangerously.

"He said the horse came home lathered that day."

"Who said? What horse? What day? Erik, make sense!"

"Well, you said you wanted me to hurry up and tell you."

Hilda stood and brushed hay off her skirt, and Erik capitulated.

"Okay, I'll tell it all. The day of the fire, the Townsends' coachman said Mrs. Townsend took out the Izzer, drove it herself, he said."

Hilda sat down again and frowned. "Why did she do that?"

"Dunno, but I guess she does it a lot. The coachman doesn't like her. Says she's a stubborn woman and high-hat."

Hilda made a face. "She can be. I know her a little. Go on."

"Anyway, the coachman doesn't like it when she takes out the buggy, because she isn't very patient with horses. And that day it was almost night when she came back with the buggy, and he said that horse had been driven so hard it was lathered with sweat, even though it was a cold day."

"Hmm. Where she did go with the buggy?"

"Dunno. Dunno any more."

"But what does it have to do with the fire?"

"Dunno. You said you wanted to know about anything unusual that happened that day."

"Oh. Yes. Thank you, Erik."

"Well, you don't have to sound so happy about it!" he grumbled, picking up the brush again and beginning to work through Donner's mane.

Hilda sighed. "It is one more thing that does not make sense. I am tired of things that do not make sense. I want things to fit!"

Erik shrugged. "Can't do anything about that. And I s'pose you're forgettin' all about the Christmas party, what with all the other things you're tryin' to do."

"Of course I do not forget! We are working very hard, the other ladies and I, to make a good party. There will be many presents, but if you will not tell me about my present from Sven, I will not tell you about the ones for the party. And there will be much food. Mrs. Clem is looking after the food herself, and she knows how boys eat, so it will be good. Now, I go home, and then to see Sven and see if he can come skating with me. Do you have to work all afternoon?"

"No! Just till Mike comes to work. Where're you going?"

"Leeper Park, I think, if it is not too crowded."

"I'll come as soon as I can! Will you stop at home and bring my skates, so I don't have to waste all that time?"

"I will, *lillebrorsan*. Don't brush all the hair off that horse."

She left before he could finish his protest about being called "little brother."

30

Man may work from sun to sun
But woman's work is never done.

—Anonymous

SUNDAY WAS, AS usual, a day to be endured. It was the Cavanaugh family's turn to serve dinner, so Hilda wore her politest face and a gown that wasn't overly extravagant and tried her best to participate in the table conversation. It wasn't easy. The Cavanaughs either treated her with painful courtesy or ignored her altogether. On the whole, she could cope more easily with being ignored. The food was strange, too. Mrs. Cavanaugh wasn't a bad cook, but she relied a good deal on potatoes.

Hilda was just choking down a bite of rather flavorless boiled potato when Patrick's brother Brian turned to her. "I haven't heard when the police are goin' to let poor Sean O'Neill out of jail. Do you know anything about that, by chance?"

Hilda was sure she didn't imagine the sarcasm in his voice. A lump rose in her throat. She took a sip of water to wash down the last of the potato, which had turned to dust in her mouth. "I do not know what the police are doing," she said, in perfect truth. "I hope they are working hard. Sean is innocent, and they must prove it soon, for the sake of Norah and the baby."

"And I suppose you'd be above doin' anything about it yourself, now that you're a fine lady and all?" This time the sarcasm was unmistakable.

"Brian!" roared Patrick in fury.

Hilda ignored him. "I do what I can, Brian," she said, trying to stay calm. "It is not easy to find out the truth."

"Not even for the girl with the best brain in town?" taunted Brian.

Hilda reached for Patrick's hand and grasped it hard, lest he explode. "Not even for her," she said with a forced smile. "But if I knew who she was, I would ask her for help. Myself, I am nearly out of ideas. Mrs. Cavanaugh, is there another biscuit? They are very good."

That changed the subject—that, and Patrick's kick at his brother under the table. On the way home, Patrick fumed about his family as Hilda had done the week before, about hers.

"Downright rude, he was!" he grumbled. " I don't know why Ma lets him get by with it."

Hilda was tired. "Every Sunday it is the same. My family is rude to you, or yours is rude to me. They will stop one day, when we have been married a long time and they have resigned themselves. Anyway, Brian did not say anything I have not thought. I should have been able to find the truth by now."

"Because you're the smartest girl in town," Patrick said, nodding in agreement. "Leave it for the day, darlin'. It's Sunday."

For once she did as he suggested. She even napped for a little while in the afternoon, after checking on Norah and Fiona, and spent the evening peacefully in front of the fire finishing her Christmas list. The sky clouded over and the temperature rose throughout the day. A light snow was falling by the time Hilda and Patrick went early to bed—but not early to sleep. There were times when Hilda was very, very glad she had not been brought up as a "lady" who was not supposed to enjoy the intimacies of marriage. Hilda enjoyed them very much indeed.

The next morning, still drugged with pleasure, she rolled over and reached out for Patrick, only to find the other side of the bed cold and empty. Oh, yes, Monday. Patrick's meeting. And much to do.

For despite her attempts to follow Aunt Molly's suggestion and stop thinking about Sean and the fire, no ideas had come to her open, receptive mind. Hilda was, as she had once heard Mrs. Clem say, completely flummoxed. Perhaps the best thing to do was to go and talk again to Andy. He might have learned some new bits of information that would lead her in a better direction. Or in any direction, she thought, yawning.

She got up, crossed the cold floor quickly, and looked out the window. Snow, but not heavy snow. Just big, pretty flakes falling slowly. She could get around in that easily enough. She might not even take the carriage, though it was nice to know she had one at her disposal if she wanted it. She rang for Eileen and jumped back into bed. What a luxury to wait until the room was warm before she had to dress!

"Eileen," she said thoughtfully when the little maid came into the room with a tray of coffee and a bucketful of coals, "we have not had time for lessons of late. I do not mean to neglect them, but there has been much to think about."

" 'Sall right, ma'am. I've been run off me feet, what with that nurse, and the new baby and all. I take that book you gave me up to bed at night, though, and sometimes try to read a little before I go to sleep."

"Good. After Christmas, when things are maybe quieter, I will start teaching you some arithmetic. I have always been good with numbers."

Eileen sighed. "Yes, ma'am," she said despondently, and began to build up the fire.

"Ah, but you must be good at arithmetic if you want to be a cook. There is a great deal of mathematics in cookery. Or so my mama and my sisters tell me."

"Then you ought to be better at cooking than you are, ma'am, bein' as you're so good with numbers," said Eileen, and then looked a little scared. "If you don't mind my sayin' so."

"You are quite right, Eileen. I should be. And one day I will be, when I can take time for lessons. Now I must have a bath. I will not need your help with dressing, and I will come down for breakfast."

"Yes, ma'am. I'll run your bath, shall I?"

"Please. And Eileen, how is Mrs. O'Neill today?"

"Oh, ma'am, she's that cheerful and bright-lookin', nobody'd think her husband was lyin' there in jail. It's wonderful how she's made up her mind to stay lively for the sake of the baby. Who's cheerin' up herself, and gainin' weight. Nurse says she'll have her fat as a little pink pig before she's done."

Hilda went to her bath with mixed feelings about Norah's improvement. "Staying lively" was all very well, but the next time Mrs. Murphy visited, she was going to know something was up. After breakfast, Hilda decided, she must go and see Norah and talk to her.

Norah apparently thought so, too. When Eileen served Hilda's breakfast, she brought a message. "That nurse has been down to warm Fiona's bottle," the maid said as she put porridge and hot toast on the table, and checked to make sure there was enough coffee and cream and sugar and butter and jam. "She says Mrs. O'Neill wants to see you when you've finished your breakfast. Says she's all excited about somethin', and Nurse had to be real firm to make her stay in bed." Eileen snickered. "I'll bet Mrs. O'Neill's sorry she got Nurse's back up. I wouldn't want her bein' 'real firm' with me."

"The nurse is doing what she needs to do," said Hilda reprovingly. Privately she agreed with Eileen. It would not be much fun to be on the wrong side of Nurse Pickerell's tongue.

Norah was indeed excited. When Hilda went into the room her friend was sitting up in the rocking chair, wrapped up in shawls and very close to the fire, but out of bed. When Hilda came in she stood up, scattering shawls over the floor.

"Now, now, none of that," said the nurse, who was folding diapers. "The doctor has said you might sit up for a bit, but he said nothing about standing and running around the room."

Norah rolled her eyes. "And who said I'm runnin' around anywhere?" She added something under her breath. Hilda didn't quite catch it, but she could guess its import.

"You had better sit down," she said hastily. "You are doing well, and I do not want you to take a turn for the worse."

"Don't want me on your hands forever, is that it?" But Norah sat, and the smile playing around her eyes took the sting away from the remark. "You took your time about getting up here."

"I was eating breakfast. What is so important, that I must hurry?"

"I've thought of somethin', that's what's so important. Somethin' you never thought of, for all your fancy brains." Norah tilted her head to one side, an impudent look on her face.

It was a look that Hilda knew well, and hadn't seen for weeks. "If you are well enough to insult me, you are getting better. See, I will sit and humbly listen to what you have thought with *your* fancy brain."

"The day you're humble is the day we'll need to take you out of church feet first," said Norah. The nurse made a tut-tutting noise in the background, but Norah paid no attention. "Now listen. You've gone all over the place talkin' to people about the fire, and askin' who knows what, and you've been gettin' nowhere, am I right?"

Hilda sighed and nodded. "I have learned things, but I cannot put them together to make a story."

"Well, if I didn't know you'd throw me out in the snow, I'd call you a dumb Swede. And me a stupid Irishwoman, as well. For why didn't we either of us think to talk to the men who were there?"

"I have talked to the firemen," began Hilda, frowning, but Norah interrupted her.

"Not the firemen, numskull. The men who were with Sean, buildin' Barry's cousin's barn. The Irishmen!"

"But—but—do they know anything? Did they see anything?"

"We don't know that till we ask, do we? Hilda Johansson, you should have thought to do that a week ago!"

Hilda stood up and began to pace. "Yes! You are right, Norah! Oh, it is stupid we have been, stupid, both of us. You I can excuse. You have been ill, and worried, and have a new baby to care for, but I!"

"You with your marv'lous brain," put in Norah.

"Yes, you may laugh at me. Norah, it is a brilliant idea you have had. I will go *now* to talk to them." She headed for the door.

"Mebbe," said Norah, "you'd want me first to tell you who they are and where to find them?"

∽

When Hilda had thought about it for a little, she realized that the police had almost certainly talked to the men already, but it didn't matter. They had got no further with their investigation than she had with hers. Therefore they had not asked the right questions. Or else…Hilda was growing more and more uneasy about the police, and particularly the sergeant in charge of the case.

At any rate, she would talk to the men herself. It could do no harm, and she might learn something important.

Fortunately most of the men worked at one of three factories: Birdsell's, Oliver's, or Studebaker's. Of these, the busiest at this time of year would be Studebaker's. The other two, which made only farm equipment, always had plenty of work for their employees, but the pace was less frantic in December than it would be in a couple of months. Hilda decided to start at Birdsell's.

There she found the men sympathetic to Sean's plight and eager to talk about that day. The foreman, who knew Sean well, agreed that the men could take five minutes off to talk to Hilda. "Not here, though," he shouted. The uproar on the factory floor was tremendous. "Better go to the lunchroom. Nobody there at this hour. I'll show you, ma'am." He escorted her and the four men to the large room where the men ate in inclement weather. "And you tell that Sean O'Neill, when you see him, that he'd have done better to stay on here. We're not laying off, like some. I'm sorry I can't hire him back, but when business picks up in the spring, if he's out of jail and still hasn't found a job, he can come back here and talk to me. He's a good worker."

"He will be out of jail, I promise. And I hope he will find a job before then, but I will tell him what you said."

"Right. Five minutes, now."

The men were so eager to tell her all about everything that she couldn't understand a word. "Please!" she said, holding up her hand. "If we have only five minutes, I must ask questions. First, one of you tell me exactly what happened when you saw the fire at the next farm."

The biggest of the men spoke up. "Name's Ryan, ma'am. I'm some kind of cousin to Sean, though I couldn't tell you just

how we're related. And I can tell you he's no thief, and no murderer!"

"I believe that, Mr. Ryan. Please tell me what happened."

They went through it all, telling Hilda nothing new. The
smoke, the idea it might be a grass fire, the worry about it going
underground. The fast run to the adjacent field, the despair when
they realized it was a barn fire. "And well alight, ma'am," said
Ryan. "Seems like it went from almost nothin' atall to a regular
inferno in just no time. We knew there was nothin' we could do
for the barn, so we tried to see if there was animals inside, but we
couldn't see none. We all wish we'd knowed about the hired man."

The others muttered assent, their heads down.

"And did any of you see Sean pick up the billfold?"

No, none of them had, but they believed his story. And yes,
he had asked all of them, once they were back at the other farm,
if they were the owner. And if that was all, ma'am, they'd best be
gettin' back to work.

"Thank you. I will leave in just one minute, but I have one
more question. Did any of you see anything unusual that day,
anything at all? Did you see anyone leave the farm next door, or
come to it?"

A man who identified himself as Neely said he'd seen the
farmer leave, early in the morning when they were just getting to
work. "At least I reckon it was the farmer. Saw somebody, anyway, leave the place in a wagon. Never saw him come back, nor
anybody else."

"So that was a waste of time," she told O'Rourke as he handed her back into the carriage.

"But it might not have been," he said, clucking to the horses.
Look on the bright side. There's two more places to try, anyway.
Oliver's now?"

They tried Oliver's. It was busier there than she had anticipat-
ed. She had forgotten that Oliver's sold plows all over the world.
Though it was winter in Indiana, she knew that there were parts
of the world that were warm in December and presumably needed plows. The noise at Oliver's was even more deafening than at

Birdsell's and the information she gathered even less useful. No one had seen anything unusual. Everyone believed forcefully in Sean's total innocence, but had no idea who, instead, might have started the fire.

"It is just like before," she said wearily as she climbed into the carriage once more, and if there was a hint of Swedish *y* in the *just*, O'Rourke tactfully ignored it. "I learn nothing. No one knows anything."

"What I say," said O'Rourke, climbing to his high seat up top, "what I say is, never give up. While there's life, there's hope. You just keep at it, ma'am. I was saying to Mrs. O'Rourke, I was saying I wasn't so set at first on workin' for a lady as pokes her nose into murders and such-like. But, I says to me wife, I says her heart's in the right place, and what she's doin' for the poor boys in town has needed doin' for a long time, so if she wants to poke, let her, I says. And there's the Studebaker noon whistle, ma'am. We'll catch the men on their lunch break, and that's a better time to talk."

Well, thought Hilda in some surprise, at least O'Rourke had unbent. Maybe one day they could all, employers and employees, look at each other as human beings, not just pieces to be moved as on a chess board.

"Yes, Kevin, let us try Studebaker's. Oh! And Kevin?"

"Yes, ma'am?" he called down.

"When we get there, why do you not try to talk to the men, too? When I have asked all I can think to, maybe. I could go a little way away. They might talk more to you than to me. You are Irish, and a working man. I am Swedish, and no longer a working woman."

"Seems to me, ma'am, as you're workin' hard enough these days. But I'll talk to 'em if you want." He slapped the reins against the horses' flanks and they moved amiably off.

And it was at Studebaker's that Hilda got, at last, her first piece of solid information, her first hint that there might be a solution to this mystery. Perhaps fittingly, it was O'Rourke who first heard the important new fact.

There were five men here who had worked on the barn with Sean and the others, five Irishmen vociferously proclaiming the innocence of Sean and the idiocy of the police. Hilda asked the same questions, got the same answers, sighed inwardly, and left the field to O'Rourke.

She was sitting a little apart, wearily trying to think what she was to tell Norah on her return, when O'Rourke came over to her. "I think you'd better hear this, ma'am," he said mysteriously, and led her back to the little group sitting on benches at a large table, their lunch pails nearly empty.

"This here's Marty Finnegan, and he's got somethin' to tell you." O'Rourke was beaming.

"It's not much, ma'am," said Finnegan bashfully. "Not as if I saw who it was, or what they were doin', or anything like that."

"But you did see something?" asked Hilda, barely able to contain her impatience.

"Saw someone leavin'. It was when we was all runnin' over there, and tryin' to see through the smoke what was happenin', and that. And I saw a buggy hightailin' it away from the farm. Movin' like all the divils in hell was after it, if you'll pardon the language, ma'am. But that's what I thought, meself, seein' it leavin' all that fire and smoke behind. And I wondered at the time why they were goin' away from the fire instead of stayin' to help. And then I figgered maybe they was goin' for help, and then I forgot all about it when we saw how bad the fire was."

Hilda took a deep breath. "Mr. Finnegan, did you see the buggy leaving the farm? I mean, driving out the drive, not just on the road?"

"Drove right through the gate, ma'am. And never bothered to close it after them, neither. Nobody brought up on a farm'd do a thing like that, so I thought, that must be a city feller. I'd forgot that part."

"And the buggy went—which way? Toward town or away from it?"

"Oh, back towards South Bend. That's why I thought maybe they was goin' for help."

"Can you tell me anything at all about the buggy? I know it was getting dark at the time, but—"

"Not all that dark, ma'am. There was still light in the sky, and then there was the light from the fire. Not that it did much good, all flickery like it was. But I could see well enough. Couldn't see the driver, but it was an Izzer buggy. Can't mistake one of them, not if you work right here where they're made, let alone livin' in South Bend where there's about a million of 'em. And it was pulled by a good horse. Gray, and some stepper."

Make them to be numbered with
thy Saints, in glory everlasting.

    — *Te Deum Laudamus*
      The Book of Common Prayer

31

MRS. MURPHY STOPPED by the house again late that afternoon, breathing fire and ready to turn things upside down again. She wanted her son-in-law out of jail. Never mind that she rather disliked him when he was free; now that he was a prisoner he was an angel of light, the best husband any daughter could have, and what was she, Hilda, doing to set him free? And as for Norah and the baby, she was taking them home, doctor or no doctor, nurse or no nurse.

Norah screamed that she wouldn't go, the nurse screamed that she would lock Norah in the room if necessary, the baby screamed on general principles. None of it touched Hilda. She spoke when spoken to, shook her head when Mrs. Murphy threatened the wrath of God and all His saints, smiled at Norah and the nurse.

"I'll have them out of here if it's the last thing I do," the frantic woman roared.

"No, I do not think so, Mrs. Murphy. If you will excuse me, I must…" and Hilda drifted out of the room without finishing the sentence.

Mrs. Murphy, deprived of her chief adversary, finally departed in confusion, so that Patrick came home to a household restored to calm and order, and a wife lost in contemplation.

"Hilda, darlin', I've asked ye three times how your day went," he said as they sat at supper. "Have ye gone deaf all of a sudden?"

"Mmm? Oh. No. I am fine."

"So did anything interestin' happen today? Are ye goin' to get Sean out of that jail?"

"Yes, soon. Patrick, I am not very hungry. I believe I will go up to bed. I need to think."

She evidently thought herself to sleep, for she made no response when Patrick came to bed hours later. But she slept only fitfully, and woke very early indeed, her heart pounding.

She wondered what noise had awakened her. No one in the house was yet stirring. Even little Eileen wouldn't get up for another hour. Hilda, having been forced for years to rise at the unholy hour of 5:30, firmly refused to allow her servants to do the same. Mrs. O'Rourke had at first insisted that she could not possibly get breakfast on the table by seven unless she rose at five. "Then we will have breakfast at eight, Mrs. O'Rourke. That will be early enough for Mr. Cavanaugh to be at the store on time. Remember you have a gas range in this house. There is no need to build up a fire before you can cook."

The cook, accustomed to her own way of doing things and privately afraid of the newfangled gas contraption, had grumbled but had finally acquiesced and now rose at 6:30 like Eileen.

So what was the noise downstairs? The morning was dark and felt drab and dreary. Her head was clearer, but she saw before her a course of action before which she quailed. Her spirits felt as dark as the sky, as dark as that indigo woolen cloth at the dressmaker's. Beautiful cloth, Hilda had seen at the first fitting yesterday afternoon, and it was going to be a beautiful gown, but would she ever feel festive enough to want to wear it?

She sat up in bed, rubbed sleep from her eyes, and listened more carefully. The muffled sounds, she decided, were outside rather than in. Muted voices, a smothered laugh, a light that shone through the bedroom window and flickered on the ceiling... Were robbers trying to break in?

Then the music began, sung in an uncertain girl's soprano to the accompaniment of an accordian. *"Natten går tunga fjät, rund gård och stuva; kring jord, som sol förlät, skuggorna ruva...."*

Hilda leapt out of bed and opened the window. Frigid air

blew in along with strains of music. Hilda joined in the chorus: *"Då i vårt mörka hus, stiger med tända ljus, Sankta Lucia, Sankta Lucia."*

Patrick sat up, shivering. "What...?"

"Get up, Patrick! It is the *Lussibrud*. Come and see!"

The song continued, Hilda humming along. Patrick pulled on his dressing gown and brought Hilda hers. They stood at the window and looked down.

A young girl stood singing, dressed all in white with a crown of lighted candles on her head. Patrick recognized her as Birgit, Hilda's youngest sister. In a semicircle around her stood the rest of Hilda's family. Sven's accordian was joined by Erik's inexpertly played harmonica, while Mama and the other girls hummed along with Birgit.

"It's pretty, darlin', but what's it all about?" asked Patrick when the song was finished. "And why so early in the mornin'?" He yawned widely.

"It is *Sankta*—Saint Lucy! This is her day, but I had forgotten. This is a custom in Sweden. I will tell you all about it, but it is too cold here, and I must go down and let them in, and make coffee. Dress quickly, Patrick. They will have breakfast for us." She called out something in Swedish, then slammed the window shut and put on her slippers.

"Breakfast?" Patrick scratched his head as Hilda darted out of the room.

When he got downstairs, a lively scene met him in the kitchen. Hilda's family crowded around the big work table, eating fragrant buns studded with raisins while Hilda poured coffee. Birgit's crown was sliding a bit on her head, but as the candles had been blown out, there was no danger. Rapid Swedish conversation was punctuated by laughter.

Patrick hesitated in the doorway, watching Hilda with her family, having a wonderful time. Would he spoil the fun if he entered? He, an Irishman who knew none of their customs, who practiced an alien faith, who understood not a word of their strange language?

He had been determined to marry Hilda from the first time
he saw her. Oh, he understood all the problems, or thought he
did. Both families would object, but he and Hilda would bring
them around.

But they were so slow to come around, slow to accept each
other's cultures. Look at the way his family, yesterday, had been
downright rude to Hilda. Hilda's family were less hostile, in part
because they owed Patrick and his uncle Dan a good deal for
their kindness, but they were not yet warmly disposed towards
the Irish, all the same. Only young Erik, to whom the dashing
Patrick was a hero, welcomed him unreservedly into the family.

Had he hurt Hilda by marrying her and separating her from
her family? The thought nagged at Patrick.

It was Hilda's mother who saw him first. "Come in, Patrick,
and have some of our good *Lussekatter.* I do not know the word
in English." Her manner was a bit stiff, but at least she had invited him into the circle, and had courteously switched to his language. The rest of the family followed suit, and Sven stood to
offer Patrick his chair.

"This is your place, at the head of the table," he said gravely.

"Ah, but you're our guest. Stay put. Erik, ye lazy scamp, give
your sister your chair. You and I can stand easy enough. Gudrun,
did you bake those buns? Whatever their name is, they smell like
a little bit o' heaven."

"Mama and I, we made them," said Gudrun, the oldest sister,
coloring a bit. "It is an old recipe handed down from *Mormor*—
Grandmother—and old before that. It is part of the custom."

"Mm," was all Patrick could reply through a mouthful of
bun. They were deep yellow in color and rich with spice.

"We will tell you about it," said Hilda. "*Sankta Lucia*—Saint
Lucy—"

"Let me tell!" interrupted Erik. "It is an old Swedish tradition," he informed Patrick, and gave Hilda a smug look, proud
of the fancy word in English. "Every year before Christmas—"

"On December thirteenth—" Hilda prompted him.

"On December thirteenth," Erik hurried on, "that's today,

very early in the morning, only we're earlier than usual because we have to go to work and school today, but very early anyway, one girl of the family gets up and makes coffee and puts on a white robe and a wreath of candles and brings the coffee and the Lucia buns, the *Lussekatter,* to the rest of the family, and she's supposed to be," he paused for a quick breath, "supposed to be Saint Lucia bringing light to the world because it's been getting darker and darker and now it will start getting light again, and so the girls sing that song about her. And it's usually the oldest girl in the family only that's Gudrun and she's too old, so sometimes it's the youngest if she's old enough, so it's Birgit this year, only she can't keep the crown on straight." Erik poked Birgit, which made the crown slide still farther over one ear, and they both started to giggle.

Freya took up the tale. "In the village in Sweden where we lived, there was a procession, with one girl from the whole village chosen to be the *Lussibrud*, the Lucy Bride, Saint Lucia. Of course all the girls who were old enough wanted to be chosen; it is a great honor."

Erik jumped in again. "And the boys, too—the very little boys are *stjärngossar*—star boys—it is a silly thing. The big boys are *tomtar*—I do not know the word in English—"

"Little demons—like you," said Hilda, reaching out to ruffle his hair. "Be quiet now and eat your breakfast."

But it was impossible for any of them to be quiet. They chattered in English and Swedish, and Erik pretended to be a *tomte* and chased Birgit around the kitchen until Patrick captured him and tickled him into submission. At some point an outraged cook stomped in, demanding to know what devilment was going on in her kitchen, followed by an equally outraged and starchy nurse, but the Lucia buns placated even them.

After an hour or more the Johanssons departed, stuffed with buns and coffee, and Hilda and Patrick made their way upstairs. "That was fun," said Patrick as he watched Hilda brush her long blond hair, braid it, and pin it into a coronet on the top of her head. "But why're you fixin' your hair? I've things I need to get workin' at down at the store, but it's not time for you to get up yet."

"There is much to do, Patrick. There is a meeting of the Boys' Club committee this afternoon, and before that—before that I must think some more."

"Seems to me you're workin' as hard as when you were at Tippecanoe Place," Patrick grumbled.

Hilda nodded. "That is what O'Rourke said yesterday. I do work hard. I wish I did not have to hunt for the murderer, Patrick. I do not like it. But I must, because of Norah and Sean."

"And the baby, and all." Patrick sighed. "Do what you have to do, darlin'. But don't you wear yourself out, now. Christmas is comin' and I've a lovely surprise for ye, and I don't want to find my darlin' girl too tired to enjoy it."

Hilda turned from her dressing table and took his hand. "I will enjoy Christmas, Patrick. I enjoyed this morning. It was good to have my family here, with you. Things are better with them, I t'ink—think. But before Christmas can be good, I must clear Sean's name, so Norah will not be angry with me."

"You gonna tell me about it?"

"Not yet. Not until—later. Soon, Patrick."

Patrick kissed her and went off to work, not sure whether to be pleased at the improvement in family relations or disturbed about Hilda's continuing involvement in crime.

32

HILDA WENT IN for a moment to see Norah, who was nursing the baby. "And I don't care what that doctor says, *or* the nurse, I'm letting her eat all she wants. And then I'm going to get up and have a bath. I'm that tired of being washed in bed, as if I was a baby meself. And then I'm goin' to eat a lot of breakfast."

"Good," said Hilda. "I have brought you something to start. It is a Swedish tradition." She handed Norah a bun, and explained about Saint Lucia and the celebration.

"So that's what that was all about," said Norah as soon as she'd swallowed a big bite. "I heard the commotion. Woke Fiona, too, and I tell you it takes a lot to wake her. Sleeps like a baby, she does."

Hilda giggled.

"And so," said Norah after another mouthful, "what are you doin' to find out who really set that fire?"

"I know who set the fire," said Hilda, her giggle silenced.

"*What?*" Norah sat bolt upright in bed, scattering crumbs and disturbing Fiona, who protested loudly. "You mean to tell me you know and you haven't told the police so Sean can get out of jail?"

"I know," said Hilda dully, "but I cannot prove it. *Yet.* I have a plan, Norah, but I will not tell you or anybody else. No one would believe me yet, anyway. Do not look at me that way. Soon, I promise you, everyone will know the truth."

She turned her back and left the room, both Norah and the baby screaming imprecations at her retreating form.

Hilda kept to her room most of the morning. She skimmed the newspapers, noting with no surprise that the Democratic-leaning *Times* deplored the rash of bank failures in the area and cited rumors that others were to follow, Henry Townsend's Farmer's Bank perhaps included. The paper predicted dire consequences for the working men of the city and fulminated against rich bankers who took no thought for the poor. The *Tribune*, Republican to the core, made little mention of local banking problems in the news columns, but mentioned those farther afield and editorialized—at length—on the irresponsibility of those who "cried wolf" and preyed on the public's fears.

Hilda nodded drearily and cast the papers aside. She thought for a long time, pacing up and down the room. At one point she sat down in front of the wash stand, opened her box of talcum powder, and took up a generous pinch of it between thumb and forefinger.

Eileen, who was making the bed, watched curiously as Hilda rubbed the powder on a piece of black leather and then blew it off. Dearly as she would have liked to ask what Hilda was doing, the little maid didn't quite dare. Mrs. Cavanaugh was a kind and understanding mistress, and had made no objection to Eileen doing the room while it was occupied, but there were limits.

Immediately after lunch, which Hilda ate absentmindedly (and alone, Patrick working through his lunch on this busy day at the store), she went upstairs again to dress for the committee meeting. This time she dressed even more carefully than for the first occasion.

"But don't you want to wear the pink, ma'am? It's your second-best for afternoon, but you can't wear the green, you wore it last time."

"No, Eileen. The black wool, please. And I will wear my hair in the coronet braids."

Eileen opened her mouth to protest, saw the look on Hilda's face, and closed it again. In her opinion, that black dress with the white trim made Hilda look almost like a maid again, especially with the braids, but it wasn't her place to say so.

Hilda chose a plain black hat, too, with a minimum of decoration, and went out the door with such a set expression on her face that Eileen whispered to O'Rourke, "She might almost be in mourning, all that black and no smile." O'Rourke shook his head—there was no accounting for a woman's mood—and helped Hilda into the carriage.

Hilda was a little bit late. That was the way she had planned it. All the other women were assembled in the library at Tippecanoe Place when she walked in. She murmured an apology to Mrs. Clem and sat down in the last available chair. Aunt Molly glanced at her, noted the sober garb, and tilted her head, eyebrows raised. Hilda gave an almost invisible shake of her head. All would be revealed soon.

"Well, now," said Mrs. Clem, "now that we're all here, we need to make sure we're ready for the party. Mrs. Elbel, you have the floor."

Mrs. Elbel, too, glanced curiously at Hilda before proceeding. "Thank you, Mrs. Clem. I believe we are very nearly ready. Mrs. Darby, have you a report for us on the decorations?"

Mrs. Darby, looking very young and pretty and just a little shy among the older women, reported that she had obtained generous contributions of a fine fir tree and money to buy the makings for decorations that were not only pretty, but practical. "Apples, both red and green. We'll tie ribbons around them and hang them on the tree, and then the boys can take them home later to eat. And all my neighbors are helping me string popcorn. And we're wrapping hard candies in colored paper and stringing them, too. We also bought candles, but I'm not sure we should light them. With so many boys around…"

She left the sentence unfinished, but heads nodded. Lighted candles on the tree were pretty, but dangerous.

"And when do you plan to put the tree up?" asked Mrs. Elbel.

"I thought on Friday. My neighbors can help, but if some of you ladies could come, too?"

Several of the women spoke up.

"Thank you. That all sounds splendid. Now, Mrs. Brick, I believe you and Mrs. Clem have planned refreshments?"

The reports went on. Hilda listened with only one ear. Her part of the planning was done; she had only to report on the gifts her brother and sisters were making. There would surely arise, sometime, an opportunity for what she had to do, but if not she would have to make her own opportunity.

"Very well," said Mrs. Elbel at last. "You ladies have worked extremely hard to get all this organized in such a short time. Let's see, now. The hall—we have Mrs. Cavanaugh to thank for that. And she has given us an approximate list of how many will attend. The refreshments sound delicious and Mrs. Darby has done a marvelous job about the decorations. Mrs. Ford, Mrs. Cushing, and I have purchased what gifts needed to be bought, although we have all, I'm sure, been gratified by the generosity of the businessmen and private citizens of the community in donating to our cause. That leaves only the entertainment." She cleared her throat. "Mrs. Townsend and Mrs. Witwer were to plan the entertainment together. Mrs. Townsend, I realize that you have—um—had other worries on your mind." An embarrassed little rustle moved around the room. The women looked at their gloves. "However, have you and Mrs. Witwer been able to come up with something to—er—amuse the boys?"

Mrs. Townsend rose. She looked, Hilda thought, as if she were about to faint. Her face was pale and her hands shook. "We have, Mrs. Elbel. We were of course not about to spend good money to entertain a passel of ruffians. We have asked Miss Collmer if she would have her piano students give a brief recital. She has agreed. One of them will also play for a game of musical chairs."

The silence that greeted this announcement threatened to prolong itself. Mrs. Elbel cleared her throat. "Yes. Well, I'm sure that the boys will—er—accept the entertainment in the spirit in which it is offered."

Mrs. Witwer looked distressed. "I did think that we might

also ask someone to do something a little—er—lighter, but…" She spread her hands and looked helplessly at Mrs. Townsend.

Hilda stood. She could keep quiet no longer. "Mrs. Townsend, I know some of these boys well. They are not ruffians, but they are not well educated, and they will not sit still for a piano recital. Miss Collmer's students are very young, I believe, and can play only simple pieces. The boys will want something more amusing, something that is fun—a clown, perhaps, or someone who does magic tricks, or—"

Mrs. Townsend was glaring at her. Now her face changed and she interrupted. "I know who you are now!" she said, pointing a trembling finger. "You didn't look like it before, in that fancy dress and with your hair all done up. You're that maid who goes around snooping into everybody's business! I don't know how in the world you got on this committee. We are a group of ladies, and we don't need the opinions of a tarted-up little nobody like you!"

The other women gasped. Mrs. Townsend sat down, her face having gone from ashy white to fiery red. She was breathing hard; her hands grasped each other tightly.

Hilda stepped forward. "I am sorry you feel that way about me, Mrs. Townsend. Excuse me, but I believe you dropped this." She proffered a black leather billfold. The initials on it, though pale, were clear enough: HT.

"That's my husband's! Where did you get that? You stole it, you dirty little thief! Give it to me this instant!"

The buzz in the room reminded Hilda of an angry hive full of bees. She stepped back, the billfold firmly clutched in her hand. "I did not steal it, Mrs. Townsend. You dropped it, or perhaps it fell out of the buggy, when you left Mr. Miller's farm after setting the fire."

"I—you—" The angry woman looked frantically around the room. Every eye was upon her, and none was friendly.

"It's all your fault!" she screamed. "You and your Irish friends and all your other precious immigrants. Everything would have worked out if it hadn't been for those stupid Irish laborers and you! You had to poke your nose in, couldn't leave the police to decide who was guilty! Who cares if a stupid lout of an Irishman—"

"That will be quite enough, Mrs. Townsend," said Mrs. Clem. Her voice was quiet, but its steel cut through the other woman's tirade. "Please go with Williams until you are able to calm yourself."

Williams and John Bolton had come into the room. They moved to Mrs. Townsend. Bolton offered his arm. "Madam? This way, if you please."

They escorted the raving woman away. Mrs. Clem spoke softly to Williams as he left the room; he nodded, his lips set in a grim line.

"He will call the police, my dear," she said to Hilda. "Such an unfortunate scene! I'm afraid some people have so little self-control. Now, Mrs. Witwer, you were going to tell us more about the entertainment?"

All's Well That Ends Well

—William Shakespeare
c. 1601

S O THEY WERE going to skip town," said Patrick, reading the papers the next morning.

"With everyone's money. What was left of it," said Hilda, cracking open a boiled egg.

"And it was Mrs. Townsend who started the fire. But why? That's what I don't quite get."

"It was Norah who started me thinking the right way, when she said maybe things did not happen as they were planned. So I thought what might happen if a fire started in a barn, and I thought about our farm in Sweden. A barn fire is very serious, so my father and mother slept in the room nearest the barn, where they could see out of the window if anything happened. If there had ever been a fire, my father would have jumped out of bed and gone to fight it, maybe not even getting dressed.

"I think that is what was meant to happen. Mr. Miller would go down to fight the fire, and then—this is not nice, but I think then Mrs. Townsend planned to shut him up in the barn with the fire. But it did not work, because Mr. Miller was not at home. So Mrs. Townsend waited and waited for him to come out, and when the barn began to burn in earnest, she had to leave in a hurry."

"And that's when the billfold fell out of the buggy, I s'pose. Though I can't think what it was doin' in there to begin with."

"Mrs. Townsend said something about that when Williams took her away. She was screaming and not making sense always, but I heard her say something about a fool leaving his old billfold in a buggy. She meant Mr. Townsend, I think." Hilda primmed her lips. "It is not a proper way to talk about one's husband."

Patrick grinned. "Of course you never think I'm a fool."

"If I think it ever, I do not say it to other people."

He patted her hand and picked up his previous thoughts. "Good girl. But why any of it? What did the pestiferous woman have against Miller?"

"Nothing. It was the farm she wanted. It was—it is—a valuable property. Mr. Miller had no heirs, or so Mrs. Townsend thought, so if he died, the bank that held the mortgage would get the farm. And the bank that held the mortgage was her husband's bank, and it was in trouble."

"The papers say it looks like he's been bleedin' the accounts for months."

"It was her, I think," said Hilda. She speared a sausage with savagery. "She is not a good woman, Patrick. She wanted fine clothes and a fine house and a social position, but she had not enough patience to wait for any of that. So she made her husband buy her these things when he could not afford them, and he had to steal money. I feel sorry for him."

"Hmph. Seems to me a man who can't stand up to his wife deserves his fate."

Hilda wisely let that pass.

"So how come she didn't burn the house down, if she wanted Miller dead? Surer way, seems to me."

"Yes, but then the farm would not be worth so much. It is a very nice house."

Patrick ate his fried potatoes for a while in thoughtful silence. "And you're tellin' me you thought all this out just because you imagined what was supposed to happen?"

"Not until afterwards. I learned two things, Patrick. I learned that Mrs. Townsend drove somewhere in an Izzer on the day of the fire and brought the horse back in a lather. And I learned that someone drove away from the fire, drove very fast, in an Izzer. I did the sum and *then* I started thinking about why. And then I was sure, when I rubbed powder into the billfold and read the initials. HT. Henry Townsend. I knew, but I had no proof. So I had to make Mrs. Townsend upset. It was not a kind thing to do, in front of the other ladies."

"And you're real sorry about it," said Patrick.

"I am not sorry at all," said Hilda, pouring herself a second cup of coffee. "She was rude about immigrants, especially the Irish. Another sausage?"

Afterword

FIVE HUNDRED AND TWELVE boys attended the Christmas party on December seventeenth. All the ladies involved regretted from time to time that they had ever conceived the idea. Four of the smallest boys got sick, either from excitement or overeating or both. Riggs made an admirable Santa Claus, and almost all the boys were happy with their presents, the exceptions being two spoiled sons of a wealthy family who got into a fist fight with Andy's little brother over a toy boat and had to be sent home. The sleds were especially popular, and two boys who helped keep the younger ones happy and occupied the whole afternoon were rewarded with the two toy Studebaker wagons, and were thrilled into speechlessness.

The ladies went home exhausted, full of the glow of good works, and profoundly grateful that it would be another year before they had to think about such a thing again. Hilda, however, was determined that they would think soon about putting the Boys' Club on a permanent, year-round basis. And then something ought to be done about the girls....

Three days later, on December twentieth, new electric street lights on attractive new cast-iron poles were turned on throughout the business district. According to the South Bend *Tribune,* "The lamps...throw more diffused rays and [are] regarded as greatly superior" to the old arc lights.

On Christmas Day, Hilda and Patrick ate two Christmas dinners, one with her family at noon, one with his family in the evening. As they had given the servants the day off, Patrick drove them himself in the new sleigh he had bought as a Christmas present for both of them. Hilda wore her new indigo gown with the Valenciennes lace trim and let Eileen put her hair up. She also wore Patrick's gift of a gold locket, but tucked under the boned lace collar, lest her family or his think she was showing off. Patrick, on the other hand, consulted the gold watch Hilda gave him at every possible opportunity.

Sean and Norah and baby Fiona celebrated Christmas with her family, saving his family's celebration until New Year's. Norah, feeling almost strong again, helped her mother serve the dinner. Mrs. Murphy drank too many toasts and spent most of the afternoon snoring on the settee. Norah and Sean sat a little apart from the others after they had helped in the kitchen, and talked about the possibility of Norah asking for her old job back, at Tippecanoe Place. Sean wasn't sure it was necessary, now that he had a fine job at Studebaker's helping make automobiles.

Hilda woke on the morning after Christmas feeling distinctly queasy, probably, she thought, from those two dinners the day before. She was disappointed, because there was a fresh fall of snow, and she wanted to try the skis Sven had made for her as a Christmas present. The next day she felt the same, and when the queasiness had gone on for a week of mornings, she began to wonder....

On April 23, 1905, Walter Miller, looking for a strayed calf, found Mr. Jenkins's billfold in a ditch not far from the farm. Having lain there all winter, it was in sorry shape, fit only to be thrown out. It contained thirteen cents.

Mary Ivancsics

About the Author

Jeanne M. Dams, of Swedish descent and a lifelong resident of South Bend, Indiana, holds degrees from Purdue and Notre Dame universities. A former teacher and university administrator, she discovered she was really a writer and has published fifteen mysteries in two series. She has traveled extensively, but lives in South Bend with her husband and a varying population of cats.

Dams has been nominated for the Macavity and has won the Agatha Award. She welcomes visitors and email at www.jeanne dams.com.

MORE MYSTERIES
FROM PERSEVERANCE PRESS
🎭 *For the New Golden Age* 🎭

JON L. BREEN
Eye of God
ISBN 978-1-880284-89-6

TAFFY CANNON
ROXANNE PRESCOTT SERIES
Guns and Roses
*Agatha and Macavity Award
nominee, Best Novel*
ISBN 978-1-880284-34-6

Blood Matters
ISBN 978-1-880284-86-5

Open Season on Lawyers
ISBN 978-1-880284-51-3

Paradise Lost
ISBN 978-1-880284-80-3

LAURA CRUM
GAIL McCARTHY SERIES
Moonblind
ISBN 978-1-880284-90-2

Chasing Cans
ISBN 978-1-880284-94-0

Going, Gone *(forthcoming)*
ISBN 978-1-880284-98-8

JEANNE M. DAMS
HILDA JOHANSSON SERIES
Crimson Snow
ISBN 978-1-880284-79-7

Indigo Christmas
ISBN 978-1-880284-95-7

KATHY LYNN EMERSON
LADY APPLETON SERIES
**Face Down Below
the Banqueting House**
ISBN 978-1-880284-71-1

**Face Down Beside
St. Anne's Well**
ISBN 978-1-880284-82-7

Face Down O'er the Border
ISBN 978-1-880284-91-9

ELAINE FLINN
MOLLY DOYLE SERIES
Deadly Vintage
ISBN 978-1-880284-87-2

HAL GLATZER
KATY GREEN SERIES
Too Dead To Swing
ISBN 978-1-880284-53-7

A Fugue in Hell's Kitchen
ISBN 978-1-880284-70-4

The Last Full Measure
ISBN 978-1-880284-84-1

PATRICIA GUIVER
DELILAH DOOLITTLE
PET DETECTIVE SERIES
The Beastly Bloodline
ISBN 978-1-880284-69-8

NANCY BAKER JACOBS
Flash Point
ISBN 978-1-880284-56-8

DIANA KILLIAN
POETIC DEATH SERIES
Docketful of Poesy
(forthcoming)
ISBN 978-1-880284-97-1

JANET LAPIERRE
PORT SILVA SERIES
Baby Mine
ISBN 978-1-880284-32-2

Keepers
*Shamus Award nominee,
Best Paperback Original*
ISBN 978-1-880284-44-5

Death Duties
ISBN 978-1-880284-74-2

Family Business
ISBN 978-1-880284-85-8

Run a Crooked Mile
(forthcoming)
ISBN 978-1880284-88-9

VALERIE S. MALMONT
Tori Miracle Series
**Death, Bones, and
Stately Homes**
ISBN 978-1-880284-65-0

DENISE OSBORNE
Feng Shui Series
Evil Intentions
ISBN 978-1-880284-77-3

LEV RAPHAEL
Nick Hoffman Series
Tropic of Murder
ISBN 978-1-880284-68-1

Hot Rocks
ISBN 978-1-880284-83-4

LORA ROBERTS
Bridget Montrose Series
Another Fine Mess
ISBN 978-1-880284-54-4

Sherlock Holmes Series
**The Affair of the
Incognito Tenant**
ISBN 978-1-880284-67-4

REBECCA ROTHENBERG
Botanical Series
The Tumbleweed Murders
(completed by Taffy Cannon)
ISBN 978-1-880284-43-8

SHEILA SIMONSON
Latouche County Series
Buffalo Bill's Defunct
ISBN 978-1-880284-96-4

SHELLEY SINGER
Jake Samson &
Rosie Vicente Series
Royal Flush
ISBN 978-1-880284-33-9

NANCY TESLER
Biofeedback Series
**Slippery Slopes and Other
Deadly Things**
ISBN 978-1-880284-58-2

PENNY WARNER
Connor Westphal Series
Blind Side
ISBN 978-1-880284-42-1

Silence Is Golden
ISBN 978-1-880284-66-7

ERIC WRIGHT
Joe Barley Series
**The Kidnapping
of Rosie Dawn**
*Barry Award, Best Paperback
Original. Edgar, Ellis, and
Anthony Award nominee*
ISBN 978-1-880284-40-7

*REFERENCE/
MYSTERY WRITING*

KATHY LYNN EMERSON
**How To Write Killer
Historical Mysteries:
The Art and Adventure of
Sleuthing Through the Past**
ISBN 978-1-880284-92-6

CAROLYN WHEAT
**How To Write Killer Fiction:
The Funhouse of Mystery &
the Roller Coaster of Suspense**
ISBN 978-1-880284-62-9

Available from your local bookstore or from
Perseverance Press/John Daniel & Co. at (800) 662-8351
or www.danielpublishing.com/perseverance.